Divine
Temptation

Nicki Elson

OMNIFIC PUBLISHING

DALLAS

Omnific Publishing
10000 North Central Expressway, Dallas, TX 75231
www.omnificpublishing.com

First Omnific eBook edition, March 2013
First Omnific trade paperback edition, March 2013

The characters and events in this book are fictitious.
Any similarity to real persons, living or dead,
is coincidental and not intended by the author.

Library of Congress Cataloguing-in-Publication Data

Elson, Nicki.
   Divine Temptation / Nicki Elson – 1st ed.
   ISBN: 978-1-623420-08-6
   1. Angels — Fiction. 2. Romance — Fiction.
   3. Supernatural — Fiction. 4. Horror — Fiction. I. Title

10 9 8 7 6 5 4 3 2 1

Cover Design by Micha Stone and Amy Brokaw
Interior Book Design by Coreen Montagna

Printed in the United States of America

*This book can only be dedicated to John Wharem,
without whose encouragement, wisdom, and honesty
this story may have never made it
from my imagination into words.*

Chapter 1

Clawed feet landed with a muffled thud atop the January snow. His balance was instantaneous. Surveying the still forest around him, he watched the pale morning sunlight filter through the bare branches, illuminating nothing but the trees, the forest floor, and him. All active life had vanished from the area moments before his arrival. To joggers along the perimeter of the preserve, the distant ruckus of fleeing animals had registered only as a minor disturbance to the music blasting through their earbuds. His entry point was good.

He shook the white crystals from his talons and stepped through the snow. As he walked, his true form mutated, adapting to the world he had entered. By the time he reached the edge of the forest, he looked like any other man, complete with a pair of black dress shoes, a wool overcoat, cashmere scarf, and fedora. His power in this world had become such that all he had to do was think it, and it was his — for such minor details, anyhow. But acquiring what he truly desired would take more finesse.

The streets along his short walk to the historic part of town were already alive with cars pushing through the slush, carrying their contents to work. It was a new year — time for humans to get back to the old routine and make more money. They had Christmas bills to pay off, after all. His mouth twisted into an unpleasant smirk. This time he wouldn't fail. This time they'd practically beckoned him forth.

He reached downtown Prairie Oaks, and as he traversed its sidewalks, a glass door swung open in front of him. Along with the earthy aroma of coffee drifted something else. He halted his steady gait and swiveled his head to peer inside. Shooting through the collection of people, his gaze landed on two women. Both of them were middle aged; one was modestly plump while the other was of a leaner build. The latter was the one he sensed. There was nothing in her appearance to set her apart from anyone else—thick waves of caramel-colored hair ending just below her shoulders, medium complexion with a dusting of makeup over straight, long features—but there was no mistaking that she could suit his purpose.

While he watched her laugh and talk with her friend, the door swung shut and then open again. This time he detected something new amid the warm air seeping out from the shop, something exceedingly unwelcome. He shuddered and moved on. He had plenty of time; there was no need to jump on the first possibility to present itself…particularly if that possibility came mixed with complications.

"I saw an angel."

Sharon's eyebrow shot up as she sipped her grande chai.

"In my dream. Last night," Maggie explained and then added, almost to herself, "I don't know why I keep thinking of him as an angel."

"Him?" Sharon asked.

"Yeah." Maggie's eyes narrowed as she strained her memory. "He was standing in my bedroom, across from the bed, next to the dresser. He was just…watching me."

"What did he look like?"

"Tall, thin."

"Fluffy wings and no shirt on?" Sharon prodded hopefully.

Maggie laughed. "No! He was fully clothed—sorry to disappoint you. And how do you possibly manage to turn talk of an angel into something perverted?"

Sharon shrugged. "A gift, I guess. Besides, you're the one who brought him into your bedroom."

"I didn't bring him anywhere. It wasn't real."

"Your subconscious brought him there. It wants a man, darlin'."

"It wanted rest. And it didn't conjure a man. It conjured an angel."

"Male angel."

"Whatever." Maggie lifted her coffee to her mouth and scanned the room. She was hardly going to engage in boy talk. Not at the age of thirty-eight. Not when divorced. And certainly not with two kids, including a thirteen-year-old daughter who was dangerously close to plunging into the world of dating herself.

Sharon sneered at Maggie's obvious closure of the subject. "Well this rots. You're my single friend, you know? I'm supposed to get to live vicariously through you, but all you ever do is go to work at that church and run your kids around to practice and lessons and whatnot. Now you finally have a sex dream and you're going to clam up on me."

"It wasn't a sex dream! Honestly, Sharon, can't those first weeks after the divorce last you for a while longer? I gave you plenty of vicarious action then."

Sharon smiled. "That you did, my friend. That you did. But those were just sleazy flings. I'm ready for some romance now. Let's find you a nice, handsome bloke that'll sweep you off your feet."

"Already happened. His name was Carl Brock, remember? And we all know how that turned out." Maggie searched for a change of subject when Sharon frowned. "So how's the Fun Fair coming along? Which committee did you get roped into this year?"

Sharon rolled her eyes and plunged into a diatribe about the grade school PTA, the invariably overeager newbie mothers, and the impossibly small budget and limited time frame. "But I'll tell you one thing," she added, "we sure do miss your mad decorating skills."

"Oh please. Do you think the kids even care about the decorations? As long as there are fun games and prizes and popcorn, they're happy."

"Well, I liked your decorations."

"Thanks." Maggie stuck out a teasing tongue.

"And I suppose you decked the hell out of those Catholic school hallways this Christmas, eh?"

Maggie took a long sip of her coffee and shook her head before gulping it down. "Nope. I'm out of the PTA business."

"What? The PTA junkie has gone cold turkey?"

Maggie laughed. "I guess it was sort of an addiction. Heaven forbid I simply join a committee—I had to run it. And I couldn't just do the job. It had to be done better than it ever had been before. These days I still clip box tops and bake brownies for the classroom parties once in a while, but mostly I keep my focus on my job in the parish office and stay out of the school's affairs. It's healthier for all of us." She glanced at her watch. "Oh gosh, I'd better get going."

"Yeah, me too." The two women stood and pulled on their coats, and then Sharon gave Maggie a big hug. "It was great seeing you, kiddo. Let's not let so much time go by again, huh?"

Maggie returned the squeeze. "You've got a deal. Tell Reggie and the girls I said hi. I'm so glad Katie and Kirsten have kept in touch." She turned to unsling her purse from the back of the chair and froze in place when she caught a glimpse of someone behind the coffee shop's counter.

"What's wrong?" Sharon asked.

"I…nothing." Maggie slid her purse strap over her shoulder and headed to the door.

Sharon got there first and positioned herself to block Maggie's way out. "Bullshit nothing—what did you see?"

Maggie knew her friend well enough to be sure she'd cause a public scene rather than miss out on the dirt. "Fine. But don't you dare say one word to him."

Sharon's mouth curled into a wicked grin at the word "him."

Keeping her back to the counter, Maggie jerked her head to gesture in that direction. "The tall, sandy-haired guy behind the counter looks just like the angel from my dream."

Sharon looked over her friend's shoulder. "That's a chick. And I wouldn't call her tall. Or dream worthy."

"What?" Maggie turned but didn't see the guy she'd spotted a few moments earlier. "He…he must've gone into the back room or something. Can we get out of here now? I'm going to be late."

"Holy crap. You're fantasizing about a Starbucks barista!"

"I'm not—Oh, forget it. We are so not meeting *here* next time." Maggie pushed past her friend and waved a mittened hand as she made her way down the slushy sidewalk to her car.

While she navigated her suv through the morning traffic, she thought about how nice it had been to see Sharon. Maggie was still on friendly terms with a few other moms from Madison Elementary, but Sharon was the only one who'd stayed steadfastly by her side and never treated her any differently throughout the divorce. Most of the other women had avoided eye contact after the news first broke. As unpleasant as that reaction was, Maggie found she preferred it to the awkward pity hugs and well-intended condolences that had occasionally come her way. Even worse were the women who'd looked her directly in the eye while a sneer played underneath their false smiles, delighted that Maggie had finally proven herself less than perfect.

She parked in the church lot and rushed into the buff-colored brick building, passing an oversized painting of the archangel Michael in the entryway to the parish office. Her lips twitched into a wry grin; perhaps she'd been unintentionally bringing work home with her.

"*There* she is," a thin, older woman with short but poufy blond hair called from behind her low cubicle walls.

"Sorry, Brenda. I know I'm a few minutes late. Met a friend for coffee."

"Well, the monsignor from Rome is coming at any minute so you'll need to reschedule all of Father Tom's appointments for the day. Might want to do the same for Father Dominic, just in case."

"I didn't think he was due in until next week," Maggie said as she hung her coat in the cubby.

"Neither did I, but we got word that he arrived in town this morning."

Maggie settled into her chair at the office's front desk and shoved aside the project she'd planned to work on in favor of the church pastor's spiral-bound appointment book.

A couple hours into her day—and still no sign of the expected visitor—a third grade class marched past the glass office doors on their way to the church, as they did every Wednesday morning at that time. Maggie looked up and smiled, waiting for a particular mop of wavy brown hair to stroll past.

Today the mop was accompanied by a huge grin decorated with peanut butter and cheese cracker crumbs. Maggie gave the boy a small wave and blew him a kiss. Liam was happy here, as was his older sister, Kirsten, and Maggie was relieved that the painful steps that had led them to St. John's had at least come to something good.

Throughout her marriage she'd maintained control over everything—her house, her garden, the neighborhood block parties, her former size-six figure. Even during the divorce proceedings, Maggie had been in command. A guilt-ridden Carl had willingly given her everything she asked for, including the house, and she'd expected that besides no longer having a husband around to leave his dirty socks on the floor or take out the garbage, the only change in her life would be having the kids gone Tuesday nights and every other weekend. She hadn't taken the time to assess the impact of her husband's infidelity on her ego until after the papers were signed. That's when she began to imagine the other moms whispering behind her back about things like the thickness of her hips, her lackluster hair which was far too often pulled into a simple ponytail. *No wonder he fell so easily into someone else's bed*, she was certain they'd concluded.

She hadn't realized she was in control of nothing until it suddenly felt like she was losing everything. After months of insecurity, less-than-satisfying sexual indiscretions, and borderline depression, she realized that she couldn't continue living so close to her old life without constantly feeling like a failure. She needed change, and she convinced herself that the kids did too.

When Maggie had approached Carl about sending Kirsten and Liam to a private school, he hadn't balked, though she knew his finances must've been severely stretched by that point. She'd also known that he was motivated by more than guilt. The caution that wavered in the deep blue of his eyes and at the edges of his baritone voice had indicated his genuine concern for her stability—that's what had given her the strength to stop spiraling downward. She didn't want him thinking she'd disintegrate without him by her side.

They'd looked at a few different schools, but Maggie liked the laid back feel of St. John's, and when she saw the posting for a part-time office secretary position—which came with a fifty-percent break in tuition—she didn't need any more signs that this was the right place for her and her children. The hunt for something away from Madison Elementary had begun as a quest to run away, but finding St. John's had felt more like being called home.

Liam's class disappeared down the hall, and the side door from the rectory opened. Father Tom stepped into the office, followed by a slight man with ash-colored hair and pointed features. Behind the two of them towered Father Dominic, the parish's junior priest, only one year out of seminary.

"Good morning, ladies," said Father Tom. The portly, gray-haired priest's customary greeting was more clipped than usual, and there was something forced about the deep crinkles surrounding his mouth and eyes as he gestured toward the shorter man. "This is Monsignor Sarto."

Maggie stood and shook the monsignor's outstretched hand. "Welcome."

He returned her greeting with a polite nod as his eyes scanned her desk. "What's your role here?"

"I'm the front desk secretary. I answer phones, coordinate use of church facilities, schedule Father Reardon and Dominic's appointments—"

"Keep the place running like a well-oiled machine," the monsignor finished, his slightly accented English backing up Father Tom's earlier explanation that the visitor was American but had been living in Italy for several years.

"I try to." Maggie let out a nervous laugh.

"Monsignor, this is Brenda Drummond, the office manager," said Father Tom.

The two senior priests stepped over to Brenda's desk, and before following, Father Dominic locked eyes briefly with Maggie, raising his eyebrows and shrugging to indicate that he still had no more clue than she did what they were all in for. Father Tom had told them that the Vatican representative's visit was routine, but word in the pews was that it was anything but. The general assumption was that Father Tom and St. John's were under some sort of review, but Maggie tried not to let her imagination wander on the issue. The pastor had never been anything but forthright with her in the past, so until she had any facts to the contrary, she'd take him at his word. Still, the stiffness of his expression as he made introductions gave the church gossip more than a touch of credence.

"Watch out," Father Tom warned after Brenda had listed off her many duties. "The moment you get settled in, Brenda here will be after you to write a weekly article for the bulletin."

The monsignor's lips maintained a polite, half smile. "I'll gladly contribute." He turned to Father Tom. "I'd like to look around the school facilities now. May we visit a classroom?"

Father Tom glanced at the clock. "I'm sure that'll be fine, but we should check in with the school principal first. Father Dominic, please run ahead and find out from Mrs. Hawk which class might be the best one to drop in on. I'll give the monsignor a quick tour of the gym and library on our way to meet you."

"You've got it." Father Dominic exited into the school hallway, oblivious to the way Monsignor Sarto's eyes had narrowed in response to the junior priest's blatant informality.

"It was a pleasure meeting you, ladies," the monsignor said before gesturing for Father Tom to lead the way. In the doorway, the visitor paused, turning briefly toward Maggie. There was no emotion in his look, but it pricked the hair on her arms and filled her with the instinct to get back to work—immediately.

That night, Maggie's consciousness clung to the wispy vapors of a dream even as her eyes opened under her satin sleep mask. She sensed his presence and pushed herself to sitting. Fumbling to pull the mask down, she looked immediately to where he stood in the corner of her bedroom, just as he had the night before. This time she noted that he didn't glow; no halo or anything else illuminated his form. Yet somehow, while her dresser and armoire stood in shadow, she could inexplicably make out his every detail.

He wore white, and she realized that was why she'd categorized this figment of her sleepy mind as an angel. But the garments weren't flowing robes. Hugging his trim physique was a pair of linen-like drawstring pants and a T-shirt.

His light brown hair had a golden cast and was neatly cropped around his ears and at his neck, but longer spikes fell across his forehead. Smooth skin stretched over his defined cheekbones and a thin, angular nose. In contrast to the straight lines of his other features was the curve of his full lips, currently pursed in concentration—or perhaps confusion. His pale eyes were earnest, and they opened wide when they landed on Maggie, as if surprised to see her looking at him.

She chuckled. "It's *my* dream. What did you expect?"

Chapter 2

Monsignor Sarto's first month in town brought more change to St. John's than Maggie had seen at the place in the previous two years. He seemed to be getting his fingers into every aspect of the parish, and Maggie could hardly keep track of all the new initiatives swirling around the church, including the conversion of an alcove into an adoration chapel, extended hours for confession, and several revisions and additions to the parish website. She knew many people considered the parish to be lacking in its forward progress and recognized that these changes were probably a good thing, but she personally loved the church's seeming imperviousness to the rapidly changing world around it. The steadiness of St. John's had been an anchor for her in those tumultuous months following the divorce.

While the monsignor's overall purpose was still a bit vague, from all the extra work Maggie had been given, it appeared he was there to assure compliance with the bishop's directives. The office staff had also learned that St. John's was merely a home base for Sarto and that he'd soon begin visits to other parishes in the area.

"Are you kidding me?" Maggie groaned one mid-February morning when she plopped herself into her office chair and read the Post-it stuck to her computer monitor. "Another new lecture?" The changes around St. John's meant the "part" in Maggie's part-time job wasn't quite so meaningful anymore.

Brenda chimed in. "I swear that man isn't going to rest until he's got every soul in the tri-cities area eating, living, and breathing their entire lives at church. Isn't it enough he's got the two of us chained here at all hours?"

Maggie huffed out an ironic sigh. "God's work, right?"

"So he says."

The two parish priests walked into the office, and Father Tom headed straight to Maggie. "Did you get my note? Sorry I didn't have many details for you. I just had the idea and got overly excited, I suppose."

Maggie looked back at the Post-it. "Oh, it's from you. Biblical archeology sounds like an interesting topic."

"Thanks. Don't worry, we won't schedule it until after Easter, but it seems like a good way to appeal to the community, even those who haven't been to church in a while. I'm considering hosting it at one of the park district meeting rooms to make it less intimidating."

"Will the monsignor allow that?" Father Dominic asked, not looking up from the papers he was rifling through at the filing cabinet.

"I am still pastor, last time I checked," Father Tom replied, a bit of the spark in his eyes dimming. "Though I suppose I should at least let him know my plans. Well, I'll get back to you with potential dates and preferred location and then we can start setting everything up."

Maggie smiled. "Sounds great."

"I'm sorry to add more to your pile—I know you've already been putting in a lot of extra hours."

"It's fine, really, Father. I'm happy to do my part."

Brenda tilted her head to look over the rim of her bifocals. "Me too. The sooner we satisfy Sir Stick-Up-His-Bum, the sooner we'll get him on a plane back to Rome."

Father Tom placed his hands over his ears and stepped toward his office. "I didn't hear a thing."

After Father Tom had closed his door, Father Dominic asked, "How are your families holding up with you two ladies spending so much more time here?"

"My kids are all out of the house, and Joe's used to it," Brenda answered.

"Kirstin and Liam are doing fine," Maggie said. "Thank the Lord Carl's current work schedule is flexible enough that he can step up and help with after-school duty though, or I don't know what I'd do."

"Sheesh, he treats his ex-wife better than most men treat their wife-wives," Brenda commented.

Maggie laughed but couldn't deny it. "I think we give each other more consideration and respect now than we ever did while married."

She smiled and returned to her work, feeling grateful that she and Carl had been able to get past the fighting and emerge at this friendlier place. For a long time she'd been convinced that the damage he'd done to the marriage was irreparable, but now that she actually liked him again, she'd begun to wonder if in time, given the second chance she'd refused him, he could've also regained her trust.

When it was time for Liam's class to head to church, Maggie's eyes flicked toward the glass doors. She always missed her children on Wednesday mornings after they'd spent the night at their dad's, but with time together so sparse over the last month, the ache was more pronounced. At the first sign of his teacher, Maggie made an impulsive move and broke protocol.

She hopped up from her desk and ran through the door, pulling Liam out of line and giving him a big smooch. Liam wasn't the kind of kid who was too cool for public kisses from his mother, and he threw his arms around her. Maggie squeezed him back and glanced over to the scowling teacher, who'd stopped the line.

"Sorry, Miss Danner. I promise not to make a habit of this. Could Liam spend his lunch hour with me in the office?"

"Sure. I'll send him down. Now, back in line, Liam."

"Thanks." Maggie waved at the line of third graders as they resumed their march. When she returned to her desk, she buzzed her daughter's classroom and asked the teacher to send Kirsten down to the office during lunch hour as well.

At twelve twenty-five, Liam strutted into the office and made himself comfortable in the conference room where he always ate when he joined his mom. Maggie heated her Lean Cuisine in the kitchenette microwave and watched for her daughter. She had to remind herself to look for the figure of a young woman rather than the skinny kid Kirsten had been when she'd first started school here.

"Where's your lunch?" Maggie asked when Kirsten arrived. "Want to grab another one of these from the freezer?"

"Gross. I'm going to eat with my friends when they come in from hanging out." Maggie hadn't heard Kirsten utter the word "recess" since fifth grade.

"Okay. Well, come join us in the meeting room and tell me what you've been up to since Monday night. Remember, your dad's taking you to piano today."

"Uh huh." Kirsten nodded, her long, straight hair dancing aside her face. "And then we're meeting Missy over at the new burger place for dinner." Her eyes went wide just before her smile disappeared.

"Kirsten, we've talked about this. It's okay. I know my initial reaction to the news of your father's new girlfriend wasn't the best, but that was four months ago. Now that I've had time to process, I'm good with it. Promise. And here's an even bigger surprise—I *like* Melissa. She's nice and seems to be good for your father. So can you please, please, please stop flinching every time her name gets mentioned around me?"

"Yeah, Mom. I know. It's just…weird."

"I know, sweetie. But it'll all get less weird as time goes on. So tell me what you've been doing. How did that history test go yesterday?"

Maggie let Kirsten do most of the talking—about school, about a friend's birthday party coming up, about a new song she was going to ask to learn on piano—while Liam wolfed down his sandwich and Goldfish crackers. When it came time for Kirsten to join her classmates in the cafeteria, she seemed almost reluctant to go.

Maggie pulled her into a hug and kissed the top of her head. "I'll see you after dinner tonight. Tell your dad I said thanks and Melissa I said hello."

Liam took the stage for the next twenty minutes and spent it trying to explain why, in real life, the Mario Bros. would be able to defeat Donkey Kong Jr.

Maggie left work in time to get home before Carl dropped off the kids. After the financial realities of being a single parent had sunk in, near the end of the kids' first school year at St. John's, Maggie decided it would be best to move to a townhouse. What the new place lacked in comparative size, it made up for with convenience—the townhouse association took care of the yard work, and the smaller interior was easier to clean, thus freeing up time as well as money. After repainting a few rooms in warm, neutral tones and hanging her favorite pieces of artwork—mostly florals and landscapes, and wrought iron wall décor—the three-bedroom, two story unit had become a pleasant sanctuary.

Upon arriving home that evening, Maggie immediately threw on her most cozy—if far from most flattering—sweats and waited for Carl to bring the kids home. She regretted her wardrobe choice the moment she heard car doors slam and looked out the window to see a perfectly coiffed Melissa get out of Carl's Lexus sedan. The woman was only a couple of years younger than Maggie, but with no kids, she had more time and money to spend at the spa and gym, and it showed from her French-tipped fingernails to the ends of her highlighted blond hair. What made it worse was the way her polished beauty complemented Carl's darker and more rugged good looks. Somehow his receding hairline and ever-more-apparent flecks of white only added to his magnetism.

Maggie gulped back her pride and opened the door. "How were the burgers?"

"Awesome!" Liam shouted.

"Expensive," Carl added.

Maggie laughed. "It's nice to see you again, Melissa. Thanks for taking the kids tonight. I really appreciate it." She turned to her children. "You two better go drop your bags in your rooms and wash up. It's getting late."

"Sorry about that," Carl said as the kids ran up the stairs. "But I think you'll forgive me when you find out what we did after dinner. I've been keeping an eye out for a good deal on a laptop for you, and Best Buy is running a special this week on a pretty decent model. So I went to check it out, and it looks good. I put one on hold for you, if you want it."

"That's great!" Now Maggie would be able to do more of her work at home and the kids could have free reign over the desktop. "You know I have no idea about electronics, so if you think it looks good, I'm sure it is. I'll go pick it up tomorrow, but…"

"You'd like me to get it all set up for you." Carl winked, and Maggie's eyes inadvertently wandered toward Melissa, wondering if it was awkward for her to witness this kind of familiar interaction between her boyfriend and his ex-wife. Recollecting herself, Maggie jerked her head toward the stairwell. "Hey, guys! Come say goodbye."

Two heads appeared over the railing at the upstairs landing.

"Bye, Dad. Bye, Missy!" Kirsten said.

"Thanks for the chup chup!" Liam called.

Carl and Melissa laughed, and Maggie turned to cock her eyebrow at them.

"Inside joke," Melissa explained. "'Night, Linus. 'Night, Lucy."

Maggie tried not to wince at the playful nicknames. She accepted that her husband had moved on romantically, and she had no right to expect him not to, but this sudden realization that her children would form relationships with this person…that was new. As Kirsten had so eloquently put it, it was just weird.

Later that night, Maggie fell into an exhausted sleep and dreamed. Melissa was with the kids at a park or a carnival, some place with swirling colors, and the three of them were having fun. Maggie watched them, and she had a choice to make: either let them be or stop them. Even her subconscious mind knew the right thing to do. But she couldn't make herself look away, and the more she watched, the angrier she became. The fury consumed her and she grew and grew until she towered above them with her head perched on a serpentine neck and her mouth laden with razor-sharp teeth. She roared and watched as the three of them burst into flames.

Her body jerked and she was instantly transported to her bed. Back to her normal size and coated in a layer of cool sweat, it seemed she was awake until the tendrils of an unearthly sensation poked at her. It was him. Pressing the palm of her hand over her sleep mask, she held it fast. She didn't want to look. She just wanted to lie there and get swallowed up by her misery—the misery she'd brought on herself. The misery she hadn't even known she'd felt during her waking hours.

The tendrils didn't let up. They poked and sank beneath the surface of her flesh. They pushed the sadness into a concentrated mass at her center so that it was no longer free to roam and spread throughout her. They asked her to open her eyes.

She pushed the mask to her forehead and sat up. He stood in the same corner of her room, but this time he met her gaze straight on, showing more curiosity than surprise. Maggie wasn't sure how long they stared at each other before she became overwhelmed with the need to get closer. But she was hesitant, wary of this man who stalked her within her dreams. She gradually leaned forward until she was on her hands and knees and crawled to the end of the king-sized bed, keeping her eyes fixed on him. Once there, she lowered to sit on her ankles, dipping her chin to indicate that it was his turn.

He returned her slight nod and stepped gingerly forward. He was being cautious too, stopping half an arm's length from her. He seemed much taller from this perspective and thinner. From this close she could see that his eyes were a pale gray, and there was something familiar in them. Something she automatically trusted.

Her breath caught. It frightened her that she would trust anything so blindly. She had an instinct to race back to the head of her bed and crawl under the covers, but stiffened when he lifted his arm, as if to touch her. Her heart beat wildly, and she stayed in place, staring up at him with wide eyes. She wanted him to touch her. In that moment, she wanted it more than anything.

He seemed to take her stationary position as permission, and his hand moved gradually but deliberately forward until his fingertips tickled Maggie's jawline. She closed her eyes at the sensation. His fingers glided across her flesh, and he cupped the side of her face. The feeling was like no other. His skin seemed to seep into hers, yet it maintained its integrity, as if he had sunken into part of her, and she into part of him.

His touch felt watery, yet solid, and it extended further into her in the form of a warm, soothing emotion. He was calming her, washing away her troubles and stabilizing her psyche. Everything was okay. She had no need to worry or be agitated. She had only to trust.

A loud crack sounded, and Maggie whipped her head toward her bedroom doorway. Liam stood there, clutching his blanket. She wasn't dreaming anymore. The overwhelming feeling of peace and safety receded, but remnants remained, successfully pushing out the hopelessness from her earlier dream. She was slightly disturbed, though, to discover that she was perched at the end of the bed. Apparently she'd gotten a little too into the angel portion of her dream. But she couldn't worry about that—she had a little boy fresh off a nightmare to comfort.

"Come here, baby," she said and scooted back to the head of the bed, unfolding more covers for him.

He crawled in beside her and seemed to fall immediately to sleep once secure in her embrace. Maggie nuzzled in close and kissed the top of his head. Keeping her arm wrapped around him, she tried to impart at least a fraction of the sanctuary she'd felt with the angel.

Chapter 3

April brought blankets of color to Midwest suburbia. Bright green lawns provided a fresh backdrop for bursts of color as various bulbs and shrubs blossomed in the opening act for three seasons of carefully orchestrated landscaping. Carl had set Maggie up with all the programs she'd need on her new laptop, and by the end of Lent, her new work duties were organized and running smoothly, allowing her to return to normal office hours. Her world fell into a steady, controllable pace.

"Anything I buy now is just going to die in the pot waiting for me to plant it," Sharon commented as she perused rows and rows of plastic containers filled with various annuals and perennials.

The Easter lilies had been cleared off the altar at St. John's, and Maggie was responsible for purchasing new spring flowers for the upcoming Sunday, so she'd called her friend for an afternoon of lunch and flower shopping. After munching down Mexican tapas, they'd driven a few towns over to Somme Park, which was hosting its annual flower show and fundraiser. Maggie had already selected several potted hostas and geraniums and asked the garden's florist to make two large floral arrangements.

"They said it would take about half an hour for the vases," Maggie informed Sharon. "So do you want to go for a walk around the grounds while we wait?"

"Sure, why not."

Maggie parked her trolley to the side of the checkout desk, and the two women stepped out of the greenhouse into the cool but sunny spring day. Somme Park was formerly the estate of a wealthy Chicago investor. Upon his death, the property had been turned over to the care of a board of directors to use as a public garden. He wanted to leave as his legacy a serene piece of Earth open to all, a place where people could come to admire God's goodness and feel a sense of quiet and harmony. Satisfaction.

The plants being sold in the greenhouse had been cultivated by the same horticulturists who designed and nurtured the extensive gardens. As Maggie and Sharon crunched through the pea gravel path around the circular pool, they took a moment to admire the elegant layout of the rose garden with its Greek statues and topiaries. The roses wouldn't make their grand entrance for months, but even without them the plot had stature.

Maggie continued to her favorite setting at the park—the prairie garden. Even though she was surrounded by pockets of prairie in her everyday life, she was fascinated by it. It wasn't just tall grasses and weeds, as Carl had often teased her; it was a kaleidoscope of hidden treasures that changed every time she looked at it. The women veered onto a narrow trail that snaked among the fading stalks of last year's prairie grasses, which were being swiftly replaced by new greenery and the beginnings of what would soon be a sea of yellow ragwort. Occasional dots of white and purple punctuated the scene as phlox and violets preened for attention. A wind whipped up, carrying sweet scents from the blooms and causing Maggie to close her cardigan and Sharon to zip up her hoodie.

"Will you have to confess to playing hookie when you go back into the office tomorrow?" Sharon asked.

Maggie shook her head. "Father Tom's great, and he knows I've been working my tail off. He's more than happy to let me have an easy day once in a while."

"Yeah, but didn't you say there's a new sheriff in town?"

"The monsignor."

"Good God. Sounds like the name of a horror film—*The Monsignor*, mwahahahah!"

"Stop it," Maggie laughed. "Though I'll admit that he's sort of stiff, and there's just something…I don't know…*cold* about him, he's nice enough. And efficient. He doesn't mess around, gets things done. I admire that about him. As much as I adore Father Tom, it's nice to have a bit more discipline around the place."

"Sounds like the two of you were made for each other."

Maggie's only response was to scrunch her nose. She wished she'd get some credit for lightening up considerably over the last couple of years, but she also recognized that order and clarity would be something she always strived for. It was just how she was made.

"Any more sexy guys come to visit you in your dreams?" Sharon asked. "Or better yet — in person?"

Maggie shook her head. "Nothing new to report in that department." It wasn't a total lie. She truly did have nothing to report — but only because she didn't want to talk about it. The angel hadn't returned since the night she'd so vividly dreamed of him touching her and filling her with such sweet peace. But that didn't mean she'd stopped thinking about him. In fact, he'd been entering her waking thoughts more prominently ever since that night. Whenever she felt her blood pressure rise from anxiety or irritation, she'd daydream about him standing with her, stroking the side of her face, and all other thought would vanish, restoring her equilibrium. But that wasn't exactly something she could explain to someone else even if she'd wanted to.

"So how about you? How's Reggie?" Maggie asked.

"He's fine. We celebrate our twentieth next month."

"You do? Sharon, that's great! Holy cow, twenty years."

"I know. Hard to believe I got married when I was only three, huh?"

They'd taken the short loop and found themselves once again at the main artery of the connecting paths. Continuing around to the other side of the pool, Sharon told Maggie about her plans for an anniversary weekend in Galena while the rolling lawn of the English landscape garden emerged on their left, taking them from the familiarity of their everyday surroundings to a foreign, almost imaginary world. Bordered by groves of evergreens, the rich green carpet swept around an oblong pond, and pockets of forsythias punched their vibrant tint into the otherwise serene palette. Half hidden by a stand of cypress was a narrow, round structure encircled by stone columns. It was a replica of a classic Greek *tholos*. Maggie stopped and stared at it.

"Thinking about getting one of those for your yard?" Sharon joked.

"Looks more appropriate for my tombstone." Maggie stepped off the gravel path and onto the lawn toward the structure.

"What are you doing? Are we even allowed to walk on the grass?"

"I think so. Yes. Look—there are people over there." Maggie gestured toward a couple walking hand in hand near the opposite stand of trees.

"Well…is it soggy? It rained last night and I just bought these shoes."

Maggie looked down and pressed the toe of her shoe into the grass. A small pool of water squished out of the dirt. "A little bit. You don't have to come. I'll just take a quick peek, and we can meet back at the greenhouse."

"Okay…but, *why* are you going?"

Maggie had already turned and resumed her trek. "I don't know." There was nothing inside the structure from what Maggie could see, and she had no particular interest in getting a closer look at the trees or pond. Yet she was compelled forward. The bottom edges of her jeans were getting soaked, but she didn't let that stop her from climbing the modest incline to where the *tholos* stood at the highest point of the garden. She stepped onto its dry surface and slipped between two pillars to discover that something actually was in there—a stone urn. It was partially filled with rain water and crumpled leaves that must've blown into the deep bowl during the past fall.

She turned and peered between the pillars, down upon the expanse of earth spread before her. When she moved to the edge of the circle, she looked upon the rose garden, and to the right she caught a glimpse of the prairie. Between them, set back, were the formal Japanese gardens leading to the mansion. Her lips spread into a smile when she imagined the large house belonging to her, and all the gardens her personal playground.

She pictured her children playing croquet on the lawn with their friends. Her parents would live with her and host tea parties in the rose garden. Everyone would be abundantly happy. There would be no more endless new projects at the church, no more jealousy or nagging sense of failure tickling the edges of her consciousness—just Maggie in her gardens. Anyone who visited her here would be free of the worries of this world.

A cloud drifted through the April sky and temporarily blotted out the sun. As the grounds darkened, Maggie's longing for the bright vision intensified. The urn. She had an urge to look into it again.

She turned and went to the center of the structure to stare down at the murky water, searching for…something; she didn't know what. Leaning to grip the edges of the urn, she felt a force coming from inside it. Calling to her. Her knees bent with the desire to kneel and ask for the sunny vision to become reality.

The cloud passed and Maggie bolted up straight.

"What the hell?" She shifted her eyes back and forth, checking to make sure no other park visitors were close enough to have witnessed her temporary hallucination. Or whatever it had been. She spotted someone standing in the trees, about fifteen feet away.

Maggie gasped. It was him. The angel, or rather the guy she'd seen in the coffee shop who resembled the angel. He stared earnestly back at her with that same questioning eyebrow slanted just as it had been in her dream. No—at Starbucks. Except he hadn't had a questioning look at Starbucks. It had definitely been in her dream. He turned and hurried away, and Maggie noticed that he was wearing all white.

"Wait!" She hopped down from the circular pavilion and followed him. He picked up his pace, and she picked up hers, trailing him deeper into the trees and out the other side into the grove of fruit trees. Without even glancing back at her, he dashed into a long tunnel covered with thick, woody vines. Maggie didn't want to look like a lunatic, so she didn't scream for him to stop or run at full speed like she suddenly wanted to.

Brushing past the fading blossoms of the cherry and apple trees, she entered the tunnel to find a handful of visitors dappled in spots of sunlight. He wasn't among them. Figuring he must've sprinted through the tunnel, she too threw off decorum and ran the rest of the way, halting once outside to scan the grove. No sign of him. She rushed to go around the high boxwood hedge that blocked her view of the main path, but just before she cleared it, a diminutive figure in black stepped out from the other side of the hedge.

"Monsignor Sarto," Maggie said, stopping in time to avoid slamming into him.

"Good afternoon, Magdelyn. Enjoying your…jog?"

"Oh." Maggie gave a dismissive chuckle and stopped her eyes from flicking around the path, where she didn't see him anyhow. The chase was over. "I thought I saw an old friend and was trying to catch up. Instead I—*literally*—ran into a new one."

Sarto's thin lips pressed into a small smile. "I'm glad you think of me as a friend. Has Father Reardon spoken to you about his upcoming presentation?"

"Not in the last couple of weeks." It struck Maggie how odd it was to be looking straight across at the monsignor. Typically she was seated at her desk with him hovering and intimidating above her, but somehow he was able to evoke a faint sense of unease even at equal level.

"You should speak with him as soon as possible," he said. "There are a few changes."

Sarto had already put the kibosh on hosting the Biblical archeology talk anywhere other than St. John's, and now it sounded like he was making changes to the presentation itself. Maggie felt a wave of indignation on behalf of Father Tom. "I'll stop in to see him tonight after I drop off the flowers," she promised. "Enjoy the rest of your stroll—it's the perfect day to be here."

The line of his mouth stretched into a wider smile. "That it is. Be sure to talk with Father Reardon."

Maggie headed in the opposite direction of the priest to meet Sharon in the greenhouse. After loading the potted plants into the back of her minivan, Maggie enlightened her friend. "You're not going to believe who I ran into out there."

"Who?"

"*Mwahahahah!*" She didn't tell her about the other visitor or the odd occurrence at the urn.

After running Kirsten and Liam to their various appointments, fixing dinner, and getting the kids settled down to do their homework, Maggie drove to St. John's to arrange the plants on the altar. Father Dominic helped her carry them in from her car.

Inside the church, a couple of people prayed in the adoration chapel, and a few parishioners knelt at the regular pews, silently reciting their penance. It was the designated evening hour for the sacrament of reconciliation, so an additional four people stood along the far wall while waiting for their turn in the confessional. Both lights were on above the doors, so Maggie surmised that the monsignor and the pastor were each taking confessions.

Up at the altar, Maggie kept her voice low and asked Father Dominic if he knew anything about changes to Father Tom's presentation. "Monsignor told me to talk to him about it."

Father Dominic set the last plant down. "What's that they say in Proverbs? Rushing into a quarrel that is not my own would be like grabbing a stray dog by the ears."

"Prefer chickens to dogs, do you?" Maggie asked with a teasing twist to her lips. "Probably a wise move though, in your position."

"Glad to hear you agree. Do you need any more help with anything?"

"Nope. I'm all good here. Thanks for meeting me."

"You're welcome—I'm always happy to help. Have a blessed evening."

"You too." Maggie tended to her work as inconspicuously as she could, sheathing the plain plastic containers in clay pots and arranging them on the altar. When she finished, she stepped back and imprinted the precise layout into her memory. She wanted to be able to pinpoint exactly which aspects of her design Sarto had rejected when she'd undoubtedly find the plants rearranged within the next day or two. A peek at her watch told her Father Tom would be occupied with confessions for another fifteen minutes, so she went to one of the pews and prayed until the door of the confessionals opened for the last time and the lights above them went out.

When the pastor exited the confessional from his side and stepped through the sacristy into the narthex, he found Maggie waiting for him. "Do you have a minute?" she asked.

"Of course. Let's go talk in the usher's room."

She followed him to the side room, located just before the doors leading into the church. Although the lounge also served as a pre-ceremony gathering place for brides and their bridesmaids, the décor was distinctly masculine with rich brown carpeting and furniture. The room was situated in the center of the building and had no windows. Rather than flipping on florescent lighting to wash away the blackness, Father Tom turned on a single table lamp. He then pulled a key from his pocket and fitted it into a cabinet at the back of the room over a narrow counter and small sink.

"I ran into Monsignor Sarto at the greenhouse today," Maggie said. "He said I should talk to you about some changes to the archeology presentation."

Glass clinked as Father Tom pulled two tumblers and a decanter from the cabinet. "I'm afraid it's no longer an archeology presentation."

"What? He changed the *whole thing?*"

Father Tom filled one of the glasses half way with a tawny liquid. "Don't get yourself worked up. We'll reschedule my original presentation for the summer. And the new topic is not an unworthy one."

"But what about all the information we've put out there about an archeological talk? Aren't people going to notice if the topic's completely changed?"

"Thus far no one outside the parish has registered, so a simple announcement of the change at the end of Masses and a blurb in the bulletin should be just fine." He tilted the decanter toward the other glass.

"None for me," Maggie said, remembering how her throat had burned after the last time she'd accepted a drink from Father Tom. "But thank you. So what's the new topic?"

"The armor of God. Monsignor Sarto seems to think we could all use a refresher on steeling ourselves against Satan." Father Tom sighed, and Maggie didn't like the forlorn sound of it. He settled into the leather armchair with his glass not leaving his hand, but not touching his lips either. The drink took on a reddish cast directly under the dim blaze of the lamp. "You have something else you'd like to talk about," he stated.

"Yes. But it can wait."

"Sit down, Maggie." He tilted his head toward the overstuffed leather chair on the opposite side of the coffee table. Maggie lowered herself into the seat, but stayed on the edge with her legs tensed. "What's on your mind, dear?"

"I've been thinking about an annulment again."

Father Tom nodded and tapped his finger on the edge of his glass. "What's changed since last year when you decided against pursuing it?"

"Nothing…and everything. I still can't see ever getting remarried myself, but Carl's been seeing someone, and it seems serious. I know he doesn't buy into the Church's position on divorce and adultery — he's satisfied that a civil divorce was enough to free us both to remarry and doesn't see the need for a decree of nullity. But I guess I buy into it enough to think I should reconsider setting him free in the eyes of the Church too, should that become important to him down the road."

"Nullifying a marriage is more than just a matter of wanting it. As we discussed before, the tribunal would need proof that at least one of you entered into the marriage without proper intention to either stay faithful or procreate."

This was the point on which Maggie had stumbled and given up last time. She hadn't wanted to face the possibility that her marriage had never been what it had seemed. "I think a case could be made that Carl never intended to stay faithful, or, at least, was ambivalent about it on our wedding day."

Father Tom set his glass down and folded his fingers together, resting his joined hands on his portly stomach. "You were married for twelve years before his indiscretion."

"Before he confessed to indiscretion. Who knows how many others there may have been?"

"He told you there've been none. Do you not believe him?"

She hesitated before answering. "I do." But she'd also believed him when he'd told her he was working late, or that he was going on a fishing weekend with the guys. Even if she could've brought herself to forgive him, she knew she'd never forget. Every time he was out of her sight, she'd have doubts about what he was really doing. She couldn't have lived that way. That's why she hadn't even considered counseling or the crisis-marriage retreat Carl had begged her to try. "The vows state until death, not a decade plus. If he'd intended to stay faithful to me for our whole marriage, he sure didn't try very hard."

"You've told me he was remorseful afterward. And he confessed without provocation. That would imply it was something that happened without prior forethought. A mistake he deeply regretted. Had he never intended to stay faithful, why would he feel such strong regret?"

In a strange way, Carl's willing confession was something she resented. She didn't understand why he couldn't have gone on living with the guilt of his nasty secret instead of burdening her with it. "Well, the regret obviously hit too late. He probably didn't realize how horrible it would feel to look at his kids and kiss his wife afterward. That doesn't mean that on our wedding day he didn't fully expect that one day he'd stray into another field when his own pasture wasn't looking so green anymore."

Father Tom stayed silent and watched her. She knew he was waiting for her to work it out for herself.

"I wasn't exactly happy in our marriage at the time either. I know I wasn't the model wife, but I *never* considered going to someone else's bed, and I just don't see how he could've done it so easily—not unless he'd always kept it in mind as an option." She shook her head and swiped at an angry tear. She hated how much pain she still felt at her husband's betrayal. "I'm sorry, Father."

"There's no need to apologize. But I think you see how this process will reopen old wounds. Are you sure you're ready for that?"

"Obviously not."

"Well, when and if you decide you are, I'd be happy to speak with Carl about it, if you like."

"Okay. Thanks." The priest smiled kindly at her, and she suddenly felt very selfish. "How are you doing? With all the changes going on around here?"

He separated his hands and waved one to brush away the question. "I'm doing just fine. It's all part of the territory—once you get too comfortable, something comes along to wiggle the rug a little." He picked up his glass and swirled it, staring at the turbulent motion within.

"He'll be gone next month, and then that rug will stop wiggling."

He lifted his gaze to her. "This too shall pass, eh? Well, I suppose you should be getting home to those children of yours."

Maggie took the cue that he wanted to be alone and said good night. When she turned to pull the door to a gentle close, she saw that he was again contemplating the thick, red drink.

Alone in her bedroom that night, Maggie let her thoughts turn toward the angel. Had she been imagining things at the garden? The guy had been masked by branches and shadow; her mind could've easily morphed his features into those of her angel. Then she remembered the almost hypnotic power of the urn, the way it had called to her, and wondered exactly what kind of herbs were in that Mexican food she'd had for lunch.

Even still, she couldn't shake the conviction that the angel was more than a dream. With determination, she propped herself up against a stack of pillows, lifted the novel from her nightstand, and settled in for some late night reading. This time if he visited, she'd know that it happened while she was lucid.

A few hours later she awoke with the light bulb blaring and a horrible crick in her neck from the way it had bent after she'd slipped half way down her pillow mountain. She flicked off the light and pulled on her eye mask, calling off the hunt.

Chapter 4

"The devil's not real," Kirsten said from the passenger seat.

Maggie kept her eyes on the road but jerked her head back. "What makes you say that?"

"Nothing *makes* me say it. It's just what I believe. I think the devil is just a made up thing that God lets people believe to keep them in line."

Maggie's insides eased when she understood that at least her daughter wasn't questioning the existence of God too. She knew sending kids to a parochial school was no guarantee their faith would remain intact forever. So rather than slam a two-ton Catechism down on their curiosity, she tried to discuss more than lecture, firmly believing that turning their own minds around an issue was what would bring them closer to God in the end. After all, it was only after decades of mistakes that she herself had started to truly nurture that relationship.

"Well, what about the people who don't stay in line?" Maggie asked. "Can they just sin and kill and turn their backs completely on God but still get a free pass at the end?"

"At the end they'll see God, and they'll be sorry, and he'll forgive them."

"What if they're not? They'll still have free will, right? What if they use it to flip God off? Is he still going to set a place for them at his table so they can spit on his food?"

Kirsten was silent for a moment before answering. "I guess I don't know how it's all going to work, but if God loves us so much, he'd never throw anyone into hell forever. Oh, I know! Purgatory. That's where he'll send them until they can get their act together."

"So, you don't believe in eternal damnation, huh? You don't need the threat of hell to be a good girl?" Maggie smiled. "That's pretty cool, actually. I'm sure he'd much rather have you follow him because you love him, not because you're afraid."

"So then I don't have to go to this stupid lecture tonight?"

"Ah, but you do believe in extra credit points for theology class, right?"

"Only like five. It'll hardly affect my grade."

"I know, smarty pants, but I have to be there anyhow and I think this'll be good for you to hear. You might not believe in the devil, but do you believe evil lurks in this world?"

"Yeah."

"Well, Father Tom's lecture is going to be all about using the protections God gave us against evil of all kinds."

"Then why doesn't Liam have to go?"

"He's too young to get it in the terms Father will be using tonight. But you're old enough and I need you to be prepared for the evils of high school next year."

"Ha ha." Kirsten rolled her eyes. They pulled into the lot, and she sulked all the way into the narthex, where she was instantly cheered when she saw a couple of her school friends. After agreeing to meet Maggie in the basement afterward, she disappeared into the church with her friends to get a seat for the lecture.

Maggie dashed downstairs to the linoleum-tiled gathering hall and began setting up for the dessert reception while greeting and chatting with the parishioners who'd volunteered to drop off baked goods and beverages. When she'd finished spreading paper tablecloths across the long tables, arranging the sweets, and brewing coffee, there were still ten minutes left of the allotted question and answer time, so she returned upstairs. Quietly entering the church, she stood at the back, behind several rows of wooden pews.

The interior walls were the same tawny brick as the outside of the building, and every few feet, the solid wall was accented by a pane of stained glass, more simple and modern in design than ornate. What gave the space a majestic feel was the high ceiling that was topped with a skylight to allow for a glimpse of the heavens. After settling into place and spotting Kirsten, Maggie was shocked to notice that Monsignor Sarto was at the lectern rather than Father Tom.

"He is always speaking to us. Always trying to get our attention. But are we listening? Or are we tuning him out in favor of earthly pleasures? What he asks of us won't be easy to do, and we will fail often; it's our human nature. But he offers the opportunity to renew and polish our armor — through confession. Someone will be here every weekday morning and every Thursday evening to hear your confessions, along with the third Saturday of every month. I encourage you to take advantage of these opportunities to strengthen your spiritual armor."

Maggie watched her daughter, who was whispering to her friend rather than listening. When Sarto paused, Maggie felt the hairs on her arms prickle. Looking up, she saw that he'd turned his attention to her.

"I take it we're ready downstairs, Mrs. Brock?" Half of the thirty or so people in the pews turned to look at her, and she simply nodded. "Excellent. Please, join us downstairs for a small earthly indulgence — coffee and dessert. Let us thank the Lord for bringing us together to learn of the powers he instills in each one of us and to now partake in the fruits of the generosity and talent of the people of our parish. Amen."

A rumbling of amens cascaded through the pews and then the guests filtered into the aisles. Maggie turned to go downstairs, and when she did, she noticed Father Tom sitting to the side of the altar — in the chairs reserved for the altar servers. His face tilted slightly downward as he stared with a hard expression toward the carpet, apparently deep in thought. If he came down to the basement later that night, Maggie didn't see him.

On the car ride to pick up Liam at his friend's house, Maggie asked Kirsten how Monsignor Sarto had come to be the one delivering the lecture.

"Father Tom talked for most of it. But I don't know, somebody asked a question, and Father Tom started to answer, but then Monsignor Sarto interrupted and, I don't know, just kept answering the questions from there."

"Huh. Well, did you get anything out of it?"

"Five extra credit points and a huge chocolate chip cookie."

Maggie was jolted from her sleep by a familiar sensation. Keeping her sleep mask on, she flipped to her other side in an attempt to force her mind into other territory. She'd decided the chase in the garden had been unacceptable and entirely caused by indulging in thoughts of the angel. After being fairly successful at blocking him from her daydreams, she wasn't about to let him back into her nighttime ones. But whenever she started to drift away toward another realm, her awareness of him would reemerge and jerk her back to her bed.

"Get out!" she shouted in frustration after the third or fourth time it happened. Ripping off the eye mask, she sat straight up to face him. He was exactly where she'd expected—standing in the corner of the room. "I said get out. I don't want you here!"

He didn't move, simply watched her, his forehead creased in concern.

Maggie threw off her covers and launched from the bed. She was done playing around. She was going to attack the intruder and beat him out of her brain for good. At least she would have if her sleep-numbed legs hadn't given out and sent her careening to the floor. The carpet burned the heels of her hands as she skidded, and she lay still for a moment, face to plush. The pain was real.

Thinking she'd once again physically acted out her dream, she lifted her head, expecting to find an empty room. Instead, she saw him kneeling next to her.

"Are you okay?" he asked.

Her mouth fell open, but she didn't respond. She only stared at him. He looked exactly the same as he had the other times—pleasant, ordinary features, but with something ethereal about him. He emanated an intensity, but also a gentleness. Both qualities had been reflected in the smooth tones of his voice as well.

She pulled herself up to all fours and then pushed back to sit with her legs folded beneath her. Rubbing the sore bits of her hands, she said in as steady of a voice as she could manage, "I'd be better if you told me who you are and why you keep coming here."

"I'm sorry. You're not supposed to see me. Or rather, you're supposed to see me if you've been allowed to, but…I can't understand why it's happening now."

"What's happening exactly?"

"I don't know. Not exactly. But it's not the first time we've appeared to humans. You're familiar with Gabriel's visitation to Mary, and it was one of us who woke Elijah and commanded him to eat while on the run from Jezebel."

"So you *are* an angel."

"Yes."

Maggie thought of the angels who led St. Peter from Herod's prison and the ones who spoke with Lot before the destruction of Sodom and Gomorra. "Are you here to warn me about something?"

"No. I don't think so…I don't know." He pushed himself off the floor and stood over Maggie.

When the silence that followed had gone on too long, Maggie asked, "Are you here to ask me to do something?"

He took a few steps away from her, turning his back. "We aren't aimless beings. We're protectors and messengers and worshipers. We always have a purpose, but…" His voice trailed off for a second before he tilted his face upward. "Lord, Father, I don't know what you want me to do here. Please tell me."

He didn't glow or cast his own light, yet Maggie again noted that he himself was more easily visible than anything else in the room—if he'd stood in broad daylight, he wouldn't have looked any different. He stayed silent for several moments and eventually lowered his gaze, studying her through tensed eyes.

"Get anything?" she asked.

He shook his head from side to side and remained silent. It was all too bizarre. If he'd given her some sort of directive, her mind would have had something to work with, but as it was, he simply stood there, expecting her to believe he was real. She accepted that she was awake and looking at him, but she couldn't believe he was actually there.

The rational portion of her brain resumed function and worked through the situation logically. The first time he'd appeared had been in January, just after the holidays. She'd been moderately resentful on New Year's Eve that Carl had someone to kiss at midnight while she didn't. Had she invented this man as a way to cope? As Carl's relationship continued, her dreams of the angel grew more vivid and she became more desperate to catch up with her figment in real life. It made sense that she'd create someone mystical after losing confidence in human men.

"I need to sleep." She thrust herself upward and walked to her bed. He followed her over as she climbed in and covered her legs with the blankets.

"What's wrong?" he asked, kneeling down to her level.

Looking directly into his eyes from this close proximity was like peering through infinite layers of swirling and flecked granite. "You really are lovely." Maggie reached a hand out to rest it upon the side of his face and smiled at the sinking sensation that once again filled her with a soothing calm. She bent her head slowly forward and touched her lips to the confused crease between his eyebrows, murmuring, "Goodbye, sweet, imaginary boy," before pulling away and lying down with her back to him.

"I'm real, Maggie." She closed her eyes and refused to let the hallucination go further, but he persisted, and she felt his breath tickling her ear as he whispered, "Go to the county building, the one off River Street near downtown." The oddness of the statement caused her eyelids to fly open, but she quickly clamped them shut again. "Go to the grounds behind the building, to the courtyard. Stand in the center of the circle. Look down."

For several minutes after his voice faded, she held her eyes closed, noting that the sensations of his presence had receded too. She lifted her lids to the dark room one last time before succumbing fully to exhaustion.

Throughout the following morning, Maggie thought of the angel and little else as she stacked and sorted non-perishable foods during her monthly shift at the local food pantry. She wanted desperately to shake him from her system but knew she wouldn't be able to until proving her internal deception by visiting the county building. Before heading into work for the afternoon, she drove there, parking in the lot out front and exiting the vehicle to stand underneath towering pine trees. Moisture clung to the ground, and the faint scent of earthworms hung in the air. A sidewalk leading to the historic red brick building branched off into a narrow trail that wrapped around the side, and she followed it, glad to see she had no company other than the clustered purple flowers she passed on the way.

Fully expecting to find nothing more than a forest or perhaps a clearing to house Dumpsters, she rounded the corner—beyond which she did, in fact, see a clearing, but no Dumpsters. The sidewalk led to a set of concrete steps that cascaded down to a circular, cobblestone courtyard. Hesitating, she wondered if it was possible that she'd seen an image of this round patio somewhere, perhaps at the historical society. But there was nothing distinctive about the site to trigger a memory. It was simply a small, unkempt patio surrounded by a nondescript strip of lawn stretching to the edge of the forest.

Her gaze traveled to the left, where in the distance, through the tops of the trees, she could see part of a stone building—the old seminary, which currently served as a retirement home for priests. Like the county building, it was considered an historic landmark, and with the parking lot full of modern cars now blocked from her view, she felt as if she'd stepped into a time warp. The angel had instructed her to stand in the center of the circle and look down, so she tightened the belt of her trench coat and descended the steps.

By the time she reached the bottom, she could barely see the top of the seminary roof. To her left was only the forest and to her right the solid wall of the county building with its glossy, darkened windows. Behind a few panes she noted high stacks of cardboard boxes and guessed these back rooms were mostly used for storage.

The rain had been heavy the night before, and the patio's stones were dark with retained moisture. Maggie stepped across the uneven cobblestones to get a closer look at the round stone in the center. It was lighter than the others and currently filthy. Tiny pools of water had gathered in the miniature valleys between raised portions of its topography, and it was worn and chipped, but clearly had been cast into some sort of image. Maggie squinted and with the tip of her shoe brushed water over the dirty parts. She could make out the form of a man in the center. He was surrounded by…something. Removing her foot from the stone, she bent at her waist for a closer look. The something was wings. The image was of an angel.

Maggie froze for a moment, leaning over the figure. Then she snapped up to stand straight and looked all around her. The haze of humidity in the air and her solitary position in this lost garden hinted at dream territory. But she couldn't retreat into the safety of chalking this up to imagination again. An angel had visited her and sent her here to prove himself. Heaven had sent her an angel, and she'd doubted him. More than once. She'd actually screamed at him to leave. She sank down to squat in front of the stone and traced her fingers over its muddy contours. While she did, she silently apologized for questioning the authenticity of this messenger, and she asked for the strength to do what God asked of her—assuming he gave her another chance.

She couldn't hide that it was more than a desire to serve the Lord that made her wish to see the angel again. She wanted to feel the tranquility he'd filled her with. She wanted the intimacy she'd felt with him on his last two visits. With her heart now opened so widely, she couldn't deny that she'd felt stirrings of a carnal, human nature. They were only slight, but they'd been there.

Her hand involuntarily pulled back from the stone, and she stood. The temperatures gave her no reason to be cold, but she wrapped her arms around herself and clung to her biceps for warmth. Forcing her eyes shut, she beseeched the Holy Spirit to strengthen her will… and to send the angel back.

His lips twisted into a nefarious smirk as he watched her through the budding branches. This one was interesting, a true child of God struggling to do right. But he sensed her transformation had only been recent, which meant her sinful desires lurked close to the surface. Entirely exploitable. She would, perhaps, suit his purposes, after all.

Chapter 5

A steady rain thumped on the roof and pinged at the window panes. Maggie sat propped against her headboard, saturated in shadow. For a while she'd stared at the pages of her paperback, but she hadn't been able to absorb so much as a sentence. Her afternoon at work had been similarly unproductive. When her digital alarm had ticked past midnight, she'd recalled that on all the other nights he'd come when the lights were out and she was sleeping—turning off her lamp had been easy, but falling asleep wasn't going to happen. Not until she saw him again. So she waited in the dark.

The moment his self-illuminated form appeared, she threw off the blankets and shot up to her knees, shuffling to the end of the bed to get closer to him. "I'm sorry. I'm so, so sorry. I believe you. I believe in you. I—" She stopped when his sudden and brilliant smile surprised her.

"Don't worry," he said, walking over. "I know this doesn't happen every day. Your skepticism in this case was rational, even admirable. But you listened to me, you followed my instructions, and now you believe."

She relaxed her position down to sitting and nodded. "I do."

It only took a few quiet moments of silently watching each other before the questions started. "Have you figured out why I can see you?" Maggie asked.

"No. Have you?"

"Me? I...no, I only just started believing you were real. Wait! Did you know the whole time that *I* was real? Did you never question it?"

"Angels only know reality."

"Yet you don't know why you're here."

His eyes narrowed slightly as he studied her. "Has anything unusual been going on in your life?"

"Well, two years ago—"

"Not the divorce. Your immediate present."

"Oh." She scanned her mind. "I assume you mean other than a wingless angel showing up in my bedroom?"

He answered by tilting his head and casting an admonishing look at her even while a smirk played at one corner of his mouth.

Maggie wrinkled her nose and almost laughed, but was stopped short by a sudden thought. "Hold on—you know about the divorce?"

"Of course."

"Of course? Does this mean…are you my guardian angel?"

"Yes and no. The human understanding of a guardian angel isn't completely accurate, but I'm the closest thing to your definition."

"So you've been watching me my whole life?"

"I've seen your whole life."

"Is that a yes or a no?"

"It's a no."

"What's the difference between watching and seeing my whole life?"

"Watching would imply that I've been lurking in the background at every moment—I think stalker is the word you'd use for it. Seeing means I'm given the knowledge of your life when I need it."

"Need it for what?"

"For various reasons."

"Including…?"

"Including times when I'm needed to intervene for protection or comfort."

"Intervene how?"

"Different ways. Most often it's through a gentle transfer of… energy is the best way for you to understand it. We don't have the power to change a person's heart, but we can plant the tiniest seeds of an idea or temper, anger, and distress."

"And sometimes you appear in front of them."

"Rarely."

"Have you done it before—with others?"

"I think so."

"You think so? Can you not remember?"

"It's…" He scowled and lifted an arm, bending it to rub the back of his neck. "It's difficult to explain."

Maggie sighed and readjusted to sit cross-legged. Patting the mattress in front of her, she said, "I have a feeling we're going to be here for a while and you might as well get comfortable."

The angel considered her gesture for a moment and then moved onto the bed, mirroring her position so that they sat nearly knee to knee. "Angels don't remember," he continued. "That is to say, we have no need of remembering because we don't forget. We know what we're meant to know, nothing more, nothing less." He lifted his fingers to brush them over the deep creases in Maggie's brow. "I'm sorry; it's not an easy concept, and it doesn't matter anyhow. You wouldn't understand. Not completely. At any rate, the moments I referred to were quick flashes of danger. I stepped in to intercede and lead the people to safety. They seemed to be able to see me and followed, but they may have been obeying an inner voice and not my physical form."

"So you didn't speak to them."

He shook his head. "You're the first I've ever spoken to."

"Really?" She liked the idea of that. "Well, besides talking to other angels, of course."

He shook his head again, and his pale eyes sparked. "First ever to anyone. We don't need to speak in the other realm."

Maggie took a moment to absorb this before asking, "You read each other's minds? All the time? Are you reading mine?"

He let out a laugh. "No. It's not mind reading. We know what we're meant to know."

"Ah, that stuff I won't understand."

"Exactly. But in this case I obviously need to speak for you to get the information you seek. You've given me my voice." As he said this, he reached his hands over to grab Maggie's where they rested on her knees.

She felt again as if their flesh was melding together, and a calming reassurance seeped into her. "It's a very nice voice," she quietly told him.

"Thank you," he replied softly.

The angel was perfectly visible to Maggie's eyes and gave no indication that he had any trouble seeing through the darkness, so she hadn't thought to turn on a light. But now the intimacy of the darkened scene occurred to her, and she slipped her hands from his touch while shifting her mind to a different direction. "Earlier today at work I was thinking, the accounts in the Bible are only summaries, really, so for all we know, it took Mary and Gabriel weeks to figure out what was being asked of her. We can do this. Maybe we should start with what we do know."

His slight nod indicated he was game.

"Okay," Maggie continued, "I've seen you twice outside of my drea—out in public. At the coffee shop and at Somme Park. That was you, yes?"

"Yes."

"Well, what could've drawn you out both times? At the coffee shop…" Her mind drifted back as she put the scene together, and she snapped her fingers. "I'd just told my friend about seeing you in my dream! Was that it? Were you coming to warn me not to tell people about you? Is this supposed to be a secret?"

He pulled his eyebrows together and shook his head. "I didn't know you'd told her about me. I felt…it was an overwhelming need to protect. There is evil in this world, all the time, and part of what we do on Earth is ward off those spirits with our presence. The evil that day was intense, apparently concentrated enough to draw me out far enough to be visible to human eyes."

A chill prickled up Maggie's arm. "Are you protecting me now? Is it, is it lurking closely right now?"

The angel tilted his face to point upward as he turned his palms out and held them slightly away from his body, staying silent for a moment before answering. "No. There's always a presence, but I don't feel anything particularly strong right now. Not strong enough to warrant my appearance. I haven't felt it the other nights I've been here either." He lowered his chin and leveled a steady gaze straight into her eyes, as if to embed the truth of what he said. "Neither have I come with a warning to not speak of me, but I do think it would be wise to keep it between us for now, at least until we've figured it out. Curiosity from others will likely only prove to be a distraction."

Maggie nodded. "I agree. I pretty much regretted saying anything to Sharon the second I opened up my mouth. Now, what about the garden? Why did you run away?"

"I wasn't running away. I was leading."

"To what?"

"Not to, from."

"*From* what?"

"The wicked forces again."

This time the hairs on Maggie's arms practically jumped out of their follicles. Something in the urn had been reaching for her. "Is something after me?"

"Difficult to say. There are concentrated pockets of supernatural malice here and there under normal circumstances. You may have just stumbled upon them. I'd say that's the most likely scenario since the two episodes occurred months apart and haven't progressed. Have you had any other sensations—instances of a strong feeling of foreboding that you can't explain?"

Maggie shook her head. "I don't think so. But I hadn't felt anything like that at the coffee shop either."

She hadn't realized that the angel had been tensed, but she now noticed the hardened muscles at his jaw relax as his shoulders sloped downward. "That's good," he said. "Either it was just coincidence, or your prayers and spiritual life are strong enough to have discouraged it. It would be best for you to remove yourself from any influences that don't feel right. But don't be overly concerned—fear will only lead you to a dark path. There's no need for worry as long as you have faith." His mouth spread into a smile. "Besides, it seems I'll come running to your rescue should it happen again."

Maggie returned his smile and gestured toward his internally-lit form. "My angel in shining...whatever that is." Her fear of the lurking evil subsided, but her curiosity hadn't. "So this brings us back to our dilemma—why are you here?"

He pressed his lips together and shrugged but didn't seem as agitated by the situation as he'd been the previous night. He touched his fingertips to the back of her hands and slid his hands around hers, folding them together. Bending his face downward, he closed his eyes and said, "Father, we ask you to grant us patience as we try to determine the path you wish us to follow. Help us trust that all will be revealed in your time. Meanwhile, may our words and actions be pleasing to you. Amen."

"Amen," Maggie repeated.

"It's late. You should sleep."

"You'll be back?"

"It's for him to decide, but I have a strong sense that I will."

"Well then, I think it's only right that I should know your name."

"Are you going to give that to me too?"

"What?"

"As with my voice, we have no need of names in heaven. They're a human thing."

"But…Gabriel, Michael…do they have names because they're archangels?"

"No. They were given their names because humans needed them. If you need me to have a name, you must give me one."

She chuckled, thinking back to all the baby name books she'd poured over when it had been time to choose names for her children. "No pressure, right?"

"None whatsoever. You'll come up with something."

"Any requests?"

"No." He pushed back from her and stood, walking toward his traditional corner of the room, but before he reached the spot, he was gone.

Over the next few weeks the angel returned many times, but not every night. Sometimes Maggie never fully woke, but was only aware of him standing there. Other nights, she couldn't stop herself from pelting more questions at him, trying to solve the mystery. But his continued prayers to grant patience seemed to be working, and she found herself content to simply accept him as a new friend, a heavenly gift, and became satisfied with waiting for the Lord reveal his plan.

"What do you think of Evan? For your name?" she asked one night. "It means 'God is gracious.' I was thinking it's also short for evangelic, and it rhymes with heaven. Too cheesy?"

He smiled. "Not too cheesy. I like it. It's nice to meet you, Maggie. I'm Evan."

Chapter 6

With Evan's visits confined to Maggie's alone time at night, she found it wasn't difficult at all to continue with life as normal while keeping her secret. The only difference was her greater sense of satisfaction as she moved about her days. The riddle of the angel's appearance had been successfully set aside for the time being, and without Maggie realizing exactly how it had happened, she'd begun opening up to him regarding certain personal struggles, namely Melissa.

Talking it out had helped Maggie accept the new woman in her children's lives as more than simply the price she'd have to pay for refusing to fix her marriage. Evan's patient listening and wise counsel led her to be truly happy that Carl's girlfriend had taken an interest in the kids. It was much preferable to the alternative—a shrew who tried to separate them from their father.

On a Sunday evening in mid-May, Carl brought the kids home after a weekend at his place. When Kirsten and Liam ran upstairs to dump their bags, he walked into the kitchen and took a seat by the island, waiting for them to come back down to give him a kiss goodbye. As usual, Maggie offered him a drink.

"A water would be great," he said.

His deep voice was flatter than usual, leading Maggie to take a closer look at him. He exhibited all his usual vitality as he perched on the stool, and nothing in his handsome features seemed drawn or tired, but his eyes, which almost always glinted with a hint of mischief, were dull, and something about him looked lost.

"Rough week?" she asked as she handed him a bottled water.

"Mediocre." He downed half the bottle in one swig.

The kids reappeared and gave their dad a hug before Liam barraged Maggie with an account of what he'd done all weekend. It seemed to come out in a single, indecipherable word. Ever since he'd started speaking full sentences, Maggie and Carl had joked that he must somehow absorb oxygen through his freckles, because he rarely stopped to take a breath.

"We went to the batting cages, and Liam here has a wicked swing," Carl translated.

"Yeah, wicked *boring*," Kirsten grumbled.

Maggie wrapped her arm around her daughter's shoulder and pulled her close. "Don't worry. Liam's outnumbered by the girls now that you're back here. What do you say we all go get our toenails painted this week?"

"Cool!" Liam shouted. "I'm gonna get Yoda painted on mine."

Maggie's eyes moved to Carl, who she knew would rather be publicly flogged than have a drop of nail polish touch his precious son's toes.

Her ex-husband cocked a teasing eyebrow. "I think we're going to have to revisit our custody arrangement and stipulate what is and is not allowed during our respective visits."

As if on cue, Kirsten's phone buzzed with a text message. "Yeah, I've got a few retroactive stipulations I'd like to get in there," Maggie retorted. The cell phone had been an unauthorized purchase during one of the weekend visits with Daddy. But that battle had been fought and was over, as reflected in Carl's smile, and Maggie thought about how nice it was to be able to joke about these things rather than scream at each other, as they'd done for so long. Kirsten disappeared into the next room, returning the text, and Liam asked to use the computer.

"Half an hour for both of you," Maggie called out loudly enough for Kirsten to hear. "Then it's up to bed. School tomorrow."

Maggie turned to Carl as Liam scampered down the hall to the computer cabinet in the front room.

"Did they get their homework all done?" she asked.

"Yes, chief. Kirsten's got that big reading project due at the end of this week. We started, but she'll probably need to spend a good two hours on the diorama she decided to make. And don't forget, Liam's third-grade sing is this Thursday, so I'll see you then. Do you want to maybe go out for pizza or something after?"

"That'd be nice." She watched Carl polish off the last of his water and smiled. "You're a good dad."

He tilted his head and narrowed his eyes.

"Sorry," Maggie said. "I'm sure I don't tell you that often enough, but I mean it."

"Thanks." He flashed a sincere smile without an ounce of cockiness in it, and then the grin faded. "Look, I may as well tell you before the kids do. Melissa and I called it quits last week."

Maggie was stunned. As far as she'd known, all had been well in paradise. She didn't know what to say — what was the appropriate response when one's ex-husband announced he'd just broken up with his girlfriend?

She settled on a simple, "I'm so sorry." And she meant it. She didn't like to see him so sad, and she worried about her children's reactions — would it be too much for them to handle after seeing their parents split? But she decided against laying that guilt on him at the moment. Eyeballing his empty water bottle, she said, "Perhaps I should have offered you something stronger, like I don't know... rubbing alcohol?"

Carl let out a dark chuckle. "I'll settle for a glass of wine. Thanks."

"Oh, okay." She'd only been joking, but okay. "Red or white?"

"Red."

She grabbed a bottle of trusty merlot and opened it. When she set a single glass on the counter, Carl said, "Please don't make me drink alone."

In addition to Carl sounding completely pathetic, Maggie noticed her arm shaking slightly and thought perhaps she could use a little nerve-soothing too. "Two glasses it is." She poured and handed one to Carl. As he took a long, slow sip, she decided her best approach to the situation was to *not* try to say the right thing. He'd see through her anyhow and might even appreciate a little honesty.

"I'm surprised," she said. "You two seemed pretty serious."

He shrugged. "Nah. I wasn't serious, anyway. She's a great girl and a lot of fun, but the fun doesn't last forever, as you well know.

When it stopped being fun, there just wasn't enough substance to make it worth the trouble. She's pretty broken up, but I thought it was better to end it now instead of stringing her along, you know?"

"Yeah, I suppose you're right."

Silence lingered in Maggie's small kitchen. She stared into her un-sipped half-glass of wine, feeling bad for Melissa and wondering about the kids. They hadn't seemed upset when they'd come into the house, but that didn't mean there wouldn't be repercussions. While she was still lost in her thoughts, Carl spoke. "You're the only girl I've ever been serious about."

Her eyes snapped up to him. He was looking straight at her wearing a small, sad smile. She recognized the expression — it was the same one he'd used so many times before the divorce to tell her he was sorry. She lifted her glass and took a gulp. Immediately after swallowing, she asked, "How'd the kids take the news?"

"They seem okay. Kirsten asked if she could still call Melissa sometimes and I told her she should wait a little bit, give Missy a bit of time, and then we'd talk about it again. I wanted to get your thoughts before saying anything definite."

"Waiting seems like the best course for now. I'll make sure to talk to Kirsten about it too."

"Thanks. Sorry to dump this on you."

"It's fine. Part of the Great Divorce Adventure, right?"

"I guess." He circled the counter to pick up the wine bottle and topped off each of their glasses. Nearly half an hour had passed, so Maggie called out for the kids to wash up for bed.

"How's work going?" Carl asked while they waited.

"Fine. A bit of a power struggle going on right now between Father Tom and the visiting monsignor."

"He's still around?"

"Yep. And apparently he'll be around for a while longer — he just announced last week that his stay's been extended indefinitely. Which seems odd because none of us are even sure exactly why he's here in the first place. How are things with you work-wise?"

"Same old bullshit. Remember when I couldn't wait to get to this side of management? What was I thinking?"

The kids raced down the stairs, with Kirsten's longer legs getting her to her father first. When it came time for his hug, Liam glowered at his sister all the way through it, but when he pulled back, his eyes scanned Carl's full wine glass. "Dad, are you sleeping over?"

Carl laughed. "No, slugger, just relaxing a little bit before I head home."

"Let's go," Maggie said, guiding the kids toward the stairs.

On the way up Kirsten pinched her brother's arm, and chastised in a poorly concealed whisper, "You're such an idiot." Maggie gave her daughter a warning look but didn't correct her.

After kissing both children good night at the top of the stairs, she returned to her guest. He'd moved to the couch, with both glasses and what remained of the bottle on the coffee table. Maggie walked over and tentatively sat at the other end of the sofa, reflexively picking up the remote. She was glad she and Carl had learned to function on friendly terms, but hanging out one-on-one like this felt odd.

"Am I keeping you from something?" Carl asked.

"No, not really. But I do have a bunch of shows recorded from last week that I haven't watched yet."

"Oh, like what?"

"Here, take a look." She went to her list of recordings and scrolled through.

"Nice selection. Hey! Where'd you find that?" He took the remote and highlighted the name of an old sitcom that had only run for a few seasons. It had been one of Carl and Maggie's favorites but had never done well in the ratings.

"On a fluke," Maggie answered. "I was flipping channels and found it replaying on some obscure cable station. Want to watch?"

Carl shrugged. "Sure." He clicked to start the show and settled into the sofa, laughing right away as he recognized the episode. Watching that show had been among the few good times the two of them had had together in those last years, and Maggie was now reminded that even though things had gotten pretty bad between them, there had always been a connection.

Instead of fast forwarding through the commercials, they started talking about old times. When the show returned, their conversation continued, stretching back to before Maggie and Carl had even been married. They drained the bottle, and Maggie felt completely relaxed with Carl for the first time in a very long while. By the time the episode ended, she was facing away from the television with her legs curled underneath her as she and Carl talked and laughed.

He flipped on the news, to which they paid no attention, and after a few more minutes of reminiscing, leaned his elbow onto the back of the couch and propped his head on his hand. "Do you know what I remember?" He gave her a sly smile and Maggie noted that the typical mischief had returned to his eyes.

"What?"

With his lips parted slightly, he imitated her moan. "*Eh, eh, oh.*" It was the sound she used to make when he stimulated just the right nerve. Maggie immediately flushed, but didn't look away. The rich blue of his irises smoldered as he took in her reaction, and her insides fluttered in response.

"Do you still make that noise?" he asked in a low, unmistakably interested voice.

Maggie raised her eyebrows. "Not that it's any of your business, but I haven't had the opportunity in a while."

"Really?" He seemed surprised, but not unpleasantly so. Lifting his hand, he ran his fingertips along Maggie's jawline, and she noticed for the first time how very, very good he still smelled. Tickling his way down to her chin, he asked, "Would you like to make that noise again?"

Maggie was taken off guard by the abrupt change in the tenor of their conversation. She'd thought they were just having fun, two friends catching up on old times. How had all of *this* suddenly surfaced? Instead of posing that question to Carl, she stared stupidly into his eyes, thinking about how very much she'd like to make that noise again…with him.

He took her hesitation as acquiescence and pressed his mouth to hers. Her arm flew around his neck, and his hands pressed into the small of her back, crushing her to him while she clutched fistfuls of the salt and pepper hair at the back of his head and pulled him closer. He felt so good. It felt right. She hadn't realized how much she'd missed him — the only boy she had ever been serious about.

Carl leaned on Maggie until her back pressed flat on the sofa cushions and he lay on top, his hips cradled between her thighs. She recognized the low growl that rumbled at the back of his throat, the urgency with which he was pressing into her — he didn't intend to stop at a kiss. Maggie pressed her hands aside his face and pulled his mouth from hers. "What if one of the kids comes down? We can't do this."

Gusts of hot breath blew from Carl's mouth onto her face. "You've got a lock on your bedroom door, right?"

His lips were only an inch away and she wanted them back on her. "Yep," she gasped back.

He rolled off her and stood, reaching for her hand. She threaded her fingers through his and let him lead her upstairs. Whenever a step creaked, he squeezed her hand and stopped, with Maggie leaning into him from behind, trying not to laugh. They finally made into her bedroom with the kids none the wiser. A thought of Evan flickered when Maggie glanced at his corner of the room. But she knew from her conversations with the angel that although he could "see" parts of her life, he wasn't a voyeur. He'd allow her privacy.

Carl locked the door and helped Maggie pull off her shirt. She returned the favor. She never thought she'd so much as see his naked torso again, yet there she was running her tongue over his lean abs and nipping at his hard chest. When their mouths met again, they were burning hot. Intertwined, they worked out of the rest of their clothing and made their way onto the bed.

When Carl pulled back to look at her, Maggie's hands went self-consciously to her stomach, which was puffier than last time Carl had seen it. He pushed her hand away and leaned down to take a sensuous bite, clearly not bothered by the modest weight gain. He stayed and played in the general vicinity, and Maggie reveled in his tenderness. Her mind traveled back to how wonderful he'd been to her and the kids during the last several months, how sorry he'd been when the marriage first fell apart, and how he'd said she was the only girl he'd ever been serious about.

He slid into her, and she was taken to a different universe, one Carl had taken her to many times before, but not in a very long time. Maggie moved with him, and they were in perfect sync. She reflected on how far they'd both come in the last two years. They were the new and improved Carl and Maggie. He smiled down at her. She was prepared to love him again, better than she ever had before. She was finally ready to truly forgive him.

Carl grasped her around the waist and flipped them so that he sat back on bended legs with Maggie straddling him. It was one of Maggie's favorite positions and one they hadn't ventured anywhere near in the few years before they'd split. The pleasure as he drove into her was intense, but she restrained her volume because of the kids. Besides, if she let herself go at full force, for all she knew her guardian angel would come crashing in there thinking someone was trying to murder her.

Maggie hung on for dear life and marveled at her husband's stamina and strength. He'd obviously increased his workout routine, and she hoped he'd keep it up after they were officially back together. They were going to have it all. Great sex. Great relationship. The separation had made them better for each other in every way.

"Eh, eh, oh." Maggie's whimpers combined into one never ending moan of ecstasy. Carl let loose a growl and gave his final thrusts.

After they'd both finished, he buried his face in her glistening breasts, kissing and suckling her salty flesh the same way he always used to. After he'd had his fill, he collapsed onto the bed, exhausted. *He should be*, Maggie thought to herself with a wry smile. She gave him a peck on his forehead and hopped off to the bathroom to clean up. She didn't want to think about the fact that they should've used protection. When she returned, she did something she'd rarely ever done before — she stayed completely naked and climbed in next to Carl. He held his arm out for her, and she snuggled into his side.

They continued breathing heavily, and didn't say much, just laughed a little at the unspoken joke that neither one of them could've predicted that this was how the evening would end. Maggie pelted Carl's neck with baby kisses and decided that they should probably hold off on telling the kids they were getting back together until everything was worked out. They could keep it as their own delicious secret for a while. She giggled to herself when she thought about how fun it was going to be sneaking around like love-starved teenagers.

Carl's hand traveled down her spine. "Baby, baby, I have missed this ass," he said as he grabbed a handful.

"I've missed this throat," Maggie said, "and this jaw, and these lips." She worked her way up to the modest bump in the ridge of his nose, then let her face hover for a moment before concluding, "And this tongue."

She kissed him deeply, trying to communicate so much through it — that she was ready to be a better wife, the wife she should have been in the first place, the best, most devoted wife any man had ever had. She pulled her mouth away and rubbed his nose with hers before lying down and nuzzling into his shoulder. For a few minutes the room was silent. Maggie wanted to tell him she loved him but waited for him to say it first.

Busying herself at his chest while his thumb tickled lines up and down her back, she walked her fingers through the thicket and spun it into tiny tornadoes. It seemed the hair that was disappearing from his hairline was congregating here.

The silence lingered.

She made her fingers like claws and scratched them through his chest hairs, mussing them all up, and then propped herself on one elbow, locking her eyes on his — she couldn't help but note that something within the vibrant blue of his irises looked vaguely petrified. "What are you thinking, Mr. Brock?"

He rolled onto his side and pressed her so she was on her back. "I'm thinking we just had mind-blowing sex."

He lowered his mouth and teased her traitorous nipple into a stiff peak. But she didn't want to be distracted. She wanted to talk about it. She wanted to hear him say that he was as eager as she was to try again. For the second time that night she lifted his head away from her. "I mean what are you thinking about us?"

After a long sigh, he said, "I don't know. Tonight was great. Wonderful. But I'm just not sure either one of us needs this kind of complication in our lives right now."

"So I'm a complication?" Maggie's heart dropped as she said it.

Carl chuckled and cradled her face. "Yes, Maggie Dawson Brock. You are a complication, always have been. It's one of the things I love most about you." He stared at her silently before adding, "I do love you, Maggie."

"To be quickly followed by the old 'But I'm not *in* love with you.'"

"No. I am in love with you." His eyes flicked over her face. "I can't imagine ever not being in love with you. It's just…I'm fresh out of a relationship and you, well, I know how independent you are, and the single life really seems to suit you. I probably haven't told you, but I'm extremely impressed with the way you've stood so firmly on your own feet these last two and a half years."

She forced herself to smile, filled with a need to not tarnish his glowing image of her as a capable, independent woman. "So then we're going to chalk tonight up as just sex?" She figured it would only take a good night's sleep to reset her mind to where it had been. She could be okay with just sex. She'd have to be.

"For now that sounds like a good idea."

As she watched the relief wash over his face, Maggie realized she'd been holding out hope for a different reaction. Something poked at her from inside, encouraging her to tell him how she really felt, to give him her vulnerability. But she couldn't. "So, since this is just sex, is it okay if I kick you out? I have an early day tomorrow." She had a sudden urge to get far away from his tender embrace.

Chapter 7

The angels sang slightly off key, but nobody seemed to mind. The occupants of the folding chairs set out in neat rows across the gym floor were more than forgiving—it was their children on stage in tinfoil halos and repurposed bed sheets after all. The chair Carl had saved for Maggie remained empty. She'd made sure Kirsten had found her father and then excused herself to help get the children into their costumes. After that she decided the view from the side of the stage was perfectly fine and stayed there for the rest of the performance. But she couldn't avoid her ex-husband after the show.

"Great job, Liam!" Carl praised as his son leaped into his arms for a bear hug.

"How do we know he did a great job?" Kirsten asked. "It's not like we could tell which screech was his."

"Kirsten," Maggie warned before turning to Carl. "I hate to say this, but my allergies have been acting up, and I feel a headache coming on."

"Probably all the screeching," Kirsten contributed unhelpfully.

Maggie shot her daughter a hard look and continued. "I think I'd better skip the pizza. And Kirsten, darling, if you can't be nicer to your brother—who did an *amazing* job tonight—you can skip it too."

"Aw, Mom." Liam pouted, triggering Maggie's maternal guilt. This night was supposed to be about her little boy, not her inability to deal with her adult issues.

"I've got ibuprofen in my car, if you think that'll help," Carl offered.

After a glance at Liam's hopeful face, Maggie agreed, and the four of them headed out to Carl's car where she swallowed the tablets dry. Since the school was on Carl's way home from the restaurant, he suggested they all drive together and then he'd drop Maggie and the kids at her car afterward.

"Yeah!" Liam shouted loudly enough to provide Maggie with a good excuse to wince at the suggestion.

"How about the three of you drive together," she said, "and I'll listen to some soothing Vivaldi *alone* in my car so that I'm feeling better by the time I get there?"

"Sounds good to me," Carl said and the kids jumped into his car.

Emilio's was fairly crowded, but Carl had made a reservation so they were shown to a booth right away, with Maggie manipulating the seating so that she sat diagonal from her ex-husband rather than straight across. He played tic-tac-toe on the back of a paper placemat with Liam while Kirsten delivered a point-by-point pitch on the virtues of getting her ears double pierced as an eighth grade graduation gift.

To anyone who didn't know better, the Brocks appeared to be a typical, happy family. The pizza came and they laughed and ate too much, and all the while a scenario played at the back of Maggie's mind — the four of them going home together, her tucking the kids into bed and then falling asleep next to Carl, listening to him snore and knowing he'd be there the next morning and every morning after that. She envisioned the reunited family packing up the car and taking the trip out West that they'd been planning right before everything had fallen apart. She'd been so focused on proving to herself that she didn't need Carl, she hadn't considered until now whether or not she wanted him — and after the other night, she couldn't deny that she did.

She finally understood that it wasn't conviction that had kept her from working on her marriage. It was fear. Even the other night when she'd lain naked in his arms, she hadn't been able to tell him how she felt. She'd only gone so far as to press *him* to open up. And when he hadn't given her the answer she'd wanted, her first instinct had been self-preservation; she didn't dare expose her heart the way she'd exposed her body. As she watched Carl across the booth, laughing with the kids and stealing glances at her, she wondered if he might reconsider "just sex" if she told him everything. But opening up to Carl would mean taking a big risk, and Maggie wasn't sure she could do it.

"You know, your mother had a nose ring when we first met." Carl looked sideways at Maggie and winked. Liam scrunched his face skeptically and Kirsten rolled her eyes. "She did! But I told her it was either the nose ring or me."

Now Maggie rolled her eyes.

"Well, maybe she should've kept the nose ring." Kirsten laughed. "You know, 'cause of how things turned out." She took a large bite of pizza, and glanced at her parents. Her smile faded upon seeing their fallen expressions.

Maggie and Carl hadn't told their children the whole story behind the breakup, just that they'd been struggling to get along for a while, that it had nothing to do with the children, and that they thought everyone would be happier if they separated—although Maggie knew it had taken a long time before Kirsten and Liam had seen either one of their parents happy again.

"Sorry," Kirsten mumbled through her food.

Maggie forced a smile back on her face. "Nah, if I'd have kept the nose ring, we wouldn't have had you two and that would've been a terrible shame."

"Wait a minute," Liam said. "Did you really have a nose ring?"

Carl and Maggie both laughed. "No, sweetie," Maggie answered. Perhaps, she thought, if not for her own sake, for the kids she could muster her courage and bare her soul to Carl.

When they left Emilio's, Carl held the door for his family, allowing Liam and Kirsten to race out first. As Maggie stepped past him, his hand found her waist, causing her to pause. "That was fun," he said.

"Yeah." She looked up at him and paused in the doorway. He was so close, and his almost possessive touch at her waist felt too natural, too good. She decided their talk better be long distance or she might end up in the same position she'd landed in the other night.

"Will you be up for a while?" she asked.

He raised a flirtatious eyebrow. "What did you have in mind?"

"A phone call," she said firmly, hoping to put any naughty thoughts out of his head.

"That works too." His smile was dirty, and Maggie shoved him lightly in the chest before joining the kids at her car.

"So what's on your mind?" Carl asked after the kids were in bed and Maggie had called him.

"I think you probably know."

"Yeah, probably." He sounded less than enthusiastic, but Maggie forced herself to stop analyzing his every intonation and pressed forward.

"I want to continue the conversation we started the other night. About us. I understand everything you were saying, and I agree with it, but…" She hesitated.

When the silence had gone on too long, Carl asked, "But what?"

She clamped her eyes shut. "But I want to try again. I'm ready for it. I want it."

Dead silence screamed between their phones.

"I know it's taken me far too long to get here," she rushed on, "but I'm here now and we love each other, so…" She again paused, needing him to pick up what she'd just dropped.

"You know I wanted it to work. I fought for us, Maggie."

She didn't miss the past tense, nor did she respond.

"Look," he eventually continued, "I just…I think you were right to be so stubborn. I never made you happy."

"That's not true! You did make me happy. You *do* make me happy. Even now. I know things have been strange, but Sunday night…it all felt so natural. Didn't you think so? We came together without effort. You made me happy."

"Until the end, when I apparently said the wrong thing. Why didn't you tell me how you were feeling then?"

Maggie shrugged in answer even though he couldn't see it and stayed silent. She didn't want to risk her voice cracking and showing her weakness.

"It's always been like this," Carl said. "We get along for a while, then I do the wrong thing and mess it all up. I can't read your mind, and I can't keep up with what you expect from me. I fail every time. It gets demoralizing after a while."

Tears broke loose and relieved the pressure that had been building in Maggie's throat. She was able to speak again. "Then why did you fight for us? Why didn't you run for the hills at your first opportunity?"

"Because I love you. And I thought we could work things out, and maybe we could've at the time. But since we've gone our separate ways, I guess I just see that we're better apart. And think about the kids. What if we got back together but it didn't work out? How hard do you think it would be on them to have to go through it all again?"

"Did Melissa demoralize you?" She hadn't registered half of what he'd just said, and her voice had taken on a hardness.

Carl exhaled roughly into the phone. "Melissa and I had a different kind of relationship. Not that I feel obligated to share this with you, but if anything, she was too accommodating, never seemed to get irritated with me enough." He let out a bitter grunt. "Guess I was so conditioned to think of myself as a failure, that when she didn't berate me, I thought there must be something wrong with her."

"Unbelievable." Maggie enunciated each syllable separately, her anger building.

"There it is," he said, baiting her.

"You know what? Thank you, Carl. *Thank you* for reminding me of all the reasons we didn't work. You're absolutely right—we're so much better apart. Because you never ever did anything wrong. Ever. It was just mean old Maggie telling you things were wrong. I just made it up in my crazy, little mind, but really, you were perfect in every way. I should've been more like wittle Missy Wissy, apparently. But wait—you ended up breaking her heart and running straight to your ex-wife's bed, didn't you? So I guess it doesn't matter. No matter how a girl acts, Carl Brock will screw her over!"

"Gee, glad we had this chat," he said flatly.

"Me too, actually." She took a deep breath and reclaimed her sanity. "It really has given me clarity. I'm sorry I was such a bitch throughout our entire marriage."

"You weren't—"

"Save it. It's okay. I know; I'm being dramatic. Just...you do get that this means we won't be sleeping with each other again, right?"

"Clear as crystal."

She rubbed her temple and closed her eyes, feeling a headache coming on for real this time. "Now that we've gotten that straightened out, can we please, please, please move forward as if this conversation never took place?"

"Sure thing." Most of the stiffness had melted from his voice, and Maggie heard that twinge of concern she so hated. She could tell he was about to ask if she was okay.

"My head's starting to throb, so I'd better go. Thanks for dinner tonight. Talk to you next week." She hung up before he had a chance to respond.

She wanted to rewind and go back to Sunday night. After he'd finished his first glass of wine, she should've sent him on his merry way. Or even tonight, she could've happily gone on the rest of her life telling herself Carl would've come around had she just been honest with him. But then she had to go and prove that theory wrong.

She needed a temporary escape, so as soon as she got upstairs, she turned on the shower. Shedding her clothes, she stepped in and let the warm water run over her. How could she have been so stupid? Why had she let herself want him again? At the back of her mind she'd always assumed she could reel Carl back in if she ever chose to. It gave her a sense of peace to think so. Stability. Control. But she'd given him enough time to realize he didn't want her. Her tears burned hotter than what was coming from the pipes, and she let them flow. It was the first time she fully acknowledged the finality of her loss.

Her tears eventually subsided, and only the tepid, saltless stream of the shower ran down her face. It was time for Maggie to get out and move on. She brushed her hair straight back, lotioned, and pulled on her fuzzy robe. Stepping out of the bathroom, the first place her eyes fell was the bed. The scene of the debacle. She couldn't make herself go there. She went instead to the chaise in the corner of the room, kicking up her legs and leaning back to stare at the quarter moon outside her window. An owl hooted. Maggie found his mournful call into the lonely night comforting — she had a comrade in her misery.

The silver glow of the moon was mimicked just to the side of Maggie. She recognized the shimmer and turned toward Evan. "Hey." She gave him a small nod and then turned back to the window. When the angel had come by earlier that week, she hadn't even brought up the incident with Carl, preferring at the time to ignore it.

"What's wrong?" he asked.

"I thought you were supposed to keep me from getting hurt." She only meant it as a joke, but there was bitterness in her tone.

"I didn't detect any danger."

"Not tonight. Sunday."

"Sunday? You seemed to be rather pleased with the situation. Did he hurt you?" Quiet anger resounded deep in his voice, grabbing Maggie's attention.

She peered at him, noting a subtle tension in his balled fists and the flickering shards in his gray eyes. For the first time, she sensed the great power residing beneath his peaceful demeanor. "No, he didn't hurt me. Not the way you mean."

The flash retreated from his eyes, but he continued studying Maggie's face, and she felt the bite of tears again. He lowered himself to the chaise, sitting beside her hip. "In what way did he hurt you?"

After releasing a sigh to loosen her tightening throat, Maggie answered in a husky whisper, "My heart. He hurt my heart."

She pressed back harder into the chaise and bit at her lip, trying to stem the fresh tears, but it didn't work. Bringing her hand to her chest, she held it there, as if clenching at her robe would somehow take the pain away. She didn't understand where these tears were coming from. She'd already let herself cry in the shower and should be dry by now. But her body wouldn't be controlled by her mind. Her release escalated into small gasps. She'd worked so hard to get her life traveling along a nice, straight path again. Then Carl showed up, said a few pretty words, and she lost control. She lost control of everything. She didn't know how to stop crying.

Evan's warm, watery-feeling hand wrapped around hers and pulled it from her chest, leaning his head there instead. Since they weren't flesh to flesh, he didn't sink into her, but the side of his face had a penetrating warmth to it, and as he lay there, still, his sweet, soothing vibe filtered into her chest. She brought her hand up to clutch his hair and held him close, her crying softening more and more until she was hardly weeping at all. She fell asleep caressing her angel's silky hair while he silently rested his beautiful head on her chest and did his very best to heal her heart.

Chapter 8

Over the next two weeks, Maggie attempted to recalibrate her mind to where it had been before her escapade with Carl. Talking with Evan helped, but when the angel wasn't present, it seemed she no longer clung to his influence very well. She considered pursuing the annulment, thinking that might help improve her emotional state, but gave up on the idea. Her marriage had happened. They'd both gone into it foolishly thinking it would last forever, and she wouldn't negate that, couldn't erase her mistakes with a piece of paper.

The end of the school year was busy for Maggie and the kids, with projects and tests and a hundred and one social activities surrounding eighth grade graduation. In between all of that, Maggie made several phone calls to her parents in Colorado. Her father had had knee surgery the day after Liam's school sing, and she could tell it comforted her mother to be able to give daily reports on the progress of his recovery. The distractions kept Maggie from dwelling too much on her melancholy state, yet when Sharon called about getting together for lunch one more time before school was out, Maggie made up an excuse and declined, not feeling ready to sit under her friend's microscope just yet.

A visit from her less invasive sister was exactly what she needed, so it was a blessing that Nancy had already planned to drive up from St. Louis to attend Kirsten's graduation. She arrived on Friday night, and on Saturday morning, Maggie's parents got adventurous on the computer and had a video chat with their granddaughter, apologizing profusely for having to miss the big day. Immediately after the call, Nancy and Kirsten disappeared into the bathroom where Nancy pulled her niece's hair up into a twist and helped her put on a light layer of makeup.

"Is this my baby girl?" Maggie exclaimed when her daughter stepped into the kitchen.

"Hey, hey, don't tear up—you'll mess up *your* makeup!" Nancy scolded.

It was difficult for Maggie not to smear her eyeliner just a little bit in the church parking lot when she saw all the graduates looking suddenly more grown up, the girls in their high heels and strapless dresses, and the boys in their button-down shirts and ties, slapping each other high five as they made their way into church for the Mass.

"There's Dad...and Missy!" Kirsten squealed and dashed across the bumpy asphalt as fast as she could in her dress shoes.

"Who's Missy?" Nancy asked.

"Carl's girlfriend." Were they back together, or had he merely invited her to the graduation for Kirsten's sake, Maggie wondered. She threw on her sunglasses to cover the only betrayal of her reaction—the tortured glint deep in her irises—and walked her sister over. Carl gave Nancy a warm, if somewhat awkward, hug and introduced Melissa. While they made polite small talk, Carl briefly locked eyes with Maggie, quirking his eyebrows in a way that told her he'd explain later.

The ceremony, led by Monsignor Sarto, gave Maggie time to quiet her tumultuous thoughts and ask for the grace she needed to get through the rest of the day without having a meltdown. She knew everything was over between her and Carl, so logically it shouldn't matter if he was back together with Melissa. But that didn't stop her from hoping there was some other explanation. All the insecurities she'd felt after he'd cheated swarmed around her, poking to get in.

After the formalities, the families were invited to a nearby golf club where one of the parents had generously reserved a banquet room. The bright space filled with a happy buzz and loud chatter as the graduates and their families arrived, and Maggie had a genuinely good time introducing her sister around while keeping an eye out for Liam, who'd found a posse to run around with. A highlight of the party was when Father Dominic stopped by to make a toast. This was the first graduating class since he'd come to the parish, and being youthful himself, he'd naturally been a favorite among the students.

While Nancy was engaged in a conversation about a reality show Maggie didn't watch, Carl came over — without Melissa. "Can I talk to you for a moment?" he asked.

"Yeah, sure. Nance, I'll be right back."

She followed Carl to the outside deck that surrounded the large room on three sides, overlooking the golf course. Placing his hand at the small of her back, he guided her to an unoccupied corner. "Missy and I are going to take off soon, but I couldn't leave without apologizing. This isn't how I would've liked for you to find out."

Maggie held her breath in an attempt to absorb the sting of knowing for certain that sleeping with her had driven Carl straight back to another woman.

"It only just happened," he continued, "so I didn't have time to warn you, but I couldn't exactly tell her not to come to the graduation."

"She doesn't know, then?"

"About us? No."

Maggie nodded slowly. "Okay. Well, I appreciate you realizing this might come as a bit of a surprise to me, but there's really nothing more to say about it, so…I'm going to go in before anything starts to look wonky." She kept nodding, and Carl watched her, nodding back as if it was infectious. Not knowing what else to do, Maggie gave him an absent-minded pat on the cheek before walking away. They were only emotions. All she had to do was keep them in check for a while.

Nancy was six years older than Maggie, just enough separation to put the sisters perpetually into different stages of life. The differences were magnified when Nancy married her high school sweetheart at the age of twenty and then got pregnant with her first child almost immediately after the wedding. The sisters found they had more in common when Maggie also became a mother, but by then Carl's job had moved his family away from Missouri, and the geographic distance plus the business of life kept the sisters from being as close as Maggie sometimes would've liked. Having her sister in town for the weekend was a treat, and Maggie wasn't going to spoil it by whining.

After dropping Kirsten off at a pool party on Sunday afternoon, Nancy suggested going to Somme Park, where her younger sister had taken her on previous visits.

Liam groaned in the back seat. "Is that the place with all the flowers?"

"Yep," Maggie answered. "And the place with a lemon ice cart right before the trails. I'll bet Aunt Cici will buy you one if you ask real nice."

"Will you, Aunt Cici?"

"Sure, pumpkin."

Within minutes of arriving, Liam took off between the rows of elms that led from the parking lot to the ice cart while the women lagged behind, strolling at a leisurely pace. A new set of blooms had emerged since Maggie had last been to the park. Her plan was to stay clear of the Greek *tholos* because of the "pocket of malice" or whatever Evan had called it. He said such pockets often occurred in random places, but she wasn't sure whether they clung to the same areas or moved around. She'd have to ask him.

"It was weird seeing Carl with another woman yesterday," Nancy said.

Maggie shrugged. "You get used to it."

"How long have they been dating?"

"Since the fall."

"What do the kids think?" Nancy asked, nodding toward Liam.

"They like her." Maggie noted the slight downturn at the corners of her sister's mouth, accentuated by thin lines that Maggie hadn't noticed last time she'd seen her. "Really, Nance, everything's hunky dory in Splitsville. You can see the kids are adjusted and so am I, so can we talk about something else? Like…you're going to have a *college* graduate this time next year. How does that feel?"

Nancy gave a slight groan. "It'll be nice to write out one less tuition check, but having him back home full time again…I don't know."

The conversation moved on as they caught up to Liam and bought their lemon ices. They proceeded to the formal garden with its geometric hedges bordering jewel-colored beds of early-blooming annuals, and then the Japanese gardens, where Liam seemed to forget his boredom when he discovered live koi flitting in the small pond. Maggie and her sister sauntered onto the arched bridge and watched him.

"It's been great having you here," Maggie said.

"It's been great being here." Nancy turned her back to the railing, leaning on both elbows as she took Maggie in with a long gaze. "You sure everything's okay in Splitsville?"

Maggie looked at her sideways. "Does it not seem okay?"

"Mmm, no, it seems fine. You just…in quiet moments you seem a little sad. And I could see that Carl inviting his girlfriend to the graduation shook you up more than you wanted to admit."

Maggie sighed. While her sister wasn't invasive, she was sometimes inconveniently discerning. "The truth is, Carl and Melissa broke up a few weeks ago, and he hadn't told me they'd gotten back together — not that he has to report to me. I was just caught off guard, that's all."

"That's all? Really?"

Maggie stayed silent and stared hard at the water.

"Look, you don't need to talk about it," Nancy said. "But just because I'm leaving tomorrow morning doesn't mean you can't change your mind and give me a call."

"Thanks." For a second Maggie considered confiding completely, but Liam was starting to pluck flower heads and toss them into the water. "Liam!"

They whisked him out of the Japanese garden and decided his attention span for the day was exhausted so they stuck to the main gravel path. As they rounded the pool and the pillared *tholos* came into view across the vast lawn, Maggie was surprised to see a small group of people gathered near it. "Wonder what's going on there."

A spray of pebbles pelted the grass, and Nancy tugged Maggie's arm, alerting her that the rock shower had originated from her son.

"Liam!"

Maggie would be forever grateful her sister had been in town that particular weekend. She had no idea how she would've reacted to Carl and Melissa getting back together if she hadn't been trying so very hard to pretend everything was okay. And with the passage of a few days, everything felt like it actually was okay. Nancy left for home late Monday morning, and on Tuesday evening, Maggie drove the kids to their father's.

Just as she was about to make a clean getaway, Carl followed her into the hallway outside his condo's front door. "I've got to ask you something," he said. "Do you have any particular plans with the kids this summer?"

"They've got some sports camps and vacation Bible school in July. And then in August we're going to see my parents—I gave you the dates for all that."

"So nothing next month?"

Maggie shook her head slowly back and forth.

"Great. Melissa's got an opportunity to borrow a colleague's camper for a couple weeks, but it has to be in June. We were thinking about trekking out West—Yellowstone. Maybe Utah too if we're up for it. So would that be okay? Last part of June? Two weeks?"

"Well…just like that? Have you been planning this?" She always gave Carl plenty of notice where the kids were concerned and didn't like being blindsided. And she was suddenly suspicious about whether he'd ever even broken up with Melissa.

"What? No, no plans. The guy just offered it up and we thought it would be a lot of fun. The kids know nothing about it, so if you want to say no, it's not a problem. I wanted to check with you first."

"You never used to be able to just walk away from work for so long."

"I never used to be so tech savvy—I'll stay in touch with the office. Plus I've got a lot of vacation days to use up before the end of the fiscal year."

"I suppose the timing's fine. But will you be able to get campsite reservations this late?"

"Wyoming and Utah are pretty big states. I'm sure we'll find something." He looked like he wanted to wink, but refrained.

Maggie scrunched her face into a tight scowl. "Do you mind waiting to tell the kids until after you've got the reservations?"

He groaned. "Fine. I guess that makes sense. I can hold off until the weekend. Actually, that'll be even better—Melissa will be here to share the news."

"Fabulous." Maggie couldn't keep the sarcasm out of her tone.

Carl frowned and reached out to grasp her elbow, which she promptly yanked away from his touch. She stepped around him to the door and pushed it open.

"Okay, babies, kisses. I gotta go."

Back at home, Maggie plopped her purse onto the kitchen counter. She intended to find something to eat, but alone and with no one to pretend for, she instead spread her hands flat on the counter and slumped her shoulders. Yellowstone had been an intended stop on the aborted family trip out West. Now her children were going to have that amazing experience with a substitute mommy. They were going to make memories with a stranger. Memories that Maggie would never be a part of.

The pain sliced through all the shoddy fortifications she'd been throwing up during the last few weeks. Inhaling deeply, she slammed her fist into the solid surface, gritting her teeth as tiny blood vessels burst in the heel of her hand. Preferring physical agony to emotional, she slammed her fist again. She wanted to hurt herself, wanted something to take the ache away from her heart. Before she could strike again, another hand covered hers, sending warm, watery sensations of comfort.

"Evan," she whispered. "What are you doing down here? Oh, never mind—you can go wherever you want."

"Wherever *he* wants."

She nodded and stared at her throbbing hand under his. "I'm sorry. I know I'm not handling anything with much grace these days. It's just…every time I think I've pulled myself up, something slams me back down. So why bother feeling better? It only seems to invite some kind of new misery." She flicked her eyes to him and a tear glided down her cheek.

He lifted his hand from hers and seemed to absorb the wet trail into his fingertip. "It's part of being human."

"Yeah, well, I'm tired of being human." She pushed herself away from the counter. "I'm tired of everything. I think I'm going to skip dinner tonight and just go to bed. Thanks for stopping by, but I suggest you find someone a little less morose to haunt."

As she turned, a flash of orange caught her eye and she looked toward the opposite counter to see a vase of fresh flowers that she hadn't put there. Her gaze slid back to Evan. "From you?"

He nodded. "I don't like to see you sad, Maggie."

She glanced back at the flowers. "They're lovely. Too bad they'll be dead in a few days." She brushed past Evan to go upstairs and collapse into bed.

Maggie passed the next morning in doldrums. At ten o'clock she called home from work to make sure the kids had gotten home safely and would be okay for the next few hours. By the time she returned to the townhouse, there was a message from Sharon asking if Maggie was available for a quick coffee one morning. She deleted the message and allowed the memory of it to fall by the wayside.

By the end of the week, her mood wasn't so much low as *gone*. She was numb. For the first time, she didn't mind that it was Carl's weekend with the kids. It was perfect, actually—she wouldn't have to force a passable mood on herself. She could stay in bed all weekend if she liked. Or drink endless bottles of wine in front of the TV. Or indulge in some combination of the two.

She didn't wake until late Saturday morning when slices of bright light cut through the slats of her wooden blinds. Pushing herself up, she threw her hair into a sloppy ponytail and did some half-hearted cleaning in between sips of coffee. By mid-afternoon, she was considering a nap. Yawning, she glanced toward the flowers Evan had brought her. The tiger lilies were already limp and paling. As she pulled them out of the vase, spotted petals drifted down to the counter. "Told you," she murmured.

After scooping them up and dropping them into the garbage disposal, she flipped the switch and lethargically watched the water swirl into the dark hole, the drone of the disposal's gears drowning out all other sound. It wasn't until after she'd turned off the switch and shut down the faucet that she felt him standing behind her. She hadn't seen him since he'd brought the flowers.

"Is the kitchen going to be our new spot, then?" she asked flatly without even turning around. Now she knew something was seriously wrong. Behind her stood an angel sent from Heaven, and all she felt was irritation.

"I had another place in mind."

"The bedroom? Perfect. That's just where I was headed." She wiped down the sink and turned, intending to avoid eye contact and scooch past him to seek the precious sanctuary of sleep, but he put himself directly in front of her.

"Not the bedroom."

She looked up into his kind, earnest face and a bit of the irritation faded. "Where then?"

"You'll have to drive there."

"Out? No. Not gonna happen. I haven't showered and I'm tired and…"

While she listed her excuses, his eyes scanned her and opened a little wider when he got to her unkempt hair. "You can put one of those — " His hand gestured in a circular motion over his head.

"Halos?" Maggie cut in.

His full mouth pulled up at one corner. "*Hat* was what I was going for."

"Ah, that'll be easier to manage. Even still, I don't want to go out."

"Please, Maggie. It's a beautiful day and the fresh air will help you sleep better when you get back."

She sighed. "Would you be coming with me?"

"I'll meet you there."

Curiosity overtook her annoyance. "Really? Will I be able to see you?"

"I don't know."

"Well, if I can, how will that work with other people around? Can they see you too?"

"You know that I don't know. Besides, that won't be a factor today. I don't expect others to be around."

Her eyes narrowed, and she studied his elegant, unflinching features before walking to the mudroom and grabbing a baseball hat from one of the coat hooks. "All right, let's do this."

He directed her to a country road she was familiar with and told her to head west until she saw a sign from him. He didn't explain what the sign would be, just that she'd know it when she saw it. As she drove further and further from civilization and the neatly rowed farm crops on either side of the road gave way to wilder land, an albino deer sprang into the middle of the road. Maggie pressed hard on her breaks, halting a few yards from the animal. She'd never seen a purely white deer before. It stared at her for a moment through its blood-shot eyes and then dashed into the trees to the right.

"I take it that's my cue," she said aloud as she pulled over and parked. Stepping around her vehicle, she noticed a path into the woods and took it.

Clusters of trees opened to patches of tall grass mixed with willowy, flowering plants, a blend of prairie and forest. She followed the path through the alternating sun and shade until it forked. One direction led to an open area, while the other curved into a thick stand of trees. As she debated which way to go, a snowy-white rabbit leaped out from the grass and took off down the path toward the trees. Maggie smiled and took a step in the rabbit's direction. Being completely removed from her normal life felt wonderful.

The trees stayed densely packed once she crossed their threshold, and the path inclined. After walking steadily uphill for a few minutes, she began to think she may have missed a clue and peered into the trees, searching for any sign of the rabbit. But the next white creature to greet her wasn't on four legs: Evan stood several yards ahead of her at the point where the path leveled off.

"Ready for this?" he asked, his radiant face tilted down toward her. Something in his expression reminded her of Liam whenever he brought home a Mother's Day craft from school that he was especially proud of.

She didn't answer, but continued ascending, and was nearly to Evan before catching a glimpse of what he wanted to show her.

Beyond where he stood, the path veered to the left and outlined the rim of a small canyon. The wide depression's sudden appearance in the serene setting was dramatic, but what made Maggie gasp were the brilliant blues and yellows that painted the canyon's floor. Hundreds and thousands of tiny flowers joined together to create a canvas more stunning than anything she'd ever seen before. Sunlight shot through the huge opening in the trees, illuminating the petals and holding them in stark contrast to the shaded forest in which Maggie and Evan stood. She turned toward her companion to find his eyebrows raised in expectation.

"Do you prefer these to the flowers I brought you last time?" he asked.

Maggie didn't even try to fight her grin, but that didn't stop her words from being obstinate. "These'll last longer, but they're still going to shrivel and die away come autumn."

"They'll retreat for a while, seek solace in the dirt, but the following spring they'll come back—stronger."

Maggie didn't respond. Instead she returned her gaze to the field of flowers at the base of the rocky walls and sank down to her knees as if to get closer to them. She twisted her baseball hat around on her head so the brim wouldn't obscure any part of her view.

Evan kneeled next to her. "These plants have seen many harsh storms and survived brutal winters. They're on their own down there. No gardener to tend them, to cover them during a frost or water them during a drought. Yet everything they need, they receive."

Maggie continued staring at the bottom of the hollow, now thinking of its occupants as tiny soldiers, on their own. But they weren't on their own. She understood that the Lord was their gardener. The moment after this thought entered her mind, she heard Evan's voice close to her ear. "These are only plants, Maggie. You are stronger. And he loves you much more. He'll take care of you."

She nodded as tears blurred her eyes. "I know he will. But I'm not strong. My problems are stupid and small, yet look how I let them crush me. He's pulled me up every time before this, but I…I don't know why he bothers. And maybe this time he shouldn't."

"He will continue to offer his hand, but you don't have to take it."

Surprised at this response, Maggie turned to face the angel. She hadn't accounted for his closeness, and the tip of her nose brushed against his. Before she could pull back, he cupped the side of her face, wrapping his fingers around to the back of her neck, holding her to him. His essence permeated her cells, but rather than the customary waves of tranquility, it was more like a rush of adrenaline. She lifted her slightly panicked eyes to his, but rather than look at her, he swiftly lifted his head and planted his warm, soft lips onto her forehead, pressing them there until his surge of energy calmed to something more familiar.

When he finally pulled his mouth away, he whispered, "I hope you'll take it."

He stood and disappeared, leaving Maggie kneeling on the forest floor at the edge of the canyon, wondering what had just happened. She turned her mind to God and said a prayer, during which she felt herself grab onto his outstretched hand with both of hers.

Chapter 9

"You miss all the good stuff on your afternoons off," Brenda said before Maggie had even sat down at her desk the following Tuesday morning.

The office manager often made little digs like this during the summer months when Maggie only worked half days.

"There's apparently been a visitation over at Somme Park."

"Visitation?"

"Yep. I got a call from a director of the foundation yesterday afternoon about some strange vines growing up a pillar on one of those structure things. Supposedly they twist to form words, but not English ones. Latin, of all things. *Peccatoribus* up one pillar, *fructus ventris* up another, and *mater* on another."

Maggie's arms prickled. She wondered if this could be happening at her particular *tholos*. "I know *mater* is mother, but what are the others?"

"*Peccatoribus* means 'sinners'; *fructus ventris* is 'fruit of the womb.' So people are freaking out, thinking this could be a visitation by the Virgin Mary."

"What else are they saying?" Maggie slowly lowered into her chair. "I mean, is it just the vines, or have people noticed anything else?"

"Of course." Brenda rolled her eyes. "A bunch of whackos are claiming to have felt, uhm...'sensations' was what I think she called it over the phone. It's apparently causing a bit of a disturbance, people showing up with candles and small religious items, so the foundation's board wanted Father Reardon to have a look around and give an official statement that it's all just coincidence. They're hoping that'll help things return to normal."

"Why don't they just cut back the vines?"

"I asked the same thing. Apparently their horticulturists threw a fit. They wouldn't cut them back all the way, only agreed to trim and reroute them. But get this — by the time the gardens reopened the next day, they'd reformed the same words! So who knows, maybe there's something to it."

Brenda shrugged as if she knew very damn well there was nothing to it, so Maggie didn't feel inclined to inform her of her personal experience at the park. Evan had told her it was an evil force — no, Evan had *surmised* it was an evil force. He didn't know why he'd been drawn to Somme Park that day any better than Maggie did. By Maggie's estimation, it was entirely possible that the Blessed Mother's vibes could've been what had pulled him into tangibility. Perhaps he wouldn't recognize that level of divine summons here on Earth. She hoped for a chance to ask him about it soon but was never sure when he'd visit again and hadn't seen him since the day at the canyon.

"So what happened? Did Father go?" Maggie asked.

Brenda glanced at the clock. "He's probably on his way there right now."

"Oh." She wouldn't know any more until he returned, so in the meantime, she'd focus on her work. Looking around her desk, she said, "He was going to put together some materials for me to type up for his presentation in two days, but I don't see anything here. Did he leave them with you?"

"Nope."

"Shoot. Well, I'll see if I can find anything in his office." When she went to his closed office door, it wouldn't budge. "Since when does he lock his door?"

"Since Monsignor Sarto started digging into all his business. Speaking of whom, looks like we're going to get a little break — check your e-mail. In the wee hours he sent a memo saying he'll be spending a good deal of time visiting parishes at the far boundaries of the diocese for the next few weeks and will only be checking in here sporadically."

"I'm surprised he didn't want to stick around long enough to look into the Somme thing."

"We sort of forgot to tell him about that. Father Tom's request. But I don't see how he could help anyhow—Monsignor's more interested in evil spirits than good ones."

"What do you mean?"

"I probably shouldn't say…do you promise it won't leave this office?"

"Brenda…" The women had shared countless off-the-record church tidbits, and Maggie wasn't in the mood to play coy.

"He's got training in exorcism."

"Really? Has he ever actually performed any?"

"I assume so, but I don't really know. Doesn't seem to like to talk about it. I only know because some of his paperwork mistakenly landed on my desk one day. Maybe it's only a hobby."

Maggie chuckled. "Yeah, given his personality, I'd say exorcism makes perfect sense as a favored pastime."

Father Tom didn't appear by the time Maggie went home, but the next morning he bustled into the office carrying a stack of books. He set them on the edge of the desk while he fished around in his pocket and pulled out a key to open his office door. "I'm sorry to have procrastinated so much on this, Maggie. But I've finally gotten inspiration for the archaeology presentation. Now I've just got to comb through these and get some notes together. How long are you in today?"

"I could stay until one."

"Oh dear." He maneuvered so he could see the face of his watch.

"Why don't you give me whatever you have ready by then, and I'll type it up at home," Maggie suggested. "Then I can finish up anything remaining in the morning."

"That would be wonderful, thank you. I'll get busy."

He stepped into his office, but Brenda stopped him with a shout. "Hey! You don't think you're going to bury your head in those books before giving us a full account of what went on at Somme, do you?"

He paused, seeming to think over his words before saying, "Nothing conclusive. I wasn't the only priest or minister called in. There were a dozen or so, all with different thoughts on what might be going on."

"Well, what do you think it was?" Brenda asked, and Maggie held her breath.

"It's not…I don't…it's probably nothing. A freak of nature. Nevertheless, we've all agreed to keep a close eye on the situation, just in case. For now the garden staff will downplay the spectacle—essentially ignore it and see if it goes away."

Maggie was relieved by his nonchalance. Surely if a priest wasn't overly concerned about it, she needn't be either. He took a step into his office, but then turned back to the women. "Before you get any ideas, I'd rather the two of you stayed away from the park for now. It's just some vines, after all. And more people showing up, particularly church staff, will only give more credence to a fluke. It's best not to get people riled up over nothing." His eyes flicked between the two women before he retreated into his office and shut the door.

"It's kind of nice the gardens don't want to use the visitation thing to lure more visitors," Maggie said.

"Not how they roll, I guess," Brenda answered absently as she returned to her work.

Maggie went home with several pages of Father Tom's handwritten notes. She was happy when Liam's friend Tommy called to ask him to the pool for the afternoon—this way she could work without interruption since Kirsten also had plans to spend the afternoon with her friends.

Deciphering the priest's handwriting was no problem, but sometimes his mind and his hand worked at two completely different speeds and his notes often ended up with arrows, asterisks, and circled text that took some figuring out. He'd bookmarked a picture of a small stone with rudimentary figures of a man and woman carved into the face that Maggie surmised he wanted included on the last page of the handouts.

She typed an outline of various archeological discoveries—capitols, palaces, and stone tablets in places such as Bogazkoy, Turkey, and Iraq—that backed up the existence of kings and societies described in Scripture. She filled another page with a list of credible tombs of biblical figures in locations that could be visited today.

Going through all the physical support—not something often explored when talking of faith and spirituality—had piqued her interest more than she'd expected, so later that evening she found herself exploring more online. Separating wheat from chaff was a bit tedious on the Internet, and she spent far too much time exploring something called the Protégé Prophecy, a supposed prediction that one of Satan's followers would father a child on this Earth. The child would bring legions of humans into the devil's fold and elevate his father's standing in the underworld. Maggie found it all fascinating, but a few additional clicks of her mouse informed her that it had all been dismissed as an unfounded hoax.

Since it was summer and there were no extra credit points to be earned, Maggie didn't push Kirsten to attend Father Tom's talk the next evening. Besides, this way she didn't have to find a babysitter for Liam. She'd promoted the presentation in the local papers and was curious to see whether the blurbs had attracted any outside folks. But most of the people she handed information packets to as they filtered in for the lecture were at least somewhat familiar, except for one reserved gentleman who took a seat several rows behind the others. Estimating him as roughly her age, Maggie noted his refined features and was certain he'd have left an impression if she'd ever seen him before. It was a decent sized showing overall, and by the time Father Tom was scheduled to begin, she had only five packets left. She set them on a table in the narthex for latecomers and stepped just inside the doors, pleased that Monsignor Sarto hadn't rushed back into town to take over this presentation too.

After greeting everyone, Father Tom started his presentation in an unusual way. "The Bible reads like a work of fiction. 'The greatest *story* ever told,' they say. And it's a story that has it all—action, sex, deception, murder. Love. So it's easy to forget that as Christians, we believe it's all true. Now, that's not to say its literal translation is always historically accurate, such as in the story of creation. The story of Adam and Eve may be literally historically accurate, or it may be a parable of sorts, but as we move beyond Genesis, and prior to Revelation, our Holy Bible becomes as much an historical account as it is a spiritual one."

He went on to delve into accounts of each of the archeological excavations Maggie had typed up.

"If I may now ask you to turn to the final page of your packet."

The swishing of paper sounded throughout the church.

"This is a picture of a seal discovered near the bottom of the *Tepe Gowra* Mound in Iraq. Would someone like to describe the carving?"

He nodded toward a man who stood up and said, "It's a woman and a man. Naked. They're bowing prostrate, like they're broken."

"And what else do you see in that picture?"

"A snake." The man's head snapped up to look at Father Tom. "It's Adam and Eve."

The pastor nodded. "Please look at the notes below and see that this finding dates back to thirty-five hundred B.C." He paused and looked out at the attendees. "It appears the fall of mankind may have a basis in history, after all. He gave them a garden. Paradise. And Satan came along and offered something else. They were tempted. They gave in. And God's been punishing them ever since."

In the quiet of the night, an elusive drip coming from somewhere in the townhouse worked like a metronome to lull and focus Maggie's mind. Yet she couldn't fall asleep. She had so many questions after the presentation, and despite Father Tom's assurances about the *tholos*, she couldn't help but wonder. She wished Evan was there to talk to about it all.

Before she lifted her head and saw him, she felt him. "Hey, stranger," she teased as she propped herself up on her elbows.

He smiled, but only halfway, and didn't make a move to approach her. "What do you need, Maggie?"

She frowned. "What do you mean?"

"You brought me here."

"Against your will?" She sat straight up.

He sighed, but didn't answer.

"I'm sorry," she said. "I just…I have a lot of questions for you. If you don't want to answer —"

"I do want to be here, and I do want to answer your questions — to the extent that I'm allowed."

"Then what's the problem? Why do you seem so…stiff?"

He gave her a long and hard look, and then the cold steel of his eyes softened to something warmer and the tensed muscles along his rigid jawline relaxed. "There's no problem. I've just not been summoned by a human before. I didn't know it was possible."

"Oh." She felt her face warm. She hadn't realized she'd been wishing hard enough for him that anyone would notice. "Guess I'd better make good use of my 'summons' then." She told him about the disturbance at Somme Park, but Evan didn't know anything about it. She asked if he thought it could have anything to do with what she'd felt there, if perhaps he'd misinterpreted the energy and it had actually been something good.

"Why would I lead you away from something good?" he asked.

"You admitted to not fully understanding what's going on here. I mean, why are you appearing to me in the first place? What drew you to the coffee shop? You don't know. So, all I'm suggesting is that maybe you were wrong that day at Somme."

Through the fringe of hair that fell across his forehead, she saw that his typically smooth brow was creased in confusion. His frown told her he didn't like the uncertainty. "Or perhaps what called me there was entirely different from the pull you felt at the urn — two conflicting spirits that appeared in the same area, either by coincidence or design. The dark shadows may have moved on from that space while the light stayed. Either way, I suggest you stay away from there for the time being."

"I was hardly planning to have a picnic there any time soon." Maggie was frustrated with the continued lack of a straight answer and let out an irritated sigh. "I'm sure there's no point to it, but let's move on to the next question. Adam and Eve — fact or fiction?" The ancient seal had seemed to prove that an Adam and Eve-like legend had existed from near the beginning of time.

"The story is true, but perhaps not exactly in the way you understand it," he explained. "To be communicated, it had to be put into human words. There is no language understood on Earth that could convey an exact account."

In response, he said, "I know it's a difficult concept to grasp — that there are things out there your mind simply can't fathom. I could try to explain, but you wouldn't understand." He spoke in gentle tones and moved closer to the bed, sitting down on the end when she shot him a dirty look for telling her she wouldn't understand. "That's where your faith comes in." He reached up and traced his thumb lightly over the tense wrinkle between her eyebrows, easing it away with his serene energy. She nodded, and his fingers moved down to rest at the bend of her jaw.

"What do you mean when you say the story is true, even if I don't understand it accurately?" she asked.

"The essentials are true—God created man, then woman. They were meant to live in perfect tranquility. But they were tempted into disobedience."

"And God punished them."

"Punishment wasn't God's purpose. His purpose was to give them what they wanted."

"They wanted to be kicked out of the Garden of Eden?"

"They wanted to be more open to sin. To bite that fruit, Eve had to overcome an enormous obstacle. God didn't make humans to sin; it wasn't in their original nature. But when Eve used her free will to surmount the obstacle—the innate goodness and obedience God had intended for mankind—and gave in to temptation, and then Adam followed, God saw what they wanted and he gave it to them."

"But everything became so awful after that; it sounds like punishment to me."

"Fear, hunger, shame, coldness—it's all a part of sin. They couldn't just have part of it; they had to take it all. But it's what they chose."

"Not really," Maggie insisted. "They wanted the fruit and the power they thought would come with it. They didn't ask for the rest of it. It seems unfair that God didn't warn them about the other stuff ahead of time."

"He did warn them."

"How?"

"With the story of Adam and Eve."

Maggie narrowed her eyes until something clicked…sort of. "This is one of those circular things, isn't it? They represent mankind and the fall, and he gives us this story as a warning, but it also really happened. So we had to live the warning in order to get the warning." She felt more confused by the end of speech and understood what Evan meant about the limitations of the human language.

He nodded, an approving smile playing upon his lips, and moved his thumb slowly back and forth over her cheek, sending a small wash of peace into her, calming her confusion and helping her to accept the gist of what she'd tried to explain without having to fully understand it.

She took in his serenity and examined his features. He didn't have any permanent lines there from worry or the harsh reality of aging. His face represented trust in and sincere devotion to something higher than himself.

"Must be nice to be free of original sin. To automatically follow the Lord's path and never mess up," she said with a touch of envy.

"Is that what you think? Do I need to remind you that the biggest sinner of all is an angel? And his most loyal followers, all angels?"

Maggie's eyes opened wide. She'd always feared Satan, but he'd also felt almost like a make believe character to her, like a villain in a Disney movie. With this very real angel sitting before her, touching her, and after Father Tom's presentation, things that had always felt vaguely mythical were brought into crisp reality. Evan brought his other hand up to her temple and touched it lightly with his fingertips, surrounding her with gentle security.

"It's true that angels are less prone to temptation," he said softly, "but when we give in, the betrayal is at a higher magnitude. It's nearly unforgivable because it's not in our nature, so it isn't weakness we demonstrate. It's willfulness, which is much worse."

His fingertips roved over Maggie's face, tracing her cheekbones, over the bridge of her nose, across her lips. She closed her eyes, luxuriating in his silky touch as he glided over her eyelids, up to her forehead, and everywhere while the sound of his rich, steady voice rolled over her.

Maggie thought of how different the sensations he now sent into her were from those she'd felt the last time he'd touched her, at the canyon. There had been an urgency then, something on the verge of losing control. He'd clearly mastered whatever had afflicted him then.

"When we overcome the lure to sin," he continued, "we're strengthened tenfold and made able to face our temptations more easily. We can come closer to that which tempts us than we previously would have dared—" he lowered his hand to rest at the side of her throat "—and resist without effort."

Maggie stared into the depths of his mesmerizing eyes and wondered how he didn't feel the throbbing vein in her neck as it pulsed in time with her thundering heart. She wasn't quite as practiced as him at resistance.

Chapter 10

Two days before sending her children on their trip out west, Maggie took a day off work and let Kirsten and Liam each invite a friend to Six Flags Great America. Nothing in Wyoming would quite compare to being flung around in tiny metal cars over twisted tracks, or having cotton candy stuck to teeth and the bottom of shoes as the small group trampled across burning asphalt on their way to the next brush with death.

They'd tackled all the major roller coasters by the time night fell and decided to take advantage of the short lines at smaller attractions. Having recently polished off a huge pepperoni pizza for dinner, the kids challenged each other to the Fiddler's Fling—last one to turn green would be the winner. Maggie sensibly abstained and stood against the fence, watching and laughing and snapping futile pictures. Most of the photos came out as nothing but blurry streaks of light.

Creating this distinct memory in her children's minds further restored her sense of security. She couldn't be the sole center of their universe, but she still played a significant role and that was enough for her. It seemed she'd become more satisfied in general since that day at the canyon, and she could legitimately call herself happy again. But she'd learned long ago that maintaining balance was a continual process, and even as she stood there, she knew this felicity wouldn't last forever. Something would come along to throw her once again into doubt and despair; it was inevitable. But this time she was going to nurture her happiness and bask in it for as long as she could.

She snapped another picture and groaned as she looked at the result. But rather than feeling the annoyance she'd just expressed, her contentment and joy received a boost of adrenaline just as someone came to stand at the fence beside her. She turned to look, and her mouth fell open when she saw Evan's attractive, flawless figure.

He laughed. "Nice to see you too. I can't stay; I'm on my way somewhere else, but I thought of you and here I am."

"I won't ask, because I already know the answer will be 'I don't know,' but this seems…we're both getting more control over this thing, as far as when we get to see each other, aren't we?"

He nodded. "Things feel different."

"But in a good way, right?"

He nodded again, and this time he smiled too. "Enjoy the rest of your evening."

He disappeared just as the ride began to slow. On one last, impulsive whim Maggie snapped a picture, and when she looked down at it, she saw both her kids' screaming faces perfectly captured as their separate cars spun next to each other.

Maggie further asserted her motherhood the next afternoon with ice cream and a walk along the river, followed by a night at the movies. When she and the kids returned home, the phone was ringing. Maggie ran to it, and after reading the caller ID, answered it in a rush.

"Sharon! I'm so, so, so sorry. I got your message but things were crazy and I didn't call back and I'm so sorry. How are you?"

"Calm down. It's no big deal. I figured you were just busy. But hey, Katie tells me Kirsten and Liam are going on vacation with their dad for a few days."

"Two weeks. They leave tomorrow."

"I thought you might want to get together while they're gone."

"That sounds great. I'm going to be working full time while they're gone to get some projects done, but maybe we can go out to dinner one night. How about I give you a call next week and we can see what works?"

"Sure. Sounds good. Tell the kids to have a great trip, and we'll talk next week."

"Okay, bye."

The next morning a huge RV pulled in front of Maggie's townhouse to take her children away. After promises of texts and phone calls and postcards, they were off. Maggie kept busy at work that day, but as she lay in bed at night, her mind was free to wonder whether her kids were comfortable sleeping in the RV, if they were homesick, if Melissa had turned into an evil shrew of a "step mother" once the children were safely out of their mother's grasp. She wished for Evan, for his soothing hands to touch her and let her know everything would be okay, but she put a halt to the yearning. She needed to sleep and didn't quite feel up to resisting him should he want to demonstrate his self-control again.

After work the next day, she went to a park by the river and sat atop a vacant picnic table, watching bikers whiz by on the paved path and fishermen wade into the water. After a few minutes, her face brightened as she watched Evan approach her. She hadn't dared hope her plan would actually work, but it had. He stopped a few feet in front of her, and for a moment they simply smiled at each other. It felt nice to exert a small amount of control over a situation that continued to baffle both of them. His pale gray irises, always beautiful, were now lustrous, shimmering in the full sunlight like cut crystals.

"Would you like to go for a walk?" he asked, breaking the happy silence.

"Can we do that?" It seemed like a silly question, but so far the two of them had only managed to remain in each other's sight when they'd stayed in one location.

He cocked an eyebrow and took several steps backward, toward the forest. "Looks like *I* can."

Maggie hopped off the table and sprinted to him. "Smart aleck."

He turned and they walked across the lawn to a path, eventually winding into the forest. Though their view of the river was blocked by tree trunks and full branches, they could still hear the rush of its currents. Maggie wasn't in the mood to get into any mystical discussions that day. She didn't want to hear Evan say he didn't know, and she didn't want to have to strain her brain cells to try to grasp concepts he'd tell her she'd never understand anyway. Instead the conversation turned to her very human issues.

She was handling the vacation just fine and understood the finality of the divorce, but that didn't mean it didn't still hurt, and Evan was such a very good listener. He let her open up without asking too many questions, without giving false encouragement, and without judgment.

"I think it's always going to be hard to see him with someone else," Maggie concluded after her diatribe. "It's not even so much that I want him for myself. It's just…it was always 'Carl and Maggie' and now it's going to be 'Carl and Melissa.' As if I, the essence of Maggie, don't matter at all. I was just one warm body easily substituted with another."

"I doubt the substitution was easy or complete — she can't fully replace what you were to him or your children. She's clearly taken up some space in all of their hearts and probably occupies parts of Carl's heart that used to be yours, but she hasn't pushed you out."

They'd reached the parking lot, and it was starting to get dark, so Evan walked Maggie to her car. She opened the driver's door, but before getting in, she turned toward him. "Thanks for putting up with me today. It was helpful to talk things out. How ironic that the very symptom of my insanity also serves as my therapist."

She was surprised when he frowned at her joke. "Do you still not believe I'm real?"

"You better be real. I sorta like having you around."

"Good. I sorta like being around."

The next several days passed quickly. Maggie's projects kept her busy at work, and Evan came around more frequently. He even showed up during Maggie's solitary nightshift at the food pantry and helped her sort donations.

"Cinnamon again?" he said out loud to himself as he unpacked bags and stocked the dry goods shelves. Then he turned to Maggie where she lined up a row of cardboard boxes to be packed with a week's worth of meals for the average family of four. "Cinnamon Life, Cinnamon Toast Crunch, apples and cinnamon oatmeal. Over there I unpacked cinnamon applesauce."

Maggie shrugged. "People like cinnamon."

"All people?"

"I'm sure not every single living person. But most, yeah."

"Why?"

"It just makes things taste better."

He pulled out another box. "Simply Cinnamon Corn Flakes," he murmured as if contemplating the wonders of the universe. "Would you say the vast majority of people enjoy the works of Mozart?"

After the last few evenings together, Maggie was getting used to his random questions and observations of humankind. He was wise beyond anything Maggie could comprehend, but apparently things like spices and classical music weren't on the list of things he "needed to know," so when he asked, she always answered to the best of her ability. She found it wildly freeing to put her mind to something other than her personal woes.

"I think most would *say* they enjoy Mozart," she answered, "but actually enjoy it? Probably a lot less."

"How about Johnny Cash?"

She chuckled as she answered, "Definitely not most."

"And yet they all like cinnamon." Evan shook his bewildered head.

"Evan, dear, I could try to explain it…but you wouldn't understand." Maggie beamed a Cheshire grin. She'd never imagined that the two weeks she'd been dreading could turn out to be so enjoyable. During the second week of the kids' absence, she found herself working as efficiently as possible at the office so she could take Friday off work.

"Oh, kids back early?" Brenda asked when Maggie told her she wouldn't be in the next day.

"No, but I've been wanting to get down to the city to see the Art Institute's refurbished Impressionist wing. The kids have never seemed enthused to go, so this seems like my best opportunity."

"Well, I guess that's fine with me now that our files are all organized. We'll be barraged with registrations for religious ed. next week, so you might as well have your fun now."

By late the following morning, Maggie stood in the Impressionist gallery at the Art Institute of Chicago, hoping to see Evan, but unsure whether he'd appear in such a populated area. If he didn't show up by the time she was through with this room, she planned to try her luck in a more isolated area of the museum.

It was as she examined a Renoir that she sensed his presence. Nodding toward the painting at a rower dressed all in white, she said over her shoulder, "Nice outfit, huh?"

"He's got panache," Evan answered, making Maggie smile. His rare and subtle dashes of humor always did. She turned and flicked her gaze around at the other patrons in the gallery, looking for an indication that anyone else could see him. She thought a woman gave a sideways glance at his unusual apparel, but couldn't be sure.

"Why don't you go talk to someone?" she suggested. "Just step up behind them, like you did to me, and make a comment about the painting they're looking at. See if they respond."

He pursed his lips into a small frown. "Is this why you brought me here?"

"No. But while we're here, what's to lose? If they don't hear or see you, no harm, right?"

"What if they hear me but don't see me?"

"Then I'm going to get a good chuckle out of it. Still a win." When he tilted his head and raised a chiding eyebrow, she added, "They'll just think whoever said it walked away."

Evan scanned the room and nodded toward a pretty young woman standing alone in front of a Degas. "Shall I try her?"

Maggie shook her head and pointed in the opposite direction at an older, balding man. "Him."

Evan sauntered over, stopping about a foot behind the man, slightly off to his side. Maggie couldn't hear what Evan said, but saw his mouth move. The man looked over his shoulder and responded. Evan stood at the painting a bit longer, and then he and Maggie subtly worked their way through the wall of paintings to each other.

"Well, now we know that I won't look crazy talking to you in public." Maggie smiled.

"He can see me. But it doesn't necessarily follow that everyone else can."

Maggie huffed. "Nothing's ever cut and dried with you, is it? Can we just assume, until it's proven otherwise, that everyone can see you? Please?"

"That sounds reasonable."

They wandered out of the Impressionist gallery and through other rooms, with nothing in particular catching their interest until they came upon a special exhibition of the institute's collection of prints and drawings. At first Maggie only glanced at the grayscale sketches and nearly moved on, but then she noticed an etching of a group of cherubs carrying a kneeling woman up to a haloed woman in robes.

Behind the women, a man sat on a cloud, holding a crown, and in the background was a dove. The description indicated that this was a depiction of a saint being greeted in Heaven.

There were only a few other people in the room, and they weren't close, so Maggie asked in a quiet voice, "Is this what Heaven looks like?"

"It conveys the feel of the place in a—"

"Yes or no."

"There's more to it tha—"

"Evan…"

"No. If you're looking at it strictly from a visual perspective, then no, that's not what Heaven looks like."

"Thank you," Maggie said and meant it.

They moved along, and Evan pulled Maggie's elbow to direct her to a pair of lithographs by Odilon Redon. They were obscure black and white drawings, with the only readily discernible figure being that of an angel holding a sickle. Maggie would have labeled the drawings "modern art," but they were both dated 1899.

She read the inscriptions. "It's from Revelation. These are part of a set." The longer Maggie looked, the more figures made themselves known among the lines. "Those look like—are those aliens?" she asked.

Evan tilted his head to examine from a new angle. "Sinners, I think. Frightened and repentant ones."

"Why are you showing me these?"

"These are a better representation of the true nature of the ethereal world."

Maggie scrunched her face. "You're telling me this is more accurate than cherubs and fluffy clouds? Come on—are you messing with me?"

"I'm not. These pieces don't capture it literally, but essentially. All art comes from God, but this artist opened himself up more fully to the transcendent parts of the message."

Maggie looked back at the pictures and frowned. "It's so…bleak."

"The end of the world will be. But don't worry—this was Redon's last set in *noir*. After this he painted only in color, and I think you'd quite like some of his heavenly images."

"So his images of the afterlife are fairly accurate?"

"*Essentially,*" they both said at the same time.

"Jinx!" Maggie pinched his arm and spun to leave the room, but stopped near the door when she spied the word "angel" in the title of a geometric piece with a gray shaded rectangle in the center and two more rectangles lying down on either side. When Evan came up behind her, she joked, "Shouldn't that say 'angle'?"

Evan stayed silent and when she glanced over her shoulder at him, she saw that he was staring wide-eyed at the etching.

"What's wrong?" she asked.

He waved his head from side to side. "Quite the contrary—everything's right. This is exactly what heaven looks like. Literally."

Maggie jerked her head back and turned to again examine the sparse drawing. She felt utter confusion until Evan lowered his lips to her ear and murmured in a teasing growl, "Now I'm messing with you."

Maggie jabbed his chest with her shoulder and laughed. "Naughty angel. So have you had enough art for the day? Want to get out of here?"

"If you do."

A few minutes later they emerged on the sunny steps leading down to Michigan Avenue, still smiling and teasing each other. As they reached the bottom step Maggie heard a familiar voice.

"Maggie Brock?"

Maggie whipped her head toward the voice. "Sharon? I can't believe I'm seeing you—this is crazy! What are you doing here?"

"I could ask you the same thing." Sharon moved closer, and Maggie saw that she had her daughters with her so she and the girls exchanged hellos. "Thanks for the phone call," Sharon said as soon as the pleasantries were over.

Maggie groaned. "I'm sorry. The time went so fast. I finally got caught up yesterday and decided last minute to take today off."

It became obvious Sharon could see Evan when her eyes not-so-subtly scanned him up and down. "The girls and I came down for Millennium Park and some shopping. What's your story?"

"Art Institute," Maggie answered, gesturing behind her.

"Okay. What's *his* story?"

Maggie flushed. She wasn't prepared to introduce Evan to anyone, much less her friend with the overactive imagination. "This is Evan. Evan, this is my friend, Sharon, and her daughters, Kate and Shelby. Evan's also a friend. He's an expert on spiritual art and has been enlightening me."

"I'll bet he has." Sharon smiled shamelessly.

"Well, I'll let you girls get on with your day," Maggie said, narrowing her eyes at her friend. "We'll talk back in the 'burbs."

"You can count on it. Nice meeting you, Evan," Sharon called as Maggie and he walked away.

Maggie turned east on Monroe and walked as fast as she could for the next few blocks, not slowing until they'd crossed Lake Shore Drive. She led Evan south, away from the crowded yacht club docks to where the view of the lake opened up into a wide, sparkling expanse.

"I'm sorry about that back there," she said. "I never expected to run into anyone I know down here. I hope it won't cause any problems for you."

"Seems more like it's causing problems for you."

"Yeah, well, you don't know Sharon. She's not going to let this go. And what am I supposed to tell her? Even if I wanted to tell her the truth, how do I explain it when even I don't know what's going on?"

"You did tell her the truth — we're friends, and I was telling you about art. Won't that satisfy her?"

"Not when I told her I had a dream about an angel and now I show up with you looking all — " she waved her hands in front of his white linen " — angelic! She's going to think you're my new boy toy and I'm making you play dress up."

"She'll think what she wants to think; your only responsibility is the truth."

"And the truth is that we're friends."

"Yes."

Maggie sighed and stayed quiet, letting herself be mesmerized by the flickers of sunlight as they caught on the tiny peaks of the restless water. She supposed Sharon seeing Evan might not be that big of a deal. Maggie had successfully fended off her friend's continual innuendo for years, and could continue to do so.

Evan slid his hand around Maggie's waist and guided her out of the bike lane as an approaching biker angrily tinkled her bell. "Thanks, guardian angel," Maggie said and wrinkled her nose, letting Evan know she was over her snit. When she looked into his eyes, admiring the way they mimicked the glittering lake, he let his hand slide. As soon as it dropped away, she wanted it back on her. Their physical contact had been rare since the night his fingers had so intimately roved her face, and Maggie was now fully aware of how much she missed his always exhilarating touch.

"So," she began as they continued their walk along the sunny lakefront, "while we're somewhat on the topic, would that even be possible—a human and angel romantic entanglement?"

"Angels and humans aren't meant for each other."

"I know we weren't created for each other, but is that all that keeps us—humans and angels—apart? There's not a...physical reason?" When he peered at her sideways, she snapped her tentative gaze away.

"When we take on the form of man, we take on his entire form, if that's what you're asking."

"Oh." They walked on in what felt to Maggie like an agitated silence. His answer had been too curt. "Should I not have asked?"

She turned back toward Evan as he lifted his arm to pull a hand through his hair, which seemed to be turning more golden as the summer progressed. When several strands sprang forward to hang nearly into his eyes, Maggie noticed something she hadn't before.

"Is your hair getting longer?"

He directed his gaze upward and tugged at a section with his fingertips, examining it. "I suppose it's a consequence of spending an extraordinary amount of time in this form."

"Back to the form thing..."

"Maggie..." His voice lost some of the stiffness it had taken on a few moments earlier, and he pushed his mouth into a regretful frown that was echoed in his eyes. "As I said, it's not meant to happen, so there's no purpose in entertaining ideas of you and I being more than what we are."

They'd stopped walking and stood staring at each other, with Maggie reading in Evan's expression something between controlled lust and mild fear—yearning. Before her imagination traveled too far down the path that the angel had just told her was closed, she returned her focus to the spots of light and resumed walking. "Don't worry, I'm not entertaining ideas. I'm obviously not in any emotional shape to get involved with a human man right now, much less a divine one. Besides, for all I know you've already got someone up in those not-clouds." She stopped abruptly and jerked her attention back to him. "Do you?"

"Do I what?"

"Have a wife or something in Heaven?"

"There isn't marriage or anything of the like in my Father's kingdom."

"Ah yes, that's right." She let out a sardonic grunt. "Poetic, isn't it?"

"There is something poetic about a happy earthly marriage too. The freedom and felicity in Heaven is ideal, but it doesn't diminish the beauty of a well-matched earthly husband and wife."

"So heavenly beings don't yearn for companionship the way humans do? You're okay being solitary forever?"

"We're not solitary. We're all one. I don't long for companionship because I have it, fully. Humans are only ever able to satisfy a part of each other's need for intimacy. Only the Lord can satisfy it completely. Even the best matched husbands and wives leave gaps of need in one another. Humans seek to fill those gaps through children, friends— "

"Extramarital affairs."

"Sometimes. It's all part of yearning for what only the Lord can truly provide. No one is complete until he's called them to his realm."

Maggie stayed quiet with her thoughts until she broke the peaceful lull to ask, "Would you like me to make you an appointment with my girl for a haircut?"

Evan flashed her a smile more brilliant than the bright city. "Don't worry. I'm sure we've got 'people' for that." He'd accentuated his words with his fingers.

"Well, well, well, looks like somebody's learned all about air quotes. Glad to see you're making such good use of that 'form.'" She imitated his finger movements.

"Cheeky human."

Chapter 11

"How long has this thing with Evan been going on, and why didn't you tell me about it?" Sharon hadn't even said hello first.

Maggie was grateful that at least this time they weren't face to face and she could cringe unseen at the other end of the phone. "It's not a *thing*. We're really just friends."

"Uh huh. How'd you meet him?"

Maggie was prepared for this one. "Through church."

"Well, nice to know you can make time for your church friends."

"Sharon—"

"Don't say sorry again. It's wearing thin."

"I know. I'm s—I mean…ah! Carl's big-ass camper just pulled in the driveway. My babies are home! I've got to go, but I'll call you and we'll get together soon."

"I'll believe that when I see it. Give those kids a smooch for me."

"I will. And I'll call. I want to hear about your big anniversary weekend."

"That was two months ago."

The sounds of kids' voices and doors slamming seeped into the house.

"Okay, we'll talk soon. Promise." Maggie rushed to hang up and ran to the front door, throwing it open and grabbing the kids into a big hug. They squeezed her back and stayed pressed into her side while Carl and Melissa unloaded their bags, so Maggie couldn't be resentful of the tears that welled in Kirsten's eyes when she waved to her father and his girlfriend as they drove away.

Melissa lowered her window and blew a kiss. "Miss you already! I'll share the pictures once they're online!"

It was already evening, and the kids looked positively exhausted, so Maggie ordered a pizza and they all got into their jammies early. Kirsten pulled a pair of polished stone earrings out of her duffel and gave them to Maggie, which reminded Liam to rifle through his bag for the Grand Teton travel mug he'd picked out for his mom. They filled her in on their western adventure until their eyelids drooped, and then, with an arm around each of their shoulders, Maggie walked them upstairs, alternately kissing the tops of their heads the whole way.

Washed up and in her own bed, Maggie was satisfied. Her children were home and she'd gotten through the dreaded trip without too much heartache. She had Evan to thank for that. But now, as she lay there with everything feeling back to normal, the angel seemed almost like a dream again, not part of her daily existence.

She'd been headed to such a dark pit of despair, and now she considered that perhaps this was why Evan had been sent to her—to pull her up. Now that she was righted, she wondered if that meant she had no more need of him…and would that mean she might not see him again?

As unpleasant as the thought was, it wasn't entirely unwelcome. She'd treasured every minute with him, had looked forward to their time together more than anything else during the last two weeks, but being with him was beginning to inspire more conflict within her than serenity. Though she'd earnestly tried to keep her feelings toward him on a high plain, her thoughts kept drifting toward something more mortal. He'd been absolutely right about the ideas she'd been entertaining—it was difficult for her to separate her growing affection for him from a physical attraction. So if he didn't come back, she had to consider that it might be for the best.

Sarto returned from his stint away from the parish and presided over late morning Sunday Mass. He wasn't always the most magnetic speaker, but on this morning he had Maggie's rapt attention.

"The devil is at work every day in this world. He's not going to jump out at you, wielding a pitchfork with his red horns flaring. He's more cunning than that. We all know the small ways he tempts us day to day, but on occasion he takes a bolder leap. And sometimes he even disguises himself in the most innocent, even most holy, of masks. He knows we yearn constantly for a connection with the higher power, so what better way to gain our trust than to pretend to be a component of the same? No doubt many of you have heard of the ruckus over at Somme Park."

A quiet murmur worked its way through the pews. The foundation's goal of keeping a low profile had worked fairly well and nothing had ever shown up in the local press about the suspected visitation at the garden, but rumors had a way of winding their way through suburbia faster than the vines had woven their way around those pillars.

"I'll be completely honest with you," the monsignor continued. "I have no idea what's going on over there, but that's exactly what concerns me. Our Lady wouldn't hide from us. So this could simply be a trick of nature. Or it could be something more sinister. And so it is my advice to each and every one of you to keep away from Somme, or if you must go, at least stay away from the site in question until such time as it can be determined that it's safe."

After Mass, Sarto broke from shaking hands with departing parishioners to seek Maggie out, saying he needed to speak with her immediately. She told Kirsten and Liam to wait for her by the front doors while she went to speak with him in the side room. An usher was setting down a stack of weekly bulletins on the counter.

"Tell the others to leave the extras on the side table. I'll put them away," Sarto instructed and shut the door after the man had left. Unlike Father Tom, he didn't go near the cabinets to offer Maggie a drink or any other source of comfort, not even a seat. The only thing he offered was a penetrating stare. "What do you know about Somme Park?"

"Do you mean the disturbance you referred to in your sermon?"

"Is that what I'm asking about? You tell me. I want to know exactly what happened to you that day I ran into you at the gardens."

Maggie knew word of the strange occurrence would eventually make its way to Sarto, but she'd expected him to forget about their little run in. She didn't see a reason to evade his question, however, especially if he could possibly shed light on what Evan hadn't been able to. "I'm sorry I didn't mention it before. I honestly thought, hoped, it was just my imagination, but then I heard about the vines and I wasn't sure any more. Are the vines still there?"

"What did you feel?"

"It was like…a pressure, drawing me to the urn that sat inside. And right before that happened, I had…a vision, the most vivid vision of the garden and everything in it belonging to me. It was beautiful, actually." Her natural impulse was to qualify her statement and again shun it as probably nothing more than her imagination, but she could see by the intent way the monsignor studied her that he believed there truly was something going on at Somme.

"Why did you run away from it?" he asked.

She wasn't ready to be entirely truthful with this answer yet, particularly not with the monsignor. The priest was too clinical and suspicious. For all she knew, he'd attempt to incarcerate Evan E.T. style to study him. "I was distracted. Heard a noise or something. And that's when I thought I saw my friend and went after him."

"Did you ever catch up with him?"

"No. So it's still happening? The vines?"

"It continues," he answered crisply. "And I discourage you in particular from going near there again. You've already shown yourself to be susceptible to its influence."

"What is 'it' exactly?"

"*It* is something for me to make a judgment on," Sarto said. "Until I do, keep clear of it. Thank you for your time, and may God bless you on this fine Sunday."

He opened the door and motioned her out. Maggie emerged into the narthex feeling as if she'd just been scolded.

"I slept with Carl."

Sharon's eyes shot wide open, and she grunted something incoherent while Maggie leaned back in her chair at the outdoor café and watched, a big grin spreading across her face. She'd purposely waited until her friend had taken a big mouthful of sandwich before delivering that piece of news.

Handing Sharon an extra napkin to catch the bits of lettuce falling out of her mouth, she said, "Go on, chew slowly while I give you the gory details. It happened late spring. He and Melissa had broken up briefly. He seemed sad, so I offered him a glass of wine, and next thing I knew we were naked and tangled up in each other."

"Was it good?" Sharon mumbled through her food.

"More like fantastic. Maybe the best sex we've ever had. But it wasn't going anywhere. Unfortunately, I didn't get that until afterward when Carl assured me that we're much better apart. And then he promptly got back together with Missy."

"Oh, sweetie."

"No, I'm done being sad about it, and I'm not entirely sorry the whole thing happened. It helped me see that I've been clinging to the marriage more than I should have, and now I can work toward truly letting go. But I'll admit, that was one reason I was avoiding you. I just haven't wanted to talk about it until recently."

Sharon peered at her for a moment. "You really do seem okay. Proud of you, kiddo. You're a lot stronger than you give yourself credit for."

"Well, I haven't done it totally alone."

"*Evan* helping you out?" Sharon winked.

"I meant my faith, but yes, Evan played a role there too. He was a gift sent right when I needed it." A gift that had an expiration date, apparently. Maggie's instincts had been right, and she hadn't seen him during the two and a half weeks since that day in Chicago.

"Go on…" Sharon coaxed.

Maggie shrugged. "Not much more to tell. We really were only just friends. But ever the idiot, my feelings were beginning to get confused, and he didn't feel the same way. So, it seemed the best thing to do was to part ways." It felt good not to have to dodge her friend's questions anymore. Evan's absence gave her a sort of freedom in that way, but the longer he was gone, the less okay she became with it. She reluctantly missed him.

"Well, too bad," Sharon said. "But realistically, it probably wouldn't have worked out anyhow. I mean, how old is he?"

"I don't actually know. I get the feeling he's a lot older than he looks though." Maggie caught her smile before it fully formed.

"Wonder if that's what all cougars tell themselves." Sharon rolled her eyes and took a sip of water as a flicker of white flashed in the distance beyond her shoulder.

"I'm not a cougar!"

"Only because he wasn't that into you," Sharon teased.

"Did he really look that much younger than me?"

"I think five years qualifies, so yeah, he looked at least that."

Maggie glanced from the restaurant patio toward the street and scanned the row of Victorian-era homes that had been retrofitted into stores and other businesses to create a quaint shopping district. The persistent blob of white that had been dancing in her periphery took form—standing on the sidewalk across the street with his earnest eyes directly on her was Evan.

"Speaking of things that are too young," Sharon continued, "you're not going to believe the new football program I just got an e-mail about from the SportsPlex. Football for eighteen-month-olds. *Little Piggies*."

The revelation was an excellent excuse for Maggie's shocked expression. She flicked her gaze back to her friend. "Stop it! Really?"

"I kid you not. Looks like suburbia's no longer satisfied with burning the kids out on their sport by age fourteen; now we're going for, what—five?"

Maggie dared a glance back at Evan. He lifted his hand and fluttered his fingertips at her while a teasing grin twitched upon his lips. She responded with a subtle nod while her insides did cartwheels.

"Well, I guess Liam's all washed up then." She forced herself back to the conversation. "Poor kid's already nine and never strapped on a cup. You think they make jock straps for babies?"

"Sure, build 'em right into the diaper."

Maggie's laughter flowed easily, the joy coming from more than the thought of reinforced nappies.

When the waitress cleared their plates, Sharon said, "We've got a couple hours before we have to pick up the girls from camp, want to do some shopping?"

"Oh, um…" Maggie shifted her gaze toward Evan, who tapped his wrist and then made an upward motion with his fingers, as if to indicate flying away. She took it to mean he had to leave soon. "I'm sorry; I've got to run." She made a show of looking at her watch. "Yipes! Right now actually. I've got a…church thing to take care of. Here." She pulled out a twenty dollar bill and held it out toward her friend. "Mind taking care of the bill?"

Sharon waved the money off. "I've got it. You'll owe me next time, all right?"

"Sounds good," Maggie said as she stood and leaned down to give her friend a peck on the cheek. "You're the best! This was fun."

She dashed out of the restaurant and across the street. Evan had moved down the sidewalk and briefly locked eyes with her before turning a corner. By the time she got to where he'd veered from the main road, he was several yards away and took another detour behind a row of tall hedges. The cat and mouse chase intensified her desire to reach him. Running down the sidewalk, she flew around the side of the hedge to practically slam into him.

"Evan!" she gasped and without thinking about what she was doing, wrapped her arms around his neck. She inhaled, and took in everything about him, including the aroma she unexpectedly recognized as uniquely his — like freshly laundered cotton enhanced by undertones of something more exotic. Coconut and spices, perhaps. She also noted that his golden hair was trimmed to the length it had been when they'd first met.

"I can only stay a moment. But you called, and I had to see you." His hands gripped her waist, the force of his touch surprising her.

"Is something wrong?"

"No, sorry, I didn't mean to imply there was." Relaxing his hold, he slid his hands to the small of her back. "I was glad to be summoned, but I have to go now. I'll be back soon…if that's what you want." His silvery eyes glinted as they intently bored into hers. "You'll have to stay open to me for that to happen."

They spoke in whispers, hidden from outsiders behind the large shrub, and Maggie tightened her grasp around his neck, as if that could somehow keep him there longer. "I didn't know I was closed to you. I kept you away?"

"I'll explain when I come back; I have to go."

His words rushed out, and before Maggie could complain, he pressed his lips firmly against hers. She sank into him, but rather than a soft and watery sensation, the pressure and tension in his kiss felt more like smashing through an iceberg. Maggie hadn't realized she'd closed her eyes until she opened them a few moments later and stared at the empty space where Evan had stood. Touching her fingertips to the tingling pink flesh of her mouth, she murmured, "What the hell was *that?*"

Her thoughts whirred on her drive home. He'd said she wasn't "open" to him, but she didn't understand how she'd kept him away. Was it because she'd recognized that she was probably better off having that temptation removed from her life? Perhaps she'd inadvertently put up a barrier against him. Then at lunch, she and Sharon had been talking about him, and she'd suddenly wished for him.

So he'd come back, and the first thing she did was press herself against him, gaze longingly into his eyes, and kiss him. She berated herself for being so weak. Though, in fairness to herself, she hadn't exactly been prepared for him to make such a move. Was it possible that he really did return her human affections? She both wanted to know and didn't. Because what difference did it make? The situation remained impossible. While attempting to sort it all out, she missed the turn to take her back home. Glancing at the clock, she saw that she had just over an hour before she'd have to pick up the kids. Kirsten's camp was on the way to Somme Park anyhow…

Ten minutes later, Maggie pulled into the garden's parking lot. The meandering trails and varied foliage were just what she needed to help unwind her jumbled thoughts. She yearned for clarity. Somme was a big place, she reasoned, big enough for her to avoid the *tholos* with no problem as she'd done when her sister had visited. She didn't have enough time to get into any real trouble there, just a quick walk around the gardens and she'd be gone.

As she strolled the rose garden, it struck her that she'd never confirmed that the scene of the vines was, in fact, where she'd assumed it was. Every description led her to believe it was at the Greek replica, but she didn't know for sure.

She only had fifteen minutes before she'd have to head to her car to be on time for kid pickup, so she skirted the round pond in record time. What she saw confirmed that the *tholos* was indeed the place. A small group of people were gathered there, and thick vines grew up the pillars, though she was too far away to make out any detail. With her purpose accomplished, she continued along the gravel path as it circled to the fruit tree grove. When she reached the opening in the hedge, she stalled for a brief moment, and then stepped through it.

Automatically, she went to the leafy tunnel through which she'd chased Evan. As she walked through it, her mind focused on the stand of trees just beyond the other end. If that was Mary in the urn, Maggie hoped to get the answers and clarity she needed. She yearned to sense something as beautiful and clear as the vision she'd seen from the *tholos* that day. The urn was a font of strength. She felt it calling to her through the trees. It was telling her to come forward to receive a reprieve from her mistakes and fortification against future error.

Or would going there, to this unverified energy, be the biggest mistake of all? She stopped before reaching the end of the tunnel, reversed her direction, and left the park.

He'd watched her enter the tunnel. As expected, telling her to keep her distance was the best way to ensure she'd be tempted. But she was stronger than he'd thought, so he'd have to find another way. This one was promising.

Chapter 12

The vines continued to grow and did so in normal, random patterns, leaving the Latin hidden underneath, and public interest waned. For several days Brenda and Maggie fielded angry phone calls and e-mails accusing the monsignor of driving the Blessed Mother away by speaking out against Somme, but by early August, that too had died down, and Maggie was glad because now she could enjoy her week-long visit in Colorado without feeling bad about leaving Brenda alone to deal with the deluge of ire.

"Dad looks good," Maggie said to her mom as they cut vegetables for the salad while Maggie's father tended the grill on the back deck. Through the sliding glass door, she could see him and Kirsten sitting on cushioned patio chairs looking down to the yard below where Liam was no doubt romping with Dusky, his grandparents' yellow Lab.

"Yes, he seems to be back to normal. Finally. Knowing you and the kids were coming was a good incentive for him to rest and keep up with his therapy. Those first few weeks were tough, though." Karen groaned.

"When you schedule the other knee, let's coordinate—Carl will take the kids so I can be here to help this time."

"Nonsense. Your kids need you. Us old coots will do just fine. Besides, next time should be easier since he'll have at least one good knee to rely on."

The glass door slid open and Kirsten poked her head in. "Grandpa wants to know if we're eating outside."

"Sure, it's a nice night," Karen said. "Come on inside to wash up, and I'll get you some plates so you can set the table."

Life slowed down at the Dawson residence in Golden, Colorado. Maggie's parents had bought the place about ten years earlier, their retirement dream home. It wasn't big but had mountain views from its open kitchen and living area and plenty of sleeping space for guests on the finished lower level. The whole area invited visitors to kick back and take a break from the rest of their lives, and Maggie was happy to oblige.

The midweek tradition on these summer visits was for Fred and Karen to take their grandchildren to Heritage Square, an amusement park filled with bumper boats, go-karts, and a huge alpine slide, while Maggie stayed back and enjoyed the alone time, reading on the deck, hiking, whatever she wanted. After she'd kissed them all goodbye, she showered, threw on a tank top and cargo shorts, and went for an adventure of her own.

Taking her parent's second car, she drove along the highway and parked in a small lot at the side of the road when she saw signs for the beginning of a trail. The day was sunny and warm, but not unpleasantly so, especially in the generous shade provided by the tall evergreens along the gravelly trail. As she walked further into the wild and away from the highway, gaps through the trees opened to reveal views of dusty brown hills nearby and sharp gray mountains in the distance. The thrill she felt at the sight of the mountains never dimmed; each glimpse was just as impressive as the last.

Armed with a small backpack filled with water, fruit, and a book, her plan was to find a cozy, secluded spot and read. She came upon a shallow river and walked next to it for a bit before finding the perfect place — a flat area with an inviting rock that was just the right height and width to sit on comfortably. But after settling in, the book didn't hold her attention. Instead, her eyes wandered to the water, rushing over low rocks and flowing around larger ones. She caught silvery flashes of fish as they glided by, and watched dragonflies dip to poke at the water's surface.

Glancing back up at the mountains, she thought she might understand her fascination with the majestic peaks. They reminded her of just what a small thing she was in the universe. Nothing but a speck. Insignificant. Unnecessary. But this thought didn't depress her. On the contrary, it gave her a sense of freedom, much like the realization a few years earlier when she'd recused herself from running the PTA and saw that it hadn't fallen apart without her. Whatever she did in this world was her choice, and whatever she chose, the people she cared about would be taken care of. Carl was obviously thriving in his life without her. Her aging parents were getting along fine living halfway across the country. And her children...yes, even they were growing in independence and had lives away from the tiny grain that was their mother.

Yet in this big world, even the smallest sliver of a human had a purpose; Maggie knew this, and her thoughts turned to Evan. Surely he must've been sent to her for a reason. He hadn't returned since the day she'd had lunch with Sharon—because the only thing she'd been able to determine with conviction was that keeping him away had made things easier. So she continued to block him, and this time it was intentional. But sitting on that rock, feeling small yet significant, she understood that by denying Evan, she was telling God no.

There was a purpose to everything, and she and Evan weren't going to be able to figure out the meaning behind his visits if they ended for good. Surely she could manage her silly heart in order to proceed and do whatever would eventually be asked of her. Various forms of these same thoughts had been swirling through her head for weeks, but now they crystallized. She could do this. She *would* do this. She was ready to see Evan again.

When the angel didn't come immediately sprinting out of the trees or rising from the river, she shook her head. Who was she to think she could snap and he'd be there? Drinking down the rest of her water, she stood and swiped dirt from the back of her shorts before stowing the empty bottle in her backpack. More than likely, her deliberate rejection had sent him elsewhere, to someone who'd say yes. The idea of having wished him away forever—and to someone else—caused pressure to build inside her chest, pressing outward like it was making room for the empty space she herself had created.

Just as that thought passed through her brain, his white-clad figure appeared on the opposite bank of the river, about thirty feet away, and Maggie couldn't have stopped the smile that burst across her face if she'd wanted to. She suddenly wondered how she'd ever mustered the will to block his radiant presence from her life in the first place.

"I see you've forgiven me!" he shouted over the hum of the tumbling river.

She cupped her hands around her mouth to project her voice. "Forgiven you? For what?"

"The kiss!"

She lowered her hands from her mouth, not knowing how to respond.

"I didn't mean it!" he said. "No, I did mean it! But not in the way you might have thought!"

"Why are you all the way over there?" she asked. "I can hardly hear you—can't you fly over here?"

"Doesn't work that way!" He scanned the body of water that rapidly coursed between them and pointed out a group of large rocks down river; they clustered together just before a sharp bend. Maggie saw that if she chose her path carefully, she'd be able to follow a haphazard trail of stepping stones to reach that cluster. Evan could do the same from his side. "Meet you there?" he shouted.

Maggie wanted to go, to stand beside him, to have him touch her and let his alluring energy become hers, but with that flash of desire, the river's speed seemed to increase about a hundred miles an hour. She hesitated, considering his proposition doubtfully.

"Or we could just keep shouting!" Evan suggested.

Maggie groaned. "Okay, I'll try, but the second it feels too dangerous I'm heading for shore!" She took a tentative step onto one of the close rocks, and then to another, each time carefully adjusting her balance before looking to the next. At the fourth stone, a particularly wide and flat one, she felt stable enough to look up and check Evan's progress. He was further down river than her and stepped across the rocks as if they were nothing more than flagstones in a neatly laid garden path. "Show off!"

He stopped and turned to her. "I'll wait here until you catch up."

"How about you just keep going and wind back to me?"

"You can do this, Maggie—you're with your guardian angel, remember?"

"No, I'm across a violent river from my guardian angel." Even with him further ahead, they'd cut the distance between them to about half as they each moved toward the river's center. "Why'd you kiss me?"

"Let's talk when we get there."

"I hear you fine from here, and I'm not taking another step until you tell me."

He tilted his face toward the clear blue sky for a moment and then locked his eyes on hers. She didn't realize how much she'd missed the intensity of his gaze until it was again wholly focused on her.

"It was an impulsive action," he finally said. "I was happy to see you again, and I didn't stop to think about how you might misinterpret it. I'm sorry."

"Well…how *should* I have interpreted it?"

"As a sign of affection from one friend to another."

"Friends." She nodded as she said it, attempting to shake her brain cells into the proper alignment, but something didn't quite tally. She'd felt more in the kiss than friendship. "Are you sure that's all it was for you?"

"Maggie…" He pressed his lips together and even from the distance she could see the muscles in his jaw tense. Five yards of pure, clear, Colorado air separated them, but somehow the atmosphere seemed to crackle as they stared at each other. Maggie stood rigid, fighting to maintain the resolve she'd talked herself into just minutes before. Evan closed his eyes for a brief moment, and when he opened them again, the fire that had been within them was quelled. "You know that's all it can be," he finally said.

Maggie contemplated the new resolution in his features, in his very posture, and understood that although he was struggling too, his goodness would prevail. And so would hers, even if she had to borrow strength from him. "Will you forgive me?" he asked.

She inhaled, calming her fluttering pulse, and steadied her balance. "There's nothing to forgive—I wasn't angry, just…confused. So thank you for explaining. I'm ready to move past it now, okay?"

Evan nodded, and then a sly smile widened his lips and eased the tension in his graceful features. Tilting his head toward the rocks in the center of the river, he challenged, "'Ready to move,' you say?"

With a small chuckle, Maggie relaxed too. "Tricky angel."

Now that they'd addressed the kiss, Maggie's barriers lowered, and she felt a new connection reach across the rushing water between them. In her mind she vividly saw herself and Evan standing on the center rock together with all worries of this world swept away in the strong current. Her longing to be there overcame her fear, and she stepped over the rocks without thinking about what she was doing until she stood on the centermost stone with her angel. He grasped her elbows, stabilizing her body and sending a wash of his gentle vibrations through her. The water was deeper here, murkier it seemed to Maggie, and even more violent than it had looked from the shore.

Turning from Evan to peer around the bend in the river, she saw that it quickly morphed into rapids. She gasped at the spray of water crashing into rock, knowing that one little slip would send her tumbling toward the mayhem. Her back was now pressed into Evan's chest, and he reached his arms around her waist to hold her steady as she crossed her arms over his and dug her fingers into his forearms. They'd come here to be able to talk, but words no longer seemed important. Evan rested his chin on her shoulder, and they stayed silent, letting the world around them rage while the charged sensations coming from Evan as he surrounded her fed a different kind of storm deep within Maggie.

Eventually, the angel murmured in her ear that she needed to be getting back to her parents' home. He walked with her across the stones, holding her hand the entire way, and through the flowing warmth of that physical connection, she too felt as if she were walking along nothing more than a garden path. When Maggie stepped onto earth, Evan's hold on her hand loosened — he'd stopped walking but didn't hold her back. He simply unfolded his fingers from around hers, and she understood that he wanted her to continue moving away from him. She resisted the urge to turn and look at him, knowing this would only make it impossible to leave, so she kept her eyes on the ground before her and slowly inched forward, feeling his fingers tickle over her palm as he too savored every last moment of contact. When the last spark of Evan slipped away, she inhaled sharply and noticed that the long pair of shadows cast by the lowering sun had become singular. He was gone. But she knew he'd be back because she wouldn't block him anymore. She couldn't.

Chapter 13

The final days of summer sped past with the usual rush of getting the kids ready for school. Kirsten was leaving behind a small, cozy grade school for a big, public high school, and although she was excited, it was still a scary prospect, so Maggie didn't want to skip out on any of the orientations. The Thursday before school officially started, she spent the afternoon helping Kirsten navigate the route between her classes one last time, ran around to three different stores to find the most elusive of the school supply requests, and then attended an evening parent meeting at the high school.

When she arrived home, she hoped to find the kids as ready for sleep as she was. Liam was in his pajamas, at least, but required two bedtime stories before his eyes began to droop. Kirsten was wide-eyed and sitting up in her bed, flipping through a magazine when Maggie finally got to her.

"Okay, sugarplum. Lights out," Maggie said.

"Why? School doesn't start till Monday."

"Right, but I've got to work tomorrow and your brother gets up early, so…you know the drill."

Kirsten shut off the light, but remained sitting. "Do you think I should text Anna about sharing gym lockers or wait until she calls me?"

"I think you shouldn't worry about that until tomorrow." Maggie half turned to leave.

"But if I text her first, I'll look desperate."

"Then there's your answer—wait and let her contact you."

"But what if she talks to someone else first and they decide to share and then I'll have to share with someone I don't even know."

"You and Anna have talked about sharing gym lockers all summer. I'm sure there's no reason to worry, but if you need to ease your mind, just text her about something else and then casually throw in a comment about the gym locker."

"What else should I text her about?"

"Kirsten! I've been running around dealing with school crap all day, and I'm done now, okay? Turn your mind to something else, get some sleep, and tomorrow morning something will come to you. Good night."

Kirsten huffed her acquiescence, and Maggie walked out of the room, glancing back to make sure her daughter was settling under her covers before heading to her own bedroom. On the way she considered making a trip downstairs to pour herself a soothing glass of wine, but smiled when she thought of something — some*one*, rather — that she found to be much more comforting.

She went to her chaise after changing into her pajamas and waited for Evan. When he appeared, she asked, "So what did you do with yourself today?"

He responded with a tilt of his head and an eyebrow cocked in a way that told her he wouldn't answer.

"Right. Angel cinnamon," she said, referring to those things he could tell her but she wouldn't understand. "Well then, I guess you're stuck hearing about my day again." Bending her legs and pulling them to her, she gestured to the open end of the long chair.

"So how did it go?" he asked after he'd lowered to sit in front of her. "Was it as awkward as you expected to face the mothers from your children's old school?"

"Not really. You were right to tell me that worrying about things that haven't happened yet was pointless. It's not like it was a big joyous reunion or anything, but we were able to say hi and smile and make chit-chat. It all felt sincere enough, with none of the old harsh feelings rising up in me."

"Time heals. And you've come a long way emotionally since those days."

"You mean I've grown up." She straightened one leg to nudge his thigh with her foot, and he grabbed it, pulling it onto his lap.

Giving her toes a squeeze through her fuzzy socks, he said, "I don't mean that in a bad way. Life is a process of constant change, and so long as that change is in a positive direction, it's good. Don't regret being who you were; be happy about who you are."

"You're like a walking proverb, aren't you?" She smiled, but as she contemplated his words, a familiar guilt tapped at her.

"What's wrong?"

"You say not to regret who I was, but how can I not when the decisions I made didn't affect just me—I forced the kids to leave their friends and change schools because *I* couldn't handle the situation. What kind of a mother does that?"

"Was the move to St. John's a bad one for Liam and Kirsten?"

"No. It ended up being a great move…for all of us, but I couldn't have known that ahead of time. I reacted impulsively and everything could've just as easily been disastrous for them."

"But it wasn't."

"But I didn't know it wouldn't be."

"But the Lord did. There is a plan, Maggie. Circumstances are often arranged in a certain way on purpose, to set us up to arrive at the place we're supposed to be—a bigger picture that we can't see."

"I get that. Sort of. It's just that the whole free will thing gets in the way. If there's a divine plan in place that's all been foreseen, then is there really free will or is it just us thinking we're making choices while God's pulling the strings?"

"Free will is genuine, and often the choices people make lead them far from their intended path, but God offers up opportunities and arranges circumstances to help bring them back to where they're supposed to be." Evan's voice was steady, unflustered by Maggie's persistent challenges.

She relaxed and leaned against the back of the chair, extending her other leg so that both feet rested in his lap. He'd begun kneading her first foot, and now moved over to the other. "That feels nice," she said, giving her toes a small wiggle as an indication that she was ready to lay the conversation to rest. As usual, she needed time to absorb the things Evan told her.

Reclining casually, almost lazily, against the wall, he turned his face toward her. Simply staring at his beautiful, serene features would be enough to reassure her on the worst of days, but he offered so much more than that—wisdom, encouragement, true friendship. "Mind if I try this without the socks?" he asked.

After thinking back to the last time she'd painted her toenails—only a week earlier—she nodded. Evan's fingertips dipped under the cuff of her loose sock, and a giggle bubbled up and out of Maggie's throat as he worked his way down to her most ticklish spot.

"Is it too much?" he asked, a teasing spark in his eye.

"No, it'll be fine. Just, maybe avoid the underside of the arch."

He complied, moving his fingers slowly over her flesh, pressing away the pockets of tightness, and caressing her with his angelic, flowing vibrations. She closed her eyes to take it all in. It was just a foot massage, no lines crossed physically, but emotionally she was bursting. She hadn't expected it to be easy to control her affection for him, but she hadn't anticipated that it would be excruciating. She needed help. But this was the one thing she couldn't talk to Evan about. If he knew the extent of the conflict he continued to cause within her, she was afraid he'd leave permanently.

Once Liam and Kirsten were settled into their school routines, Maggie went to Father Tom. He was the only person she trusted with her secret, and she could no longer ride this teeter-totter of emotions by herself. It was a quiet evening with the church empty save for a few people in the adoration chapel. Father Tom had again led her to the dimly lit usher's room, where they sat across from each other on the overstuffed leather chairs. The priest took a swig of his red liquid and set it on the side table. Maggie, meanwhile, played with the knuckles of her empty hands.

"Are you certain the confessional wouldn't be a more appropriate spot?" Father Tom asked. "It seems you have something to get off your chest."

"No, it's not exactly a confession. But I do need your guidance."

"All right, I'm listening."

"I don't think I need to ask this but…to be sure, can I count on you to keep our discussion confidential? You're the only one I want to share this with."

"Of course."

Maggie stared down at her hands and took a breath. "I'm being visited by an angel."

She was surprised to hear a small gasp come from the priest and looked up. "What makes you think it's an angel?" he asked.

"Many things, but he also tells me that he is."

"And you're certain it's not just your imagination? Is he coming to you in your dreams?"

Maggie recounted her brief history with Evan, emphasizing the parts that made it clear he was not of this world. Father Tom listened intently, nodding at each new bit of evidence. When she'd brought him up to date, he leaned forward with his elbows on his knees and his hands clasped together. In a low voice, he said, "And you have no idea why he's here? What he wants from you?"

"No. And neither does he."

The priest sat back and rested one arm across his stomach while he propped the other elbow on it and curled his fingers over his lips. He seemed to draw his gaze within while he contemplated the situation. Maggie remained silent, not wanting to disturb his thoughts. After several moments, his eyes snapped to her. "When did you say he first appeared to you?"

"Early January."

He nodded. "And he's visited continually since then?"

"Not continually. There've been…complications."

He raised an eyebrow. "Such as?"

"Such as I'm human and a woman and apparently much more vulnerable than I pretend to be. He's been an amazing support to me, and we've developed a friendship. But I've also developed…deeper feelings for him."

The priest's eyes opened wide. "Romantic feelings?"

"Yes, but I've not acted on them, and I won't! I accept that he and I can be nothing more than friends."

"What does this have to do with him not continually visiting you? Did he stay away after you confessed your affections?"

"It was more like I kept him away, mentally blocked him."

"And that was enough to keep him away physically?"

Maggie nodded.

Father Tom's features melted into a relieved smile. "So you see? You're controlling this."

"In that respect, yes, but I've prayed and prayed about it, and every time I get the feeling that I'm supposed to stay open to him. So I need your spiritual advice on how to handle this responsibility."

While she'd spoken, the priest's expression had tensed, transforming his smile into a tight frown. He again leaned forward and dropped his voice to almost a whisper. "Maggie, I'm afraid my advice is that you continue to block him. What you see isn't real."

Maggie's throat constricted. Despite everything she'd told him, he didn't believe her, and these were exactly the words she didn't want to hear. Blocking Evan was no longer an option she'd give herself, and now it seemed she was entirely alone in dealing with her conflicting emotions.

The creases in Father Tom's forehead went deeper, causing Maggie to regret coming to him. He didn't have the magical answers she'd been hoping for, so disturbing him had served no purpose other than to make him worry for her sanity. She wanted to apologize and rush out of the room, but her disappointment held her temporarily paralyzed, unable to get up and face her dilemma all on her own.

Father Tom's eyes suddenly sparked. "Hold on — I know a man. Raymond Fender. A widower. He's active with the men's ministry, and his children went to St. John's. Surely you must know them."

"Jason Fender was in Kirsten's class. His mother died about a year before we started here." Maggie had no idea what this had to do with they'd just been talking about, but was grateful for the change in subject. "I may have crossed paths with Raymond at school events, but I've never met him. How's he adjusting?"

"Better. Much better. I've heard that he signed up for one of those dating websites. I'm sure he must be lonely after losing his wife, and I've sensed the same loneliness from you at times. That could be what's affecting you now. I wonder…if Raymond is open to dating someone from the parish, would you be interested?"

"That's your solution to my problem — a blind date?" Maggie laughed. This certainly wasn't where she'd expected the discussion to end up, and she was surprised to find she didn't hate the idea.

Father Tom smiled. "Yes, I suppose it is." Then his features clouded with concern, reminding Maggie a little too much of Carl during her shakier days right after the divorce. When the priest spoke again, his voice was low and had a darker edge. "But should your angel continue to appear, I caution you to keep an arm's length from him at all times."

Raymond Fender had dark eyes and short, wavy brown hair that was graying only at the temples. His face was classically male, with a squared jaw, strong chin, and long dimples that creased both sides of his face when he smiled. He was very tall, a few inches higher than Carl's five-foot-eleven, and had wide shoulders, so Maggie wasn't surprised to learn during their first coffee date that he'd played college football. He had a gentler disposition than Maggie would have expected from an ex-athlete, and the one word she'd have used to describe him after their first meeting was "kind."

As they left the coffee shop Tuesday, he'd asked if Maggie had plans for the coming Saturday evening, and since she didn't, they set up a second date for dinner. At the popular steak place, which extended out over the river with stellar views through floor-to-ceiling windows, Maggie learned that in addition to Jason, Ray had two other sons away at college. The loss of their mother had been a blow to all of them, but it sounded like strong faith and the support of family living close by had pulled them through. Financial concerns didn't seem to be an issue—Ray was a vice president with a large insurance firm. With his two oldest out of the house and his youngest now in high school, he felt like it was time to pay attention to his personal life. All this he conveyed to Maggie as they amiably conversed over salad and then filet. Maggie likewise brought him up to speed on her story.

"I haven't really dated since the divorce," she explained. "Life seems to have been filled with enough craziness that I just…I don't know, put it off or just haven't felt the need. But this is nice. I think Father Tom might know me better than I know myself."

"He's a wise man," Ray said. "I've enjoyed working with him on some of the men's conferences. I like the trust he puts in the parishioners—lets us work autonomously without having to get his hands in every little thing."

Maggie thought she might detect an unspoken addendum: *unlike the monsignor*, and wanted to let him know she concurred, but figured it would be bad form to talk church politics so early in the relationship. He picked up the bottle of pinot noir and refilled her glass.

"It's a little strange getting back into dating," he said. "And in our stage of life, it pretty much has to be a conscious decision rather than it just happening, like when we were in our twenties."

"Have you thought about Internet dating sites?" Maggie asked. Of course she knew the answer, but this seemed like the diplomatic way to ask. Plus, she wanted to see if he'd be honest.

"I've actually got a profile on one—for forty-somethings. It seems to make logical sense, zero in right away on people with similar interests and values."

"True. Assuming people are being honest on their forms. But I guess why wouldn't they be? It's to their benefit, right?"

He nodded. "I suppose."

"You don't seem too enthusiastic."

"I trawled through some profiles, and it just felt odd. Like I was stalking them. I don't really have any experience in social networking, never bothered setting up a profile on any of the popular sites, so as much sense as it made, I wasn't comfortable with it. But I was committed to at least giving it a shot."

"So did you go on any dates?"

"I chatted with a couple women and set up a date with one."

"What happened?"

He turned his eyes to his steak and cut as he answered. "I had coffee with you." Maggie titled her head questioningly as he slowly raised his gaze to her and shrugged. "I was supposed to have dinner with her tonight. But after Tuesday, I knew there'd be no point having dinner with her if I was wishing it was you instead, so I cancelled."

Maggie smiled but chastised him. "That's so mean!"

"Not really. It isn't like she even knows me, and wouldn't it have been more mean to have led her on even after I knew I wouldn't be interested?"

"You didn't even give her a chance. You might've liked her."

"Might have, but I *know* I like you." He raised his glass and indicated for Maggie to do the same. "To Father Tom, who beats iDate any day."

They clinked glasses, and Maggie shook her head but couldn't keep the goofy grin off her face. She'd never imagined that catching a man's attention could still make her feel downright giddy.

"Stop acting so innocent," Ray teased, his long dimples accenting his smile. "Did you honestly think I could get reservations at this place on a Saturday night in less than a week?"

"Raymond! Are you telling me I'm sitting in another woman's chair and eating her meat?"

"All I'm trying to tell you is that I'm glad you're here."

"Me too."

The conversation continued to flow easily throughout the rest of dinner, and Maggie started to think Father Tom's distraction tactics just might work after all. The first awkward moment didn't happen until the end of the evening, after Raymond had driven her home and walked her to her front door. To kiss or not to kiss. Maggie was warm from the wine and feeling nothing but good things about the man in front of her, so her vote was for kiss. She was pretty sure he felt the same, but he fidgeted and seemed unsure of how to go about it, so she decided to make things easy for him.

Even in her high heels, she had to lift up on tiptoes to rake her fingers through the thick hair at the back of his head and bring her inviting lips within inches of his. "Thank you for dinner," she murmured, not breaking eye contact.

He answered by lowering his mouth to hers.

That could've been it. A simple, light kiss. But when he began to break away, Maggie pulled him back to her. She wanted a man's mouth crushing onto hers, needed it. He responded by wrapping his large hands around her back and giving in to her need.

When he finally came up for air, he gasped. "Wow. It's been a long time since…wow."

Maggie didn't say anything, but leaned the side of her face against his broad chest so she wouldn't have to meet his eyes. The entire time she'd been kissing him, she'd been thinking of Evan.

Chapter 14

Maggie met Raymond late in the following week for lunch. She really did like him, and even though she continued to feel a pull toward Evan, progressing with Ray seemed to be her best shot at keeping the angel where he belonged in her heart.

"So how are your kids adjusting to school?" Ray asked after he'd finished describing a roommate issue one of his sons was having at college.

"Fine. Great, actually. Kirsten seems to like being at the high school as much as your Jason does. And Liam's doing okay too, but he's been bummed this week. One of his friends is being nasty to him."

"It'd sure be easier to raise our own kids if we didn't have all those other kids to contend with too, eh?"

"Sometimes I think so. But his friend Tommy is usually such a sweet kid, so I don't know what's gotten into him. I'm wondering if it has something to do with when he got sick at our house at the end of summer. You know how the last thing you eat right before you get the stomach flu becomes unappetizing for, like, ever? Do you think he could've made that association with Liam? The two of them were playing, I walked in to see if they wanted a snack, and the next thing I knew Tommy was puking all over the place. Oh, sorry," Maggie added with a slight laugh when Raymond lowered his spoonful of broccoli cheddar soup back into the bowl.

He gave her a teasing scowl and moved on to his sandwich.

"The really tough thing," she continued, "is that I can't decide whether or not to give Tommy's mom a call. My experience has been that no parent ever thinks it's their own kid's fault."

"That's a sticky situation for sure. Have you talked to the teacher about it?"

"No, not yet. But that's a good idea. I'm sure Liam's not lying, but I never know how much he might be exaggerating. And if he's not, well, then maybe the teacher can handle talking to Tommy's mom." She smiled. "Thanks for the advice."

"You're welcome."

Tommy Wilson didn't show up to school the next week; his mother had called him in sick. By Wednesday, the boy's condition was severe enough that his mother called the church office and spoke to Brenda, asking to have a priest sent over.

"For an anointing? Is it that bad?" Maggie gasped when Brenda told her.

"No. He's not in the hospital or anything, but she did sound freaked out," the office manager explained as she dialed the rectory. "Hello, Monsignor. It's Brenda. Grace Wilson just called in hysterics. Her son is ill, and she asked for a priest to visit them ASAP."

A few hours later, Sarto stalked into the office from the front entrance and went directly to Maggie's desk. "Mrs. Brock, can you make arrangements for your children tonight? I need you to accompany me."

"Does this have something to do with Tommy?" An ill feeling pooled in her stomach.

"It does. Can you arrange it?"

"I…yes. Kirsten's old enough to stay with Liam. What time do you need me?"

"Just after dusk, seven thirty. I'll pick you up at your home."

He exited the office before Maggie could ask any more questions. He'd seemed angry, and she was certain the Wilson kid must be pinning something on Liam. She felt immediately guilty for thinking that about a sick child, but as far as she knew, he wasn't sick at all and was just being dramatic.

To be better prepared for whatever she was about to face, she had a good talk with Liam before the monsignor picked her up. Her son only repeated the same things he'd been telling her all along, and part way through the interrogation he teared up. The only thing he confessed was that he missed his best buddy.

"Okay, baby, don't cry." Maggie hugged him and stopped her questions. "I'm going to help Monsignor Sarto figure things out and we'll get your old friend back."

At precisely seven thirty, Sarto's car pulled into the driveway, with Maggie waiting at the door. "To bed by nine if I'm not back by then!" she called to the kids.

It felt strange sitting next to the priest in his compact sedan. He always emanated an almost otherwordly presence, so it was odd to see him doing something as normal and everyday as driving an ordinary car. She'd halfway expected him to show up in a pope-sized Batmobile.

"Are we going to the Wilson's?" she asked.

"Not right away," he answered curtly. They drove a little further in silence before he spoke again. "We're going to Somme Park."

Maggie's chest tightened. "I thought you wanted everyone to stay away from there."

"I did. But not everyone listens."

Maggie was confused — was he saying he wasn't listening to himself? "Isn't the park closed?"

"They know we're coming."

Those were the last words he spoke before pulling into the parking lot and exiting the car. The night seemed to grow darker as the pair crossed the expanse of asphalt and walked past the night guard with no more greeting than a nod by Sarto. Street lamps along the main path shot cones of white light onto the gravel, leaving everything beyond in a dark gloom.

After curving past the fruit tree grove, Sarto motioned for Maggie to step off the path. They were going directly to the *tholos*, and the closer they got to it, the faster Maggie's heart beat. This didn't feel right. Why would he bring her to the very place he'd warned everyone to avoid? She peered sideways at the acute angles of the priest's profile as they walked, not noticing until then that he'd grasped the back of her arm, as if afraid she might run away otherwise. His face was stiff as always, but his typical coldness was replaced by a burning intensity. He flicked his gaze to her.

"Monsignor, I'm sorry, but can you please tell me what this has to do with Tommy?"

"You'll see soon enough." He quickened his pace so that she had to move into a slow jog to keep from being dragged. When they reached the structure, she planted her feet firmly in the grass and refused to step inside. Sarto stood directly behind her, tightening his grip. "What do you feel?" he asked in a low, controlled voice.

"Fear," Maggie answered.

"That doesn't sound like what you felt last time."

"Last time I didn't have someone forcing me inside," she said through clenched teeth, her wariness of the monsignor's connection to the energy growing.

He relaxed his hold. "I apologize for frightening you, but we're working with a limited timeframe. Please, Mrs. Brock, for the good of the Wilson boy, you must do what I ask without resistance."

"I don't understand. How does this help Tommy?"

"His family started noticing the changes in their son after they visited here last July. They didn't want to admit this to me at first, but once they did I began to form my theory. I think he became infected during his visit; he may have taken something from the urn that wasn't meant for him."

Maggie stared at him, showing the confusion she felt.

"You felt stirrings here," the priest continued. "I suspect the spirit in the urn was attempting to connect with you as well. I need you to be very brave right now and approach the urn, telling me exactly what you feel at each moment. I need to determine exactly what type of influence we're dealing with. Are you ready?"

"To tempt a demon? What if it infects me too?"

"I'm trained to deal with these things."

She considered breaking the priest's grip and running away, but where would that leave Tommy Wilson if he truly was possessed?

Maggie wasn't sure she could make her feet step into the *tholos* no matter how much her mind willed it. That's when she saw a soft wash of white through the tree branches. Evan stayed hidden, apparently not wanting to reveal himself to Sarto, but the glimpse was enough to give her the courage to walk slowly, with the priest by her side, to the urn. She inhaled deeply and attempted to calm herself, opening to the energy.

After a few silent moments, she said, "I don't sense it. It just feels empty."

Sarto's hand moved from her arm to the back of her neck, where he applied a forward pressure. Maggie resisted and shifted her eyes toward Evan. He'd moved noiselessly forward, and she could now see the rigid features of his solemn face. Slowly nodding, he kept his steely gaze on hers, silently assuring her he'd be right there should anything go wrong. Maggie attempted to swallow but found that her throat had gone completely dry. She closed her eyes and bent forward so that she hovered directly over the urn.

"Perhaps I should step outside," Sarto whispered. The pressure of his hand lifted.

Maggie stayed still, trying to clear her mind of everything. She wanted to pray, but was afraid that would only keep the spirit at bay.

Minutes passed, and Sarto lost patience. "Nothing?" he asked.

"Nothing." Maggie stood straight and opened her eyes.

"It's gone then. The boy may have taken it all. This is worse than I expected. Come, there's no time to drop you back at home."

They ran to the car, and Monsignor Sarto sped along the roads to the Wilson residence. "Should I wait in here?" Maggie asked when they pulled into the driveway.

"No. You'll stay with me. I may need your help."

They got out of the car, and he pulled a black satchel from the trunk before motioning for her to follow him to the house. Grace Wilson flung the front door open within seconds of Sarto rapping upon it. Her puffy eyes indicated she'd spent a good deal of time crying. "He seems better," she said, the high-pitched squeak in her voice betraying her lack of faith in these hopeful words. "I tried keeping him in bed like you said, but he was getting restless, so I let him go into the basement to play his video games. Ken's with him, but Tommy seems just like normal."

"Because it knows we're coming," Sarto said and headed straight to the basement stairs.

Maggie didn't say anything, but reached out and grabbed Grace's hand, rubbing the back of it with her thumb as they descended the basement stairs. Tommy stared forward at the television monitor with his fingers busy at the controls, completely ignoring their approach.

"Tommy," his dad said, "it's time to stop the game."

"Aw, just let me finish this level. I'm about to beat it."

Sarto nodded toward Ken, indicating it was fine to give the boy a few more minutes. The priest set his bag on the air hockey table and pulled out a long, purple stole, placing it around his neck. "Where are the other children?" he asked.

"We sent them for a sleepover at their grandma's," Grace explained.

"When this is all over, I'll want to spend some time with each of them, as well. Just to be sure."

"Of course," Grace said in a husky whisper pulling her hand from Maggie's to cover her mouth as she began to weep.

Maggie took a step closer and gently rubbed Grace's back. The act of comforting the other woman helped to allay her own fears. Sarto meanwhile unloaded his bag of tricks—a Bible, a bottle of holy water, and two rosaries. He handed a rosary to each of Tommy's parents and murmured for Ken to sit next to his son and be at the ready to restrain him should that become necessary.

"Okay, buddy," Ken said to Tommy as he sat down. "Time to stop the game." When the boy ignored him, Ken laid his hand on the remote.

"Don't touch it!" Tommy shrieked, causing Grace to flinch.

Ken gripped the remote and pried it from his son's hand. Tommy slumped back onto the couch and crossed his arms, scowling, while Sarto kneeled down in front of him and placed the ends of the purple alb onto each of the boy's shoulders. The priest tipped the bottle of holy water onto his finger tips and crossed himself before reaching out and tracing a small cross on Tommy's forehead.

Tommy stayed silent and watched the priest. His lower lip began to quiver. Monsignor Sarto kept his hand at Tommy's forehead and rested his palm upon it as he spoke words in Latin. A prayer. When he finished, Sarto's hand remained where it was, and he closed his eyes, the corners crinkling. "Why are you here?" he asked.

"You know why," Tommy said in a voice that sounded like his, but there was something more mature in the tone.

"Why have you entered this boy? How can he possibly help your ends?"

"He's a vehicle."

"To…?" Sarto prompted.

"Her." The word came out in a guttural hiss, and Maggie's fear crept back in. A year ago she would've suspected this was all an elaborate ruse, but now she didn't question it. The boy was possessed.

"Why do you stay so long?" Sarto asked the demon. "Have you given up on your objective? Lost sight of it?" Sarto asked.

Tommy clamped his mouth shut and set his jaw stubbornly. Sarto began chanting, again in Latin. He moved both hands to the boy's shoulders on top of the purple cloth and continued his incantation, his voice becoming lower and lower until it was a barely audible hum.

At last, Tommy spoke, and his voice had resumed its childlike quality. "He doesn't want to talk to you anymore. He's afraid."

"Will you talk to me, Tommy?" The priest likewise modified his tone to something more soothing. "Why is he with you?"

"Because I was bad. And he tricked me. He told me no one would ever find out and I could have whatever I wanted if I let him in. I wish I just would've told Mom and Dad that I made the scratch on their car." He clenched his eyes shut and tears leaked out. "But he said he wouldn't stay. He doesn't want to stay, and he's going to get in real big trouble if he doesn't get out soon."

"Why don't you let him out?"

Tommy opened his watery eyes to look at the priest. "H-He's so mean. I want him out but—" Tommy swallowed hard and flinched. Then he groaned and started to whimper. "I can't. Every time he tries to leave…I get sick."

Maggie's stomach lurched, and Tommy began to sob. His shoulders shook, and Sarto gripped them, attempting to hold the boy still. "Let him out, Tommy. It's okay. Just relax and release him."

Tommy took several deep breaths. And then he screamed. His father's arm flew around his shoulders, and Grace ran to him, but Sarto shouted for them to stand back and not touch the boy. "Pray your rosaries—both of you. Now!"

The priest resumed chanting his incantation while he closed his eyes and held Tommy firm. Both Grace and Ken gripped the beads in their hands and seemed to do their best to recite prayers while their eyes burned on their shaking son. Maggie, meanwhile, stood helplessly by watching Tommy struggle with the demon. He suddenly looked so small, so very small as his body trembled and his eyes rolled back, revealing only the white.

Strings of vomit spilled out the sides of his mouth. The demon was trying to get out. A flash of fear ripped through Maggie, and then eased. Everything was going to be okay. She could take the pain from this child. She had the ability. All she needed to do was open up to accept the spirit into herself instead. She'd be a savior. As an adult, she'd be much better able to handle the gifts this being would bestow upon her. Of course a stupid child had failed to deliver. But she wouldn't. She was so much more worthy than this sniveling creature and his insipid parents clutching their trinkets. As if those could ever save them.

Maggie gasped. These thoughts weren't hers. She shot her gaze desperately at Sarto and saw that his eyes were opened, watching her with an odd expression of expectation. She stumbled to the air hockey table and reached into the priest's bag, pulling out the first thing she touched. A wooden crucifix. She put it to her chest and attempted to recite the Our Father or the Hail Mary, anything, but no verses came to her.

Her knees slammed onto the concrete floor of the basement as she murmured, "Help me Father, help me, help me." They were the only words she could muster.

She was still whimpering on the ground when Grace shouted her son's name. Maggie slowly opened her eyes. The sensation that had gripped her was gone, and her thoughts were her own. Lifting her head, she saw Tommy slumped into Ken's embrace with Grace hovering over them.

"He's fine," Monsignor Sarto told them. "He'll probably sleep for a long while, but he's out of danger. I'll leave you with the rosaries—blessed by the Holy See himself—and this vial of holy water. Bless him with the sign of the cross every night and every morning. I recommend the whole family fast for the next three days. Only a small breakfast, lunch, and dinner with no eating in between. For Thomas, I leave this." He pulled a pewter charm on a chain out of his pocket. "It's the medal of St. Benedict. He should keep it on his person going forward. I'll be by at least once a day for the next week to check on him and to pray over your other children. It appears the demon has fled, but one must proceed with caution in these matters. If you notice any odd behavior, call me at once."

The Wilsons were shaken, but expressed their gratitude. After the monsignor packed his bag, they all went upstairs, with Ken carrying his sleeping child, and said their goodbyes at the front door. During the entire exchange, Sarto never once made eye contact with Maggie, not even when he pulled his crucifix from her hand.

Maggie sat awkwardly next to Sarto in the small vehicle. He didn't appear inclined to speak, but she had to ask. "Did I do something wrong in there? You seem so angry with me."

He stared out through the glossy black window, and for a moment, Maggie thought he was going to ignore the question.

"I didn't tell you to take the crucifix," he finally said. "You don't understand the rite of exorcism and it wasn't your place to interfere."

"I understand, Monsignor. But the spirit—it seemed like it was trying to enter me as it left Tommy. I felt the same sort of euphoria, or promises, that I did at the urn. It's hard to explain. But isn't that what you sensed when you were looking at me so intently?"

"It had formed a root in the boy. It needed a strong enough incentive to be able to release its grip."

"And I was the incentive? Is that why you brought me there?" Sarto kept his eyes on the road, and Maggie exhaled sharply, zoning her gaze onto the beams of the car's headlights as they shot into darkness. Folding her arms over her chest, she murmured, "I can't believe this."

"My methods may veer from the norm, but you can't deny they were effective."

"Were they? You seem disappointed I was able to escape with my soul fully intact. Shouldn't you be glad I grabbed the crucifix?"

She glanced sideways at him and saw his thin lips press together before he said, "That cross is formed around a splinter of wood from his cross at Calvary. It was an excellent choice of weapon." Maggie narrowed her eyes while he kept his stiffly trained on the road with not so much as a flicker in her direction. "At any rate, you have nothing to worry about. The extraction was too simple—meaning it was a lesser demon and not one that can do much damage on its own. It merely weakens the host's resolve against larger evil."

That new knowledge didn't exactly comfort Maggie. "What happened to it? Is it still out there?"

Sarto inhaled. "The energy is out there, but weakened. If weakened enough it may dissipate entirely. It hardly matters now. I hope you realize the importance of keeping the details of tonight's events to yourself, out of respect for the family's privacy."

"Of course."

They stayed mute for the rest of the drive while Maggie tried to concoct a plausible story with which to appease Brenda. A fabricated account would probably strike the office manager as more realistic than what had actually happened anyhow. When Maggie walked into her dark home with only the dim light above the kitchen sink providing bleak illumination, her first thought was to rush upstairs and kiss both of her children, but she didn't want to wake them. The evening had been so completely surreal that Maggie had felt almost as if she'd been walking through a movie, or a very dark dream. It was only when moving along the familiarity of her hallway that the reality of it hit her.

She jumped when the phone rang and rushed to it, her first thought being that it would disturb the children, her second being that she needed to talk to someone—anyone more communicative and less morose than the monsignor. The caller ID told her it was Sharon.

"Hi!" she said, letting herself take a full breath for the first time in what felt like a while.

"Are you working out? This late?" Sharon asked.

"No, no, I just…" Maggie's throat clenched. Everything that had happened that evening rushed at her and she couldn't even begin to explain.

"Oh no, did I wake you up? I'm sorry; this was the first chance I had to sit on my ass all day." While Sharon rambled on, Evan appeared across from Maggie on the opposite side of the kitchen island. She covered the receiver so Sharon wouldn't hear the tiny gasps that she suddenly didn't seem able to control. Evan watched her through cautious eyes, with the corners of his mouth curved into a compassionate frown.

Maggie jerked herself back into control, and when she was able to steady her voice, interrupted her friend. "Hey, Sharon, I'm sorry. I should've just let you leave a message. I'm actually not feeling very well. Could we talk another time?"

"Oh, yeah, sure. You okay?"

"I will be. Thanks."

The second after she clicked off the phone, Evan was at her side, holding her while she buried her face in his shoulder and released her sobs. He stroked her hair and scooped his arms behind her knees, lifting her. She clung to him, feeling as if she were emptying herself—all her fear, confusion, anxiety, and conflict. She needed someone to take it from her, at least for a little while. "Don't leave me," she whispered.

He pulled her closer and carried her upstairs, where he laid her on the bed, then climbed in behind and wrapped his arms around her, cradling her in his peace.

Chapter 15

The blurred, red numbers told Maggie her alarm would go off in twenty minutes. She'd slept solid the whole night through and had never felt the need to pull on her sleep mask. Closing her eyes again, she reflected on what had happened the night before. It was all still so eerie, but no longer overwhelming.

She flipped to her other side, keeping her eyes shut, and inhaled Evan's mellow and enticing scent. When she lifted her lids, he was only inches away, with his head on the pillow and his crystalline eyes wide open and crisp, not dull and puffy like Maggie was sure hers must be.

"Have you been here all night? Watching me?" she asked.

He reached up to push her hair from her cheek. "I was with you, but not watching you."

"You slept too?"

"No." His fingers stayed on her face, lightly tracing over her forehead, lulling her eyes back closed.

Stifling a yawn, she murmured, "You didn't watch me, but you were with me, and you didn't sleep. What did you do?"

"You wouldn't understand," he said and tweaked her nose before bringing his hand to rest on her hip, molding over it.

"It's a little early in the day to be torturing me with your cryptic answers, isn't it?" she said as she nuzzled into the pillow.

"Are you feeling better?" he asked.

"Isn't that something you can sense?"

"I want to hear you say it."

Maggie opened her eyes. "I'm still a little freaked out, but I'm feeling better. Is it still out there? The thing that was in Tommy?"

"Most likely. Men of the cloth have certain powers and rights entrusted to them, but obliterating any of God's creatures from existence isn't one of them."

"One of God's creatures? It sounds so strange to call it that."

"If you believe he's the Great Creator of all things, then yes, even spirits turned evil were initially created by him."

Maggie gave a small nod. "Before it left Tommy, it felt like…like it wanted to enter me."

"I know, Maggie. I know everything about what happened last night. You don't need to talk about it unless you want to."

"Do you know that the thing, the demon, may have made an earlier attempt to get to me? When Tommy was here playing with Liam, after his family had visited Somme, he got sick—he vomited, which is what he said happened whenever the demon tried to leave him."

"I'm sure it tried to leave many times. That doesn't mean it was targeting you. But either way, there have been enough close calls that I'm going to stay closer to you from now on. I won't interfere, and I promise to stay in the background. But you'll have to be careful about blocking me again, Maggie."

She pulled her hand from under the covers to rest it along the side of his face. "I wouldn't have made it through last night without you. I want you close. I won't block you again."

They stared at each other, silently sealing their pact. It had been weeks since Maggie had felt their flesh meld the way it did now with her hand pressed against his face, and she knew no matter how many times she experienced it, the sensation would always take her by surprise. "Father Tom said I should keep an arm's distance from you."

"Should I move away?" Evan's silvery irises flicked back and forth, studying her expression, while his hand tensed on her hip.

Maggie shook her head no as best she could with half her face against her pillow, and she lightened the pressure of her hand on his face so that her fingertips barely skimmed its surface, gliding over the contours of his jaw and cheekbone. "I can handle this. You're my friend. My blessed, divine friend, and I can keep the lines straight. Plus, I've got a burning hunk of man now to direct my earthly passions at."

"Raymond?"

"Yes, Raymond." She tweaked his nose and brought her arm under the cover, snuggling in closer to her platonic friend for the last few minutes before the alarm would sound and she'd have to begin her day.

"Just be careful, Maggie. I'll be around, but that doesn't mean I can protect you from everything."

Maggie could hardly breathe. Her heart throbbed at double time as Ray's weight pressed into her. Her skin burned despite the fact that her blouse was now open and hanging half way off of her. Although Evan might be lurking somewhere near, she felt no sense of her guardian angel. But just the thought of him was enough to rally her force of will. She pushed back Raymond, inching him away. Her sudden resistance seemed to surprise him, and he sat all the way back in the driver's seat of his truck. Once she'd caught her breath, she climbed over the console to straddle him.

"I'm sorry," she whispered. "I'm sorry, I'm sorry, I'm sorry," she repeated as she feathered small kisses onto the side of his neck. She'd entered into the make-out session willingly enough—instigated it, if she was being honest—but she hadn't expected it to get so heated that quickly. Ray didn't say anything, just breathed hot, heavy gusts onto Maggie's bare shoulder. She pulled back and readjusted her shirt, slowly buttoning it back up as she tried to explain herself. "This all just kind of took me by surprise, and there's something I want to talk to you about before we get too far down this road, okay? I'm not sure how you're going to feel about it."

Raymond brought a hand up to smooth his disheveled hair. He seemed to be more bewildered than angry. "Feel about what?"

"Carl and I never got an annulment. So, if you adhere strictly to the church's rules, then having sex with me would make you an adulterer. And I just, I didn't think it would be fair of me to pin that scarlet letter on you without at least warning you first."

He turned his eyes to the window, and she kicked herself internally for not having told him earlier. He probably figured she was free and clear of marital encumbrances when Father Tom set them up.

Raymond returned his gaze to her. "Is that really all this is about?"

"Isn't that enough?"

"Maggie, I know this could become an issue if we went as far as getting married and wanted a church wedding, but even then I'm sure it could be worked out. Red tape as far as I'm concerned. So no, it doesn't bother me. Does it bother you?"

Maggie shrugged. "I'm not sure exactly where I stand on it. And believe me, I've given it a lot of thought. But I just can't bring myself to negate my marriage to Carl as if it was never real. And the more I've thought about it, an annulment just seems like a way to avoid admitting to a mistake. Isn't it unfair for the church to deny me a second chance just because I'm willing to own up to my mistakes rather than ask for a free pass?"

While talking, she mis-buttoned the top of her blouse, and Ray's long fingers followed behind, putting the buttons into the correct holes. "It sounds to me like you know exactly where you come out on the issue. Listen to his word, and listen to your heart — it'll all come together." He finished buttoning and ran his fingertips along the inside edge of her collar, ticking her skin. Maggie smiled in appreciation of his straightforward simplicity.

"So where does this leave us?" he asked.

"It leaves you as a very good kisser." She leaned down and gave him a soft peck on the lips. "And me needing to get into the house before the kids start getting suspicious about what Mommy and Mr. Fender have been doing out in the driveway for so long."

He laid his hand over hers and held it to his chest. "That's not what I meant."

"I know." She sighed. "I guess I've still got some internal wrestling to do. But I'm getting there. And when I arrive, you'll be the first to know." They finished off the evening with a long, slow kiss that brought Maggie a little closer to clarity.

It had been more than a week since the incident at the Wilson's before Maggie thought to call Sharon. Kirsten and Liam were both occupied in other rooms, so she grabbed the phone and dialed, planning to chat with her friend while she straightened up in the kitchen.

"Hello," Sharon said.

"Hi! It's me, Maggie."

"Yeah, I know. Saw your name on the phone." Sharon's tone stayed flat.

"Right, of course. Well, I was calling to see if you're free next weekend. The kids and I — and this new guy I've been seeing — were hoping you'd join us for Boo at the Zoo. I know it'll be crazy crowded being the last weekend before Halloween, but — "

"Can't. Busy next weekend."

"Oh, shoot. I really want you to meet Raymond, the new guy. He's great."

"I'm sure he is, and sorry to shock you that I, too, have a life. May not be the thrill ride that yours is, but it's mine, and I've got plans."

"Oh, something exciting?" Maggie asked in an attempt to allay whatever had put her friend in such a sour mood.

"Probably not to you." Sharon left her answer clipped, causing Maggie to suspect her friend's irritability was purposely being directed toward her.

She proceeded, babbling now that she was somewhat nervous, under the hope that she was just being paranoid. "Well, if it's an adult-only thing that's got you tied up, Katie and Shelby are welcome to join us. Actually, Kirsten's sort of counting on Katie being there. Raymond's bringing his teenaged son, and she's just absolutely mortified by the thought that the outing could be construed as a double father-son, mother-daughter date. Apparently she doesn't think Jason, who I haven't met yet but sounds like a great kid, is cool enough for her."

"Ah, okay, now I get why you called. Sorry, can't help you out. Katie's coming with us."

"Okay, well, I figured it was worth a shot. So how's everything else with you?"

"If you really gave a rat's ass about how I was doing you'd probably call more often, and not just to ask a favor."

"Aha, so you *are* mad at me."

"Frankly, yeah. I'm tired of being hung up on and rushed out on. You're making me feel like the clingy best friend, and I guess I'm just done with it. You're not obligated to be my friend, and I'm not obligated to be yours. We don't have to pretend just because our daughters are close."

Maggie was stunned into silence.

"Look," Sharon continued. "I'm most likely perimenopausal, and I've had a shitty week. It's best to hang up now before I say something I'll really regret. Have a good time at the zoo."

Maggie heard a click at the other end of the line, but continued to hold her phone, staring at it even after she'd also clicked off. She couldn't deny she'd been neglectful, but she had a lot going on under the surface that Sharon had no idea about and felt unfairly blindsided. She was completely oblivious to how richly she'd deserved her friend's reproach.

By the time zoo day arrived, Maggie had decided it was better that it was just the five of them for their first "family date." This way they could get to know each other without being distracted by others. Every year, Maggie had thought about coming to the zoo for its autumn festivities, but it took Ray suggesting it to get her there. The day was cool and slightly windy, sending orange and yellow leaves swirling through the park at random intervals, and the animals were so much more alert and energized in the crisp weather than during the hot summer months. In contrast, Raymond was noticeably more reserved. He didn't grab Maggie's hand or show any other type of physical affection, and she appreciated his respect for any conflicted feelings the kids might have about the new relationship.

It turned out that Kirsten didn't need live people for a distraction and spent most of the day texting her friends and glancing up once in a while at a particularly playful rhino or baboon. Jason seemed bored at first, but as the day progressed, it became clear that every word he said was like gold to Liam—particularly when the topic of video games came up—and the two boys started palling around, with Jason taking Liam off on side expeditions to the bear wilderness and the reptile house. As Maggie had suspected, Jason was a very nice kid, but he wore his insecurities on the outside—in the form of dark, nondescript clothing and long bangs that shrouded his eyes. She was pleased that Kirsten hadn't been outright rude to the boy, but she made a note to talk to her daughter later about making more of an effort to be nice.

Things got busy for Ray the following week, and Maggie only heard from him sporadically. She was disappointed when he didn't answer her last-minute phone call inviting him over to drink wine with her while she handed out Halloween candy. It tended to be more drinking than candy giving since few trick-or-treaters ventured into her neighborhood of townhouses.

She'd already gone out with Liam, dressed as Super Mario for the second year in a row, for an hour before Carl came to take him to what they called the "rich neighborhood" where houses gave out full-sized candy bars and cans of soda. Then she'd driven Kirsten to the annual Halloween scavenger hunt party at Katie's and stubbornly stayed in the car when she'd dropped her off instead of accepting the customary open invitation for the parents to come in for a mug of Sharon's specialty Halloween grog.

When Ray responded via text that he couldn't make it, Maggie sighed and filled her glass, resigned to drink alone as she smiled at the random goblin or princess on her door step and tossed fun-sized candy bars into their bags. After a particularly adorable spider left, she kept the door open and leaned against its frame to watch the arachnid, its parents, and their baby ladybug amble down the sidewalk.

"It's safe to come in, you know. I'm all alone," Maggie said when the family was too far to hear.

"You knew I was here?" Evan asked, his lean form coming into full view as he stepped from the shadows.

"I always know."

"And yet this is the first time in weeks you've invited me in…"

"Sorry." She smiled and stepped back to motion him through the doorway. "I've been busy."

"So I've seen," he remarked as he strode past her. After Maggie shut the door, he asked, "And everything feels…normal?"

"Remarkably normal. Is that why you've been sticking so close to the shadows? To restore normalcy? Do you think that'll help keep me away from the evil influence?"

"Possibly. Sometimes these things are drawn to those closest to our Lord. Being a constant companion of an angel could make you a target."

"Then wouldn't it make more sense for you to not come around at all?"

"Do you want me to stay away?" Evan asked.

"No, definitely not. It's just that, if you're not fooling me, surely you're not fooling it, them, whatever. So is a true separation something we should consider?"

"I have considered it." Evan examined her, his eyes roving over her face and down her length, as if searching for something. It made her uneasy.

"What is it?" she asked.

"I don't appear to have any choice. I've not been allowed to take my focus off you. The best I can do is stay in the background."

"So you *want* to leave me?"

"No. But I also don't necessarily want to be around to witness... everything."

The silver of his irises looked more leaden than usual as he glanced away, and Maggie blushed, thinking of that night in Ray's truck. Perhaps she hadn't been able to sense the angel's presence as accurately as she'd thought. A subject change seemed in order. "We haven't talked since that phone call to Sharon, the one where she told me I'm a horrible friend. I was thinking about how Liam's friend had started being nasty to him because he'd been infected—do you think that could be the case with Sharon too, maybe to a lesser extent?"

"I can't say for sure, but this seems like a strictly human problem to me. It's entirely possible for friends to get angry at each other without being possessed by demons."

She narrowed her eyes. "Look, I know I haven't been the most attentive to her, but I can't believe she'd come down on me like that. And honestly, she's been pretty damn rude to me throughout the years—always prying into my business, making snap judgments about my personal life—and I've never once railed on her. She can just stew on this one for a while."

Maggie took a long sip of wine and drained her glass, ignoring the arch in Evan's eyebrow that accused *her* of being the one who was stewing. As she reached for the bottle, Evan laid his hand on hers. "Be careful with your anger, Maggie. It feeds them. You and your friend have issues to work out, but giving evil purchase on your souls isn't going to help either of you."

The doorbell rang, and Maggie laughed at the timely arrival of a miniature, horned Beelzebub standing on her doorstep.

Chapter 16

On All Souls Day, Maggie let Brenda know she'd be taking an extra long lunch break and drove south along the river to meet Raymond at a new gourmet sandwich place. She found him already there, seated at one of the high-backed booths. He stood and greeted her with a stiff kiss on her cheek and stayed quiet while they looked over their menus. At first Maggie thought he was probably preoccupied with the work that had been keeping him busy the last several days, but when he laid down his menu and didn't look directly at her as he asked how she'd been, she knew something wasn't right.

"What's going on?" she asked.

He met her gaze and gave a chagrinned half-smile — it didn't even cause the slightest dent in the sides of his face. "I was planning on getting into this after we'd had a chance to eat, but I apparently need to work on my poker face."

"Is it bad news?" she asked.

He reached his hands across the table and touched hers with just the tips of his fingers. "Maggie, I've been seeing someone else."

The entire restaurant may as well have fallen into a dark pit and left Maggie perched amidst a gray sea of nothing, because that's exactly how she felt. She hadn't seen this coming from eight million miles away.

"I know we've never talked about being exclusive," he continued. "So for all I know you're seeing someone else too, but we've progressed far enough that I feel like I owe you an explanation. I guess what

I've realized about myself is that I'm just not the type of guy who can handle dating two women at once."

"And you're choosing her."

Raymond watched Maggie and cautiously nodded just as the waiter approached to tell them all about the soup of the day.

"You know what? I'm not hungry, but thanks," Maggie said, handing the server her menu.

"Give us a few more minutes," Raymond interjected.

The confused waiter looked down at Maggie's menu and seemed to consider giving it back to her, but after a nod from Ray, he left with it.

"A restaurant, Ray? Really? You think this is a good place to break up with someone?"

"I'm sorry, you're right. This wasn't the right place to do it. Come on." He set his menu down and stood, reaching for Maggie's hand. "I don't blame you for being shocked. But I think it'll benefit you just as much as me if you'll let me explain."

Maggie ignored his outstretched hand, but stood and led him out of the restaurant. The day was overcast, but with mild temperatures, so Maggie continued down the sidewalk.

When they passed a coffee shop, Raymond said, "At least let me buy you a coffee."

"Hot chocolate. The biggest they've got. With whipped cream." A few minutes later, armed with her warm cup of security, she was ready to hear him out. They'd walked onto the main bridge and stood on one of the curved lookout points over the shallow river.

"I wasn't looking for someone else. I dropped off the dating site and felt very grateful to have met you. But then she came back in my life, a former college girlfriend. After graduation we'd gone our separate directions, and even at university our timing had never been quite right, but it looks like we've been given a second chance."

"How long has this been going on?"

"She first called me about a month ago. She moved back into the area. For a while it was honestly just a reuniting of old friends—a phone call here, a lunch there, but in the last couple of weeks the old flames reignited. I suppose it's because we've got all that history to build on that it's moving so fast."

Maggie saw the gentle glow under his surface as he spoke of this other woman and noticed something missing under her own — there was no nagging sting of jealousy.

"The only negative is having to end things with you," Ray said.

"Yeah, her timing's still rather sucky for me." Maggie stared hard at him. His downturned mouth and the glassiness of his warm, brown eyes gave his otherwise sturdy face a somewhat pathetic air and convinced her of his sincerity. Softening, she said, "I appreciate you being honest and not stringing me along."

"I'd never do that. I respect you too much." He chanced a small smile.

"Thanks." She nodded but couldn't quite smile back. Ray was a good guy, and she could see that he was already beating himself up over hurting her, so she shrugged and added, "Who am I to mess with fate?"

He cocked his eyebrow. "You believe in fate?"

Now Maggie was able to smile as she glanced down and confessed, "No."

"Didn't think so."

When she lifted her eyes back to his, one side of Ray's mouth lifted in a regretful half-smile. "I didn't believe in it either, but I wouldn't be doing this unless I was sure, and I think my certainty can only be explained by fate, as if an angel carried her on his wings and brought her back into my life."

Maggie turned her gaze toward the rushing river and murmured, "Interesting choice of words."

Once safely back in her car, she drove around for a bit and let the tears flow, afterward blaming her red eyes on late-season allergies. At the end of the day, with the kids in bed, she thought she'd cry again, but didn't. Instead she pulled a load of whites out of the dryer and sat cross legged on her bed folding clothes while watching TV.

Evan appeared, and a quick glance at the careful way in which he regarded her told Maggie he knew what had happened. "Relax," she said. "I'm fine."

"Does your heart hurt?" he asked.

Maggie paused in her folding and considered his question. After a few moments, she shook her head. "Not my heart this time. Just my ego. Getting kinda tired of being the rejectee."

"Good," Evan answered. "Egos are much easier to heal."

Maggie balled up one last pair of socks and set it on top of the pile in the basket. "Might be nice to get to see your face around here more often—and not only when I'm feeling sorry for myself."

"I think I can arrange that. Right now, however, I'm going to let you get your rest."

Maggie nodded, wanting nothing more than to curl up under her blankets for a long, solitary sleep.

Ever since the exorcism, an unspoken tension had flickered between Maggie and Monsignor Sarto. She avoided interaction with him even more than usual, but often felt him scrutinizing her. Yet the moment she turned her head in his direction, his eyes would dart away.

"I'm not saying he's evil or anything. I just find it a little hard to trust him after he used me as demon bait," she explained to Evan one evening in the quiet of her bedroom. She hadn't been able to let go of the hostility on her own, so she was bringing her concerns to the angel.

"It was an effective plan," he responded.

"Seriously? You're taking his side?"

"There are no sides, Maggie. Only truth, and the truth is that, although you may not like them, his tactics worked."

"And what if they hadn't? What if the demon had entered me? Would you still be defending him?"

A playful smirk danced across Evan's full lips and into his shining eyes. "Then it would've been my turn to play exorcist."

"You can do that?" she asked from her seated position on the bed.

Evan, standing above her, tilted his head and leveled a teasing glare that was both charming and challenging. "Do you doubt me?"

Maggie smiled, intrigued by this new aspect of her angel. "I'm quite sure you're capable, but…how would you do it? I don't picture you walking around with a little leather bag full of goodies."

"I don't need goodies."

Maggie laughed. "How then?"

Evan clasped his hands together behind his back and made a show of pacing alongside the bed while he examined her through narrowed eyes, sizing her up.

"You're a fighter," he declared.

Maggie opened her mouth to deliver a quip, but before she could utter a sound, he'd climbed onto the bed and laid her flat, pinning her hands over her head and trapping her hips between his thighs. She made an instinctual move to break free, but he didn't budge a millimeter.

"So my first act would be to subdue you," he said. "Then I'd ask—politely, of course—for the demon to come forth. We'd have a conversation, he'd see he didn't stand a chance, and he'd leave."

"That easy, huh?" Maggie asked, doing her best to match his nonchalant demeanor rather than give in to the rush of adrenaline fluttering dangerously close to her surface.

"True, they're not all cooperative. Some can be irritatingly stubborn. *Those* get threatened with an angel's kiss."

"Doesn't sound so bad." Maggie's voice sounded very small to her own ears.

"That's because you're not a demon." His eyes left hers to wander down to her parted lips. "If you were, you'd flee at the first graze."

Maggie held her breath as he lowered his face and pressed his lips softly against hers while inhaling the air from her mouth into his own. Any negative thoughts she'd had, any unpleasant feelings she'd clung to throughout the day drifted away.

He lifted his mouth from hers, holding his face only inches away. When he exhaled, his breath cooled the moisture he'd left behind on her lips.

"What if that doesn't work?" she asked in the barest of whispers.

He answered by pressing his mouth more earnestly onto hers. The blending sensation that occurred whenever they pressed flesh to flesh was hardly discernible as they melded in a gentle, yet all-encompassing kiss. As they moved together, Evan pulled all malevolence out of her, leaving behind only the purest sentiments, untainted by anything corrupt or shameful. Her thoughts merged into a translucent and feathery cloud.

His pressure eventually eased, but he lingered over her mouth, not seeming inclined to pull fully away, and Maggie noticed the inexplicable absence of the questions that should have been swirling in her mind. She didn't worry that the sensual encounter was wrong; she somehow knew it wasn't. She also understood that this was as physical as things could ever get between them. But that knowledge didn't leave her aching for more—her dominant emotion as he pressed his mouth one final time to hers was satisfaction.

He released her wrists and removed his weight from hers, lying on his side and looking down on what she was sure must be a dazed expression. "Are you okay?" he asked.

She shook herself into focus and murmured, "That was amazing. The demons must run screaming from that level of...of...bliss."

Evan smiled. "Consider it a taste of what you can expect in the next life." He trailed his fingertips along the side of her face, and for a long while they simply watched each other.

Inevitably, however, Maggie's curiosity returned and she reluctantly broke the enchanted silence. "Can all angels do that?"

"We all have the ability, but it takes a certain level of training."

"So you're a trained demon hunter?" She pushed herself to sitting, and now looked down on his agile form as he reclined on a propped arm.

"It's not my specialty, but I've received some training."

"And why are you showing me this now?"

He glanced away and sat up, his mouth pulled tight.

"Evan, tell me."

"I've been concerned about Tommy's demon. No signs of it have appeared in the vicinity, and I started thinking that perhaps it had, in fact, entered you and gone immediately dormant, biding its time until my attention went elsewhere. You've been holding more grudges than usual lately—that's often a sign."

"I thought you said my problems with Sharon seemed like a human issue."

"True, but now I see you're holding onto your animosity toward the monsignor too, so it seemed like a good idea to check, just in case."

"So this was a sneak attack?"

Evan chuckled. "I guess you could say that."

"And you're sure it couldn't still be in there, hiding in some dark corner?"

"I was pretty thorough."

Maggie smiled and nodded in agreement as her face flushed. It only took a moment away from Evan's touch for her human instincts to kick in, and her reflections on the kiss were already twisting it into something slightly naughty. The way the white linen stretched across his chest when he sat up, giving a hint of the lean but defined muscle beneath, wasn't helping. "What about the last time you kissed me, the quick one behind the bushes? Were you checking then too?"

"No. I told you, that was a spontaneous reaction because I was happy to see you."

"What about the time you kissed my forehead, at the canyon? I was pretty low then, were you worried that evil influences were involved?"

"That was…something else." His gaze fell for a moment before he lifted it to her again, the muscles between his jaw and cheekbones flexing.

"What, exactly? You've never really explained it."

"I was tempering a random spark of something I'd not felt before. An urge, most likely lust." His resolute focus on her didn't waver. He didn't smile, but his look wasn't harsh either. He was merely stating facts. "That kiss was done as an act of self-control."

"The control you didn't exercise behind the bushes." She wanted to coax out a warmer reaction to his confession.

He tilted his head and raised his eyebrow in warning. "Technically, that's correct, but that was a kiss of friendship and what I was demonstrating prior to that was control over my lust, which I've contained ever since."

Maggie nodded and kept her smug smile internal—he'd said "contained" not "extinguished." Satisfied with the answer, she was ready to move on. "Have you ever actually cast out a demon?"

"That was my first attempt on a human."

"So that's a no?"

He pushed himself back to lean against the headboard, raking his fingers through his hair. "Not exactly."

"What then—cows? Sheep?" She'd only been joking, but became concerned when a dark shadow crossed his face. "You don't have to answer that," she quickly added.

"I cast them out of my Lord's kingdom."

"Out of…do you mean you…" Maggie thought she should've been numbed to new revelations by that point, but each one continued to astonish her, and this one most of all. It was impossible for her to picture her gentle angel in the midst of the great battle in Heaven.

He sat with knees bent and forearms resting on them while he stared at the fingers of one hand twisting over the knuckles of the other. Crawling to him, Maggie took both his hands into hers. He stopped fidgeting and turned his palms up to grasp onto her, letting his breath drain out in a slow exhale.

He didn't look at her as he said, "I lost brothers that day. Lucifer had been doing his work discreetly. The signs were there that something was going on—unexplained fires, strange symbols; it was how they communicated—but no one on the other side understood it. It was a brilliant strategy. We had no idea who'd been recruited to his side until weapons were drawn." Evan's fingers wrapped tightly around Maggie's wrists, and a new kind of energy flowed into her. It was cold and trembled at the edges. "Angels who'd been by my side for ages, whom I'd trusted and served with, suddenly held their blades to me. We didn't have time to sort it out. We had to react immediately."

Maggie shuddered involuntarily, and Evan's eyes snapped up. He dropped his frozen hold on her and clutched his hands into fists on his knees. "I'm sorry."

"Don't be sorry." Maggie moved to sit beside him, resting one hand protectively on his shoulder and reaching the other across to cup his jaw. "How many times have you patiently listened to my petty drama? This is so much bigger. You can tell me. I'll listen. I want to."

He pressed his mouth into a straight line before whispering, "I don't want to relive it."

"You don't have to."

He ducked his head, and Maggie instinctively guided it to her chest. Leaning back against the headboard, she slid her hand from his shoulder to the side of his head and let the other drop to his back as he rolled into her and wrapped his arms around her waist. With her knees pulled up on either side to fully cradle him, she stroked his back and combed her fingers through his hair as she'd done so many times to comfort her children.

They lay wrapped in each other until the vibe coming from Evan warmed enough for Maggie to fall asleep. She only half woke once during the night to find herself alone under her covers and hear Evan murmur, "Thank you," before he left.

Chapter 17

The next day at work, Maggie received a text from Carl asking her to call him that evening to discuss Thanksgiving. It was his turn with the kids so she wasn't sure what there was to discuss—unless this time he wanted to usurp the whole weekend and take them to Disney World or somewhere else fabulous without her.

She never would've been able to predict what Carl actually said: "Melissa and I were talking, and we'd like to invite you to join us for Thanksgiving dinner."

Maggie didn't respond.

"Mags? You still there?"

"Yes. So…is this a we'll-ask-her-to-be-nice-but-hope-she-says-no invitation?"

"If it was, would I tell you that?"

"Guess not." She twisted her lips and bit them. It was all she could think to do in her utter confusion.

"Seriously, we want you here. It would be nice for the kids to be able to celebrate with both parents, don't you think? And I know she'd never tell you this, but Kirsten worries about you when you're left alone on holidays."

"Yeah, she does the same about you."

"So come on, it'll be fun," Carl coaxed.

Maggie exhaled. She knew she was about to give in, so she threw up one more barrier. "Does Melissa still not know about our little escapade last spring?"

It was Carl's turn to be silent.

"Carlicious, still there?"

"She doesn't know, and I'd like to keep it that way. She and I were broken up at the time, so you and I didn't do anything wrong, but I don't imagine she'd be thrilled with the news. I don't see what the purpose would be in telling her."

"Relax, I agree one hundred percent."

"Good. So are we on for Thanksgiving?"

"Yes. And…thanks for the invite."

"Words are cheap, Magpie. Know how you could *show* me your appreciation?"

"How?" she asked cautiously.

"By bringing your famous sweet potato casserole. I told Missy you would."

"Aha! I knew there had to be an ulterior motive." Maggie laughed, thinking perhaps this would be fun after all.

After helping Liam with a science report and then getting him into bed and securing a promise from Kirsten to only stay on the computer for another half an hour, she ran out to the store for peanut butter and other lunch supplies, and then decided to take a quick run by the church to see if Randy, the janitor, had delivered the giant cornucopia and silk florals she'd asked him to retrieve from storage. When she could, she preferred to arrange the altar in the later hours when the church was typically vacant.

On her way into the narthex, she passed by a man heading out. He tilted his head in greeting and she recognized him as the handsome newcomer at Father Tom's archeology presentation the previous summer. It was the first time she'd seen him since, but he'd obviously continued on at the church in some capacity, even if it was just to visit the adoration chapel, where she assumed he was coming from.

Maggie found the boxes she wanted stacked in the coat closet and smiled. Picking up the two bulkiest, she carried them to the church, pushing the door open with her back. When she turned and faced the front, she stopped abruptly. The altar was in disarray, with its tall, brass candlesticks knocked over and strewn across the twisted cloth. The glass surrounding the hanging lamp had been shattered, and the flame, ever-burning to indicate the presence of Christ, was dead.

Maggie swallowed and set the boxes on a pew in the back row, thinking she should run to the rectory to alert the priests, but she held still when a muffled sob sounded from the altar. Taking a breath and stepping into the aisle, she peered through shimmering dimness, with the glow of electric votive candles casting an eerie motion throughout the large, open space. A dark, hunched figure kneeled at the side of the altar, directly beneath the fractured lamp.

Maggie walked cautiously up the aisle and about halfway she saw that it was Father Tom. He appeared to be picking up the glass shards, and even in the gloomy church Maggie could see he was shaking.

"Father! What happened?" She quickened her pace to reach him, but he sat back on his knees and held a hand up for her to stop. She did as he requested, but insisted, "You're bleeding. Please, let me help you clean that up."

She took another step, but now another figure emerged from the shadows. It was Monsignor Sarto, and his face smoldered with quiet fury as he hovered over Father Tom. She now noticed the overturned wooden pillar that typically held the paschal candle at the monsignor's feet. The candle itself had rolled nearby.

"You can't help him." The monsignor's voice was cold and his words final. "Please leave us and lock the doors on your way out."

"But I don't mind —" She dared another step.

"I said leave!" The monsignor demanded.

Maggie halted, but turned her worried gaze on Father Tom. He nodded and attempted a reassuring smile. "Go on, dear. It'll all be fine." When she still didn't move, he added, "Please."

"You're sure?" she asked quietly, as if the monsignor wasn't standing right there, glaring at her.

Father Tom nodded again, his eyes pleading for her to just do as she was asked, so she retreated, picking up the boxes on her way out. When she reached the doors into the narthex, the monsignor called out to her.

"I advise you not to say a word about this to anyone. For Father Reardon's sake, at the very least."

Maggie nodded and left. After ensuring no one was in the adoration chapel, she locked the church doors and prayed throughout her entire drive home. She checked on the kids, got ready for bed, and waited for Evan. But he didn't appear that night.

All the next morning, Maggie was tempted to tell Brenda about what she'd witnessed in church the night before, but first she wanted to talk with Father Tom. When the door from the rectory opened, she whipped her head around to greet the pastor, but instead she saw Monsignor Sarto. He was closely followed by Father Dominic, whose eyes remained steadfastly fixed on the floor as the two men made their way to the conference room.

Sarto paused in the doorway. "Mrs. Drummond, Mrs. Brock, please join us."

Brenda shot Maggie a questioning glance, and as they both stood and walked together, Maggie's mouth went dry. Sarto stood at the head of the long table and motioned for the women to sit down. They took chairs next to each other, opposite from where Father Dominic sat.

"There has been a significant development," the monsignor said. "I've also requested the presence of the principal, school secretaries, and our financial consultant. We'll wait for them."

Maggie stared at the glossy tabletop, attempting to manage the dread gnawing at her gut. Within minutes, nearly all the seats were taken, but the room remained disturbingly quiet. Sarto continued standing. "Thank you all for coming on such short notice. I don't doubt you'll be surprised to learn that Father Reardon has voluntarily applied for mental health leave, which the bishop has granted." A low murmur went through the room, and Brenda's hand shot to her mouth. "This morning I drove him to St. Paul's Retirement Home for the Religious, where he'll be staying indefinitely. For now it's best to operate under the assumption that he won't return to St. John's."

"No!" Maggie shouted and stood. "This isn't right! He can't…he's not ready to retire." She felt Brenda's hand on her arm, coaxing her down, but she stood firm, her glare aimed straight at Sarto.

"I understand how surprising this is," Sarto said calmly to the group at large before turning to Maggie. It was only for a flicker of a second, but Maggie was certain his lip had curled when his eyes fell on her. "Your loyalty is commendable, Mrs. Brock, but this outburst won't help any of us to move on and address the ongoing operational and spiritual needs of St. John's parish."

She saw there was no point in arguing with Sarto and sat down. She'd find another way to get Father Tom back. The meeting continued with everyone volunteering to fill in the gaps until either Father Tom was reinstated or a new pastor was found.

Maggie and Brenda stayed busy the entire day rearranging schedules and notifying committee heads and other parish leaders of the new development. Every time Maggie delivered the news, her heart ached. When Father Dominic came in to gather some things from Father Tom's office, he said that he was as shocked and bewildered as everyone else, and his somewhat dazed expression backed this up. After school, Maggie drove the kids home from school and went immediately to the retirement home.

Most of the leaves had fallen from the tall oaks that peppered the hilltop home of the former seminary. The three story structure with its thick stone pillars had a solid, formidable presence, even with the peeling trim and fogged windows. Inside, the place had a less clinical feel than Maggie had expected. The front doors opened to a cozy sitting area with upholstered chairs and a throw rug. Framed artwork hung on walls painted in rich, warm colors that calmed the panic that had been clambering within Maggie all day.

A slight, elderly woman sat at a small desk to the side of the room. "May I help you?" she asked.

"I'm here to see Father Thomas Reardon."

"Ah, our newest resident," the woman said. "Let me see if I can find him for you. What's your name, dear?"

"Magdelyn Brock."

The woman got up and went through the double doors at the far end of the room. While waiting, Maggie walked over to inspect one of the paintings more closely. The brass tag on the frame said it was a reproduction of a painting by Henry Ossawa Tanner in 1898. *The Annunciation.* A young Mary sat cautiously on her bed, covered in robes, with her feet on the floor and hands clasped on her lap. Her head tilted in question, but her eyes held fast on the luminous figure at the left of the canvas.

Maggie was torn from her study when the double doors reopened. The woman gave her a kind smile, but her eyelids crinkled downward in apology. "Father Reardon has requested privacy and is currently taking no visitors."

"Did you speak to him? Did you tell him it was me?"

The woman's mouth curved into a sympathetic frown. "I'm sorry, dear. Perhaps you can try again next week."

Maggie nodded and walked out. On her way to the row of parking spaces, she kept her neck craned, unsuccessfully searching every window for signs of her beloved priest.

"Can you please go check on him?" Maggie asked Evan when he finally came to see her a few days later. She'd immediately filled him in on what had happened since he'd been gone.

"Priests aren't in my sphere."

"You don't have to talk to him, just…just go float into the old seminary building and see how he looks, what he's doing." She paced across her bedroom floor in front of the angel.

"That's not how it works."

"Well, talk to your angel friends, then. Network and find someone who knows."

"That's not—"

Maggie leveled a glare that stopped him from completing his sentence. "This is driving me insane! There has to be something I can do. Bringing pumpkin bread to that gatekeeper when I tried to see him again yesterday didn't help. I just need to know he's okay. And I want him to know he's got someone on the outside who cares."

"The outside?" Evan's lips twisted into a half smile. "You make it sound like he's in prison."

"How can you be so sure he isn't? It's all very strange, don't you think? I still don't know what that scene in the church was all about. Maybe I should go have a chat with Sarto."

The angel's smile faded. "I'm not sure that would do any good. He doesn't exactly seem to be forthcoming with information."

"Yeah, Pot, and you are?"

"Pot?"

"Calling the kettle black. Never mind. My point is that you're not helping either, so what am I supposed to do?"

"Wait until Father Tom is ready to see you, and pray for him in the meantime."

The boiling air seeped out of Maggie like she was a popped balloon. "Always supremely logical, aren't you?" She looked down to the plush carpet as she squished it through her clenched toes and contemplated what he'd said, concluding, "Well, I guess that's all I can do — for now." After a few moments of silence, she tilted her head to look at him. "Where've you been these last few days?"

"After verifying during our experiment the other night that you are not, in fact, inhabited by a demon, the aura of danger surrounding you lessened. It appears this lower level of risk translates into me resuming my other duties."

"Oh. I hadn't even thought about you neglecting other things while spending so much time watching over me."

"They weren't neglected — they were being taken care of, just not by me."

"Does this mean you'll fade away and not come back at all if the 'aura of danger' stays away?"

"I don't know."

"Great. So I can lose you and Father Tom both at the same time."

"You wouldn't lose me. I've always been around and will continue to be."

"It wouldn't be the same. I want to see you, talk to you. Touch you." She reached to his sides and slid her fingers between his. "I don't know how I would've gotten through these last few months if you weren't right here."

"You've gotten through many tough situations without me. You'd have been fine."

Frowning and shaking her head slowly, she curled into him, wrapping her arms around his waist and nuzzling into his chest. She didn't want to have to get through things by herself anymore. In the quietness and the closeness, she inhaled his mildly spiced scent and noticed things she hadn't before. "Your heart beats," she murmured. "Fully human form…" Spreading her fingers, she traced up and down his lower back with her thumbs.

"Maggie…" he warned, and the hands he'd molded to her back stiffened. She didn't miss the corresponding increase in his heart rate.

She stopped moving her fingers, but remained pressed to him. With fabric between them, he felt firm and solid, exactly like a man.

"I know humans weren't made to be with angels," she said, "but humans weren't made to travel into outer space either, and yet we still do it. We weren't made to glide over water either, but we figured out a way. Maybe you and I can figure out a way too."

When Evan didn't answer right away, she let her fingertips resume roving ever so cautiously along the indent of his spine. She only got halfway up before he reached his hands behind to grab hers and hold them still. "That isn't why I'm here," he said, though the tremor of his tone conflicted with the certainty of his words.

"You don't know why you're here." Pressing her fingertips resolutely into his muscle, she pulled her face away from his chest to level a challenging look at him. She was tired of waiting for answers. And she was tired of fighting these feelings.

A hint of fire glinted in the shards of Evan's irises, but the cool gray surrounding them tempered the urgency, and when he spoke again, his voice had become steady and determined. "It's not for that. Do you remember Father Tom's advice? To stay an arm's length away from each other?"

She nodded, her stubbornness receding with the pastor's name being brought back into the conversation.

"He's a wise man, Maggie. We should've listened to him. So maybe now, to show how very much we respect him, we can follow his guidance."

He knew just which buttons to press. She let her hands drop to her sides, with his following along as he intertwined his fingers with hers. They stood only precious centimeters apart, his head tilting down while hers angled up so they were nearly cheek-to-cheek. It would have been so easy for Maggie to swing her face over to rest against his smooth, extraordinary flesh, to sink into him, but she knew that would be too much to pull back from, so instead she closed her eyes and stayed still, absorbing his essence as she attempted to siphon from him whatever resistance he could spare.

His warm breath cascaded along her jaw and down her neck. "I have to go," he whispered, and without Maggie being prepared for him to leave, he squeezed her hands, then stepped back and faded from view before she'd fully reopened her eyes. She was afraid it would be the last time he ever touched her.

Chapter 18

The day before Thanksgiving, Maggie stopped by St. Paul's Retirement Home to drop off a small dish of sweet potato casserole. "It needs to be refrigerated," she said to the woman at the front desk, "so if someone could let him know."

"Maybe you can tell him yourself. Would you like me to try again?"

Maggie smiled, thinking perhaps the pumpkin bread had done the trick after all. A few minutes later, she was given directions to Father Tom's room and at last allowed beyond the sitting area. Upon reaching his room, she rapped her knuckles lightly on his half-opened door.

"Come in, Maggie," he said in a gravelly voice that sounded too tired.

"Hi!" She was determined to stay cheerful throughout the visit. "How are you feeling?"

Sitting in a chair by the window with a light blanket over his legs, he merely shrugged in answer.

"I brought you some sweet potatoes for Thanksgiving. I was making it for tomorrow anyhow, so I figured why not make a little extra? I used lots of sugar, so it'll make a good dessert if you don't get enough at the meal they serve here. And if you'd prefer a home cooked dinner, I could bring you a whole plate full tomorrow night."

He nodded and then his eyes wandered toward the window. "That sounds nice. But…no. Please don't."

"Okay." She looked around the sparse room and spotted a small dorm-sized refrigerator next to the desk. "I'm going to put this in your fridge. They're pretty good cold, but if you want to heat them up I'm sure you can just ask somebody to do that for you."

"That will be fine."

Maggie bent and turned from him to put the potatoes away, cursing the tears that stung the corners of her eyes. He seemed so lost and she didn't want to admit to herself that he might belong here. Once she was sure her smile was firmly in place, she again faced him.

He slowly swiveled his head toward her, and his droopy eyes met her gaze. "Perhaps it was too soon for me to receive guests. I must look pretty old and worthless."

"No, no, you don't." She pulled the desk chair over and sat facing him, taking his hands in hers. "But, Father…what are you doing here? What happened that night in the church?"

His shoulders lifted as he took in a deep breath. "I'm too ashamed to say."

Maggie waited, giving him the opportunity to continue, but when he didn't, she asked, "Did the monsignor do something to you? You can tell me. I'm on your side. No matter what, I'll back you up."

He squeezed her hands. "People…are not always what they seem. Don't be quick to judge, and don't trust blindly." His grip tightened until it almost hurt as he peered at her through eyes that were suddenly more clear and wide. "Be wary of strangers. Anyone who's come into your life this last year. And pray, Maggie. *Pray*. Keep your heart with the Lord. Promise me!"

Her head bobbed as if she thought she could reassure him with the velocity of her nod. "I will."

His grip relaxed and he settled back into his chair, but his brow held tight in concern. Maggie closed her eyes, and began to recite the Our Father and then the Hail Mary. He joined in and they recited a few more prayers together. When they finished, he thanked her for coming and wished her a happy Thanksgiving. Then his focus once again turned toward the window, and she knew it was his way of dismissing her.

The kids ran off with Carl as soon as they arrived at his place so he could demonstrate the capabilities of his brand new, monstrously huge TV, and Maggie carried her bag of food into the kitchen, where Melissa busily tended the various pots and dishes.

"I brought some wine," Maggie announced. "Figured the two of us could use it, so I bought the big boy." She pulled an oversized bottle of Chardonnay out of the bag and plopped it on the counter. "I brought food, too."

"Ah yes, the oven's all ready for your world famous sweet potatoes."

While the two women went about their work, Maggie asked, "So how's the real estate biz?"

"Always slow this time of year, but I've got a client who absolutely insists on being in a house by Christmas, so I'm in the market for a motivated seller."

"Too many of those these days."

"That's sadly true. But I'm seeing fewer and fewer. So, how's the church biz?"

"Eh, kind of weird lately."

"Oh yeah, your favorite priest got put to pasture. Carl told me." Melissa's eyes moved to the doorway. "Speak of the devil."

"Carl told you what?" the devil asked, walking into the kitchen.

Maggie quirked an eyebrow. "Were you just standing outside the doorway waiting for your name to come up?"

"Afraid of a little girl talk, are ya?" Melissa teased.

"Girl talk, no. Woman talk—that's a whole other story."

"We were talking about Father Tom," Maggie said. "I was able to visit with him yesterday."

"So you see, everything's fine," her ex-husband assured her.

Maggie shook her head. "No, something doesn't feel right. He was too quiet, and when he did talk, he was almost panicked, paranoid. But I still say he doesn't belong there."

"He's not exactly a young man, Maggie," Carl said. "Sounds like he could use a mental break, and you don't know, he might relish the opportunity to kick back and play chess or whatever it is retired priests do. Why don't you just let him rest and enjoy it?"

Maggie stayed quiet as Carl walked over to the oven and pulled out the rack to baste the turkey. Nobody else seemed to share her suspicions. Even Brenda, though she was upset, had accepted the circumstances at face value. Perhaps it was time for Maggie to do the same.

She walked to the far end of the counter and uncorked the wine. As she poured three glasses, she watched Carl and Melissa working in unison, crossing paths and exchanging little smiles as they prepared the meal. He'd apparently gotten more in touch with his domestic side since the divorce. It felt strange to Maggie to feel happy for him in his new life, but she did.

Dinner with her children, ex-husband, and his new girlfriend was surprisingly comfortable. At least it was until Melissa asked Kirsten how things were going with Carter — a name Maggie's daughter had never before uttered to her mother — and Kirsten's eyes shot wide open in what she'd obviously meant to be a subtle warning glare at Melissa.

"I assume she's not talking about Jimmy," Maggie said wryly, staring directly at a flushed Kirsten.

"Who?" Kirsten asked.

"U.S. President. That song you learned in third grade," Carl said and started singing "The Presidents Song" — a diversion tactic if Maggie'd ever seen one.

"Cut the crap, Carl. Who's Carter?" Maggie demanded, turning back to Kirsten.

Huffing and looking at her plate while she pushed her fork through her mashed potatoes, Kirsten mumbled, "He's a boy at school who I think is cute. And he's nice to me."

Liam started making fake retching sounds, and Maggie smiled, liking that, after cute, nice was the first quality her daughter appreciated in a boy. "Why didn't you tell me about him?" she asked.

"I don't know. You said I'm not allowed to date until sixteen so I guess I just didn't want you freaking out."

"Are you dating?" Maggie asked.

"No! He doesn't even know I like him. God! Can we change the subject?" Kirsten's pleading eyes vacillated between Carl and Melissa.

"After I say this, sweetie," Melissa said. "I'm with your mom on waiting to date. Don't be in a rush; there'll be plenty of time after you turn sixteen."

Kirsten sat back in her chair with a dramatic exhale. "Yeah, I guess. I mean, look at the three of you. You're still dating and you're so *old*."

Carl sucked his lips in over his teeth to look like gums and croaked, "What? What'd she say?"

Everyone laughed except Kirsten, whose eyes risked getting trapped in a permanent roll. But she did at least smile.

"So you've got someone?" Melissa asked with an encouraging nod toward Maggie.

"Oh…"

While Maggie fumbled around for what to say, Kirsten sat forward, giving her mother an intense stare. "Yeah, mom, tell everyone about the new guy."

Maggie flicked a questioning glance at her daughter before answering. "I was seeing a man from church earlier in the fall, but he got back together with an old flame, so our story was cut short."

"Oh, I'm sorry," Melissa said.

"Not as sorry as me," Liam chimed in. "His son was like awesome, and he was gonna sell me his Alienware PC really cheap as soon as he bought a new one."

Maggie felt a twinge of guilt. It wasn't fair to bring people into her children's lives who could so easily disappear. Suddenly, anonymity was another point in Evan's favor.

After dinner, everyone helped clean up the table and pack the food away. Then Carl and the kids retired to the family room to watch TV while Maggie stayed in the kitchen to help Melissa do the dishes. As soon as two women were alone, Melissa poured each of them another glass of wine, saying, "Might as well make an event of it."

Maggie threw a dishtowel over her shoulder, and they dug into their work. Melissa was easy to talk to, even more so as Maggie sipped down yet another glass of Chardonnay, and before she knew it, she was telling her husband's girlfriend about Sharon. "I'm perfectly willing to apologize and do what I can to redeem myself," she explained, "but I left a message a week ago, and she hasn't returned my call. I'm not going to grovel."

"Mmm, yes, girlfriends are so much more difficult to crack than the guys," Melissa mused. "With men, all you've got to do is make 'em a meat loaf, throw on something sexy, and all's forgiven."

Maggie scowled. "I haven't exactly had a lot of success with that half of the species, either." She was caught up on her drying duties, and stood next to Melissa, waiting for her to finish washing another bowl.

"Aw, come on, it can't be that bad." With two rubber-gloved hands busy in the sink, Melissa playfully bumped her hip into Maggie's just as Maggie lifted her glass to her lips.

"Oh, yes, it can be!" Maggie laughed, taking a step away and then a gulp.

Melissa narrowed her eyes and looked her boyfriend's ex up and down. "When's the last time you got laid?"

Maggie held the wine in her mouth for a moment before letting it burn down her throat. "Too long?" she answered carefully, not knowing what kinds of confessions Carl may have made in the last few days.

Melissa jabbed a sudsy finger at Maggie. "That's exactly what I thought. At least tell me you have a decent vibrator."

When Melissa resumed washing, Maggie wandered back to the sink, relieved that the identity of the counterpart to her last "lay" was still secret, but knowing she must seem rather pathetic. Ego plus wine encouraged her next statement. "*Please* don't say anything to the kids, but I do kind of, sort of, have a man in my life."

"Is that what that hesitation was about?" Melissa grinned and gave Maggie a sideways glance.

"What hesitation?"

"At dinner, when I asked if you had a guy. You hesitated."

"I did? Do you think anyone else noticed?" She looked toward the entrance to the kitchen.

"That's doubtful. So, tell me about him."

"Well, he's wonderful, first of all. Supportive, smart, funny—but not in a life-of-the-party kind of way, more subtle. And he's very interesting. I swear we could talk forever."

"Good looking?"

Maggie nodded. "But it's so much more than that."

"So what's the problem? Why haven't you introduced Kir and Liam to Mr. Wonderful?"

"It's complicated. He's not…" *Human?* "He's playing hard to get."

"How do you mean?"

"Well, there's an obvious physical attraction, and at times we've gotten quite close, but he throws up a barrier. He doesn't think we're a good match, that there's no future, and so he doesn't want to lead me on."

"Not a good match—why? Because you have kids? Doesn't sound so wonderful to me."

"No, that's not why." Maggie exhaled, kicking herself for making Evan the subject of girl talk. "It's just really complicated, and I'm sorry, I don't want to talk about it anymore." Maggie scowled at the pale truth serum lying innocently at the bottom of her wine glass. "I think I'd better switch to coffee."

Melissa pulled the plug on the drain and peeled off her gloves. "Persistence, my dear. I have faith you'll bring him around. If not, dump his ass — 'cause you really need to get laid." She winked while she rubbed lotion into her manicured hands and let the subject drop.

The five of them finished off the evening curled up on Carl's comfy furniture, eating pumpkin pie and watching *It's a Wonderful Life*. The kids were staying at Carl's for the long weekend, so after the movie Maggie kissed them good night, and then Carl followed her into the hall to thank her for coming.

"You were right," she conceded. "It was fun. Thanks for having me over."

He smiled and pulled her into an unexpected bear hug. "Kiddo, I think this is the start of a great friendship."

Maggie laughed. "You just butchered Bogart, but I have to say I agree with you."

Back at home, all alone and with no sign of Evan, Maggie slid open the deep drawer of her night stand. She reached in and fished around before landing on what she was looking for. "Hello, old friend," she murmured as she pulled out a long, slender, vibrating toy.

It had been a while since she'd seriously considered using it. On nights the kids were home, concern that they'd hear the low hum in the small townhouse always overshadowed any pleasure she'd hoped to derive. And ever since Evan's unpredictable appearances, she didn't dare use it when the house was empty either. Tonight, however, she ran her finger along its length, and thought perhaps letting Evan watch wasn't such a bad thing. Her lips curled into a wicked smile. If he was determined to stay an arm's length away, what choice did he give her?

He listened to her heavy breathing and watched her back arch off the bed the moment the device hit its mark. Her sharp gasps delighted him. She was ready, but he'd have to move quickly. He couldn't deny daughters of God were beautiful, and he'd always found the daughters of man to be ravishing—but something in between was precisely what he was after.

Chapter 19

If Evan had been watching Thanksgiving night, he gave no indication, and Maggie didn't press him to find out. He was entitled to his secrets. And she was entitled to tease and entice him — without touching, of course. Just enough to tickle the edges of her desire.

It was the first Saturday in December and three days since Maggie had last seen the angel, but he'd been coming by regularly every few days, so it seemed he wasn't set to be banished from her world just yet. By Maggie's estimation, he was due for another visit and with Liam away at a sleepover and Kirsten out at the movie theater, they'd have a couple hours to themselves if he arrived soon. She exchanged her T-shirt for a gauzy printed blouse and threw on a pair of dangling earrings. Ignoring the first candle on the Advent wreath, she went around the kitchen and great room lighting spiced mulberry candles to wash the walls and surfaces in sensual movement. After hitting play on Tchaikovsky's *Nutcracker Suite*, she had a thought and pulled a box from the cabinet under the TV. When she turned, Evan stood behind her.

"Scrabble?" he questioned, reading the box.

Maggie smiled. "I'm tired of playing figurative games, so I thought, for a change of pace, we should match wits at a real one."

He tilted his head and pursed his lips, not appearing enthusiastic.

"Unless you'd prefer Ouija," she teased. "Maybe then we'd finally get some straight answers about exactly what it is you and I are supposed to do with each other."

"Scrabble will be fine. You'll have to tell me how to play, though."

She went to the kitchen table and spread out the board. "It's a word game. Sort of like building your own crossword puzzle." His brow furrowed. "Which you're not familiar with either. Okay, I'll start with the basics." She gave him a cursory explanation with a promise to address the finer details as they went along.

They selected their first set of letters, and as Evan laid his squares on the wooden ledge, he asked, "When do you expect the children home?"

"Liam's gone all night. And Kirsten's at the movies with Katie—they couldn't decide which one to see, so they're going to make it a marathon and see two back-to-back. Here, pull a tile out of the bag—whoever draws the earliest in the alphabet goes first."

"*A* for angel," Evan said, revealing his letter and waggling his eyebrows up and down.

Maggie laughed. "You go first then. One letter of your word has to be laid over this center star, and you'll get double points on the whole word."

He studied his tiles, and laid down *ORION*.

"Ooh, sorry, can't do that."

"It's a word."

"Yeah, but proper nouns aren't allowed. Sorry I didn't explain that before. I suppose since you're a first timer, I could let you have this one."

"No. I'll play by the rules." He swept his tiles off the board and took a bit longer to come up with *NOIR*.

Maggie wasn't entirely sure that word was allowable either, being French rather than English in origin. Normally she'd challenge her opponent, but this time she decided not to draw attention to his potential infraction. It was only worth eight points anyway, and she saw a way to make the most of it.

While she set down her tiles, Evan asked, "If you're serious about making amends with Sharon, wouldn't tonight have been the perfect opportunity to meet up with her? Go see a movie of your own or out to dinner?"

She'd laid a *W* and a *Y* on either side of Evan's *R* to spell *WRY*, earning double points for each of her letters. "I made my gesture weeks ago, and if she's not willing to return it, that's her choice. By the way, that's seventeen points for me."

With a troubled expression, Evan intently scanned his letters. His eyes flicked to the board, and then his lips twitched into a smirk. From the *N* he formed *NAKED*, with triple points on *K*. "Twenty points for me." He grinned.

Maggie narrowed her eyes, and couldn't prove it, but suspected he was happy about more than just his impressive word score — perhaps he *had* been watching the other night. She mentally rearranged her row of letters, and after things clicked into place, pulled six from the ledge. Points weren't her objective this time. She used Evan's *K* to retort with *STALKER*.

"Thirteen." She winked.

He focused his eyes downward until he'd formed his next word on the board, and when he looked back up it was with a challenging gaze. Using Maggie's *S*, he'd responded with *SUCCUBUS*. Apparently, their figurative games could meld quite easily into their literal ones. "With triple points on this *C*, that's another twenty points for me," Evan announced.

Maggie slid a *P*, *R*, and *E* from her ledge and was about to use them with his top *U*, but then spotted the open *D* at the bottom of the puzzle. A quick calculation told her she'd be even with the angel if she chose *PURE*, but she'd have more fun with the other option. She sacrificed the two points and laid down *PRUDE*. "Sixteen." She smiled, figuring she'd have plenty of time to make up for the lost points later.

The phone rang, and Maggie jumped up to answer it.

"Mom?" It was Kirsten, and even from just the one syllable Maggie could tell her daughter was upset.

"Did you get caught sneaking into a theater?" She'd warned the girls to buy tickets to both movies.

"No. But, Mom, please, could you just come pick me up? I'm not at the theater."

"Where are you?" Maggie's tone had hardened.

"Look, just don't yell at me yet. *Please*. I really need you to come." Kirsten's voice broke, and short, squeaking sobs came through the phone.

"Sweetie, I will. Just…calm down. I'll be there. Where are you?" Maggie's heart began to pound. Breaking down like this wasn't like her daughter.

"Hold on a second," Kirsten said in a shaky voice. The phone was muffled and then she said, "It's off of Foxgrove, about three miles south of downtown. Go west on a road called Hutchens. It turns gravelly, and you'll see the police cars."

Maggie had to stop herself from shouting. "Police?"

"I haven't been arrested or anything," Kirsten explained. "Just please come now."

"I'm on my way." Maggie clicked the phone off and grabbed her purse from the counter. "I've got to go," she called to Evan as she went to the closet to snatch her coat before speeding out of the house.

How in the hell did she get all the way out on Hutchens? And why in God's name are the police involved? She fought off thoughts of possible scenarios the entire way. She'd just have to find out when she got there. The moonlight was blotted out by thick clouds, so she'd expected to be plunged into complete darkness after turning onto the gravel road, which was bordered only by farmers' fields. Instead, bright punches of throbbing light vibrated in the distance, revealing smoke, blacker than the night and billowing high into the sky. The sharp scent of ash penetrated the car.

As she drew closer to the flashing lights, Maggie saw the police and fire vehicles they were attached to. A black and white was turned sideways across the road and an officer waved for her to stop. "Sorry, ma'am. This road's been closed."

"My daughter's in there. I just got a call."

"Can I see some ID please?"

She dug her driver's license out of her wallet and handed it to him.

Shining his flashlight, he briefly examined it before handing it back. "I'm going to have to ask you to park here, off the road. You'll find your daughter straight up that way." He indicated the road behind him.

"What happened?" she asked. "Is everyone okay?"

"The officers with your daughter can tell you more."

Keeping her hands as steady as she could, she pulled her car alongside a minivan parked diagonally in the faded grass. The land was brittle and dry as it awaited the first snow of the season. Maggie practically ran down the rocky road until she came upon a group of teens standing between two police cars. Three fire trucks stood on the left of the road, and just beyond them streams of water gushed from long hoses into the smoking field.

"Mom!" Kirsten called out from the group, but was held back from bolting to Maggie by the police officer who was apparently watching over them.

Without needing to be asked, Maggie whipped out her driver's license again and said, "That's my daughter. Can you please tell me what's going on?"

The officer let Kirsten come to stand by her mother and explained that the police had been called in when the resident of a farmhouse nearby reported seeing flames in the field. The fire department had responded immediately and contained it, but several minors had been caught attempting to flee the scene. Upon questioning, the teens had revealed that they'd started a bonfire in the field, but they'd lost control of it and it spread.

While he explained, a couple more parents arrived, and he addressed them as well. "As of right now, we believe we have all the minors in attendance accounted for, and thankfully none are injured. Because they're all minors, no arrests have been made, but they're guilty of trespassing, damages to property, and violation of burn laws. All misdemeanors, but nevertheless, I suggest you each get yourselves an attorney. They've all been processed and questioned, so you're free to take your children home."

Maggie looked at her daughter. "You're okay?"

Tears filled Kirsten's eyes, but she nodded. "Yeah. I'm sorry, Mom. I really thought we were going to see the movies, but Kate got a text from these guys and they picked us up at the theater and took us out here. I'm so sorry!"

Maggie pulled her into a hug. This wasn't the time to lay into her, yet she couldn't quite conjure up any words of comfort either. She was in shock. "Does your father know?"

"He wasn't home and didn't answer his cell." Of course Kirsten had tried him first.

"Let's go," Maggie murmured and began walking toward her car. On the way, they crossed paths with Sharon, and Maggie glared at her.

"Oh my God, Kirsten!" Sharon shouted. "Where's Katie? Is she okay?"

Kirsten nodded and shrank into Maggie, who jerked her head back and said tersely, "She's back there with her other friends. Don't plan on seeing Kirsten around your house for a while."

Sharon's mouth fell open, and Maggie tightened her grip over Kirsten's shoulder and continued walking. She didn't speak again until they were back on Foxgrove and heading home. "Now, how about you tell me exactly what happened."

"It was just supposed to be a bonfire," Kirsten said. "We were only going to stay for a little while, and then they'd bring us back to the theater for the next movie, so I didn't see any reason to call you."

"Don't feed me that bull. We'll talk about all the ways you're in trouble with *me* tomorrow, but tonight I want to figure out exactly how much trouble you might be in with the law. How did the fire spread? And tell me the truth — did some of those kids do it on purpose?"

"No! It was all an accident. Someone threw a full can of pop in there and we were taking bets on what would happen, and then it exploded. At first it just seemed like ash flying out, but then we saw sparks turn into flames so a bunch of us started stomping them out. It was fine. But all of a sudden all these other explosions started happening — I swear I don't know why. I didn't notice anyone else throw in cans — but the fire was exploding and we all started stomping out the flames, but they kept coming, and then some got really big and just, like, took off into the field. I guess we all panicked and just started running. It was really scary, Mom."

Her voice trembled, and Maggie reached a hand from the wheel to grasp her hand as she continued with the story. "It didn't seem like a regular fire. It was, like, alive, sort of. I was running with Katie and Jake and Carter, but then it felt like the fire shot in a line straight through us and I got separated from them. I kept running farther away from them because it seemed like the flames were chasing me. Every time I swerved one way, they followed, and then finally, somehow Carter got back to me and just tackled me to the ground, out of the way, and the fire kept going but didn't spread out to us. We were able to walk away, and then the firemen and police were there."

Maggie returned both hands to the wheel and gripped it. The thought of how this story could've ended differently was too frightening, too horrible, to contemplate. And there would've been nothing Maggie could've done about. "Do you have any idea how lucky you are?" she found herself shouting at her daughter. "What in the hell were you thinking? Trespassing! You think it's okay to just light a fire on someone else's property?"

"It was already lit when we got there!"

"And why were you even there? Don't lie to me again and tell me it was Katie's friends who called—this Carter is apparently *your* boyfriend! Correction, 'was' your boyfriend. You won't be seeing him anymore. You won't be seeing anyone for a while."

Kirsten pulled her arms up and crossed them over her chest, staring out the windshield as tears streamed down her face.

Maggie exhaled. "I'm sorry I lost my temper, but I assure you, the rest of your friends there tonight will also be grounded—at least the ones with parents who care about them."

Kirsten blew a derisive laugh. "Yeah, right. Like you care so much."

"Don't turn this around on me. Of course I care about you. And that's why we need to tighten up the rules now that you've proven your intent to stretch them."

"Well, if I'm home all the time, won't that make it more difficult to sneak around with your new boyfriend? Or will you just keep him up in your bedroom all the time?"

Maggie stared straight ahead. She felt her daughter's eyes on her but was too stunned to respond.

"I'm not stupid," Kirsten continued. "I can hear his voice coming from your room at night. I can't make out what he's saying or anything, but I know it's a man's voice. And lately it's obvious all you really care about is getting me and Liam out of the way so you can be with him. At least Dad includes us on the stuff he does with Melissa."

"I...I brought you along to the zoo with Mr. Fender—and you were kicking and screaming the whole way."

"So you admit you've got someone else now?"

They'd arrived home, and Maggie pressed the button to open the garage door. As they waited for it to open she said, "I've got a television in my room and have started watching it when I have trouble sleeping at night, so that's got to be what you're hearing. The closest thing resembling a boyfriend is a rather handsome doctor in a new show I've become addicted to." She hated to lie to her daughter, but there was no other option. And after what Kirsten had pulled that night, she figured she was owed a chance to lie.

They got out of the car and entered the kitchen to find candles still flickering all over the place. Kirsten sneered at her mother. "Is this all for the rather handsome doctor?"

"Wash up for bed," Maggie ordered as she snuffed the candles. "We'll talk about all of this in the morning. For now, I honestly am just happy to have you home and safe." She planted a kiss on her daughter's head and wrapped her in a tight hug.

After Kirsten was safely in bed, Maggie threw her coat back on and paced along the front porch, attempting to invoke whatever summoning powers she was allowed. "Would it really have been so difficult to snuff the candles?" she muttered to herself while she waited.

"You're angry about candles?" Evan asked skeptically from behind her.

She pivoted and huffed. "Well, they sure didn't help our case. Kirsten's heard you in my room and asked me about my new boyfriend."

"What did you tell her?"

"That you play a doctor on TV." Maggie pressed her icy hands into her closed eyes and sank onto the wooden rocker. "Everything's such a mess."

Evan left her alone with her emotions for a few moments, and then said, "She's okay though. Unharmed. What did she tell you about the incident?"

Maggie lowered her hands. "So you already know about it?"

He nodded.

"She said some stupid kid threw an unopened can of soda into the bonfire and it exploded. Apparently there were a lot of other idiots there who did the same thing because the fire kept popping and caught the surrounding dried stalks, spreading out like...wildfire, for lack of a better word. She said a line of fire chased her until the little bastard that brought her there in the first place pushed her out of the way."

Evan's face tensed. "Is that all?"

"Essentially. Then she told me what a horrible mother I am."

He kneeled in front of her. "Are *you* okay?"

She frowned and ran the back of her fingers down the side of his face. "Just please tell me my kids have guardian angels too and that I won't have to rely on that twerp Carter to protect her."

"They do," he answered.

She shook her head, feeling only slightly relieved. "I just wish we could infuse her with all the things I had to learn the hard way, you know? Now that she's getting older and more independent, I'm just so scared about what can happen to her. Can't the Lord give teenagers an extra layer of protection?"

"He does."

Maggie tilted her head questioningly at him.

"He gives them parents."

His sober look when he said this was like reflective glass, causing Maggie to see herself through someone else's eyes. But they weren't Evan's eyes she was looking through, they were Kirsten's. When she'd confronted her mother about her new boyfriend, Maggie's first concern had been to protect her secret. But looking back on it, she only now realized that Kirsten had been telling her something else—she'd been feeling neglected, pushed aside by the mystery paramour. Pushed aside by her mother.

Maggie's head waved from side to side. "And I wasn't there. I was with you, playing a game." She locked eyes with his and held his gaze. "Evan, I've been pushing a lot of things aside for you." His gaze held steady, giving nothing away as she carefully watched him, and she pulled her hand back from where it had been lingering at his chin. "Kirsten does tend toward the dramatic, but I admit there've been nights when I've rushed through getting the kids to bed in the hopes of seeing you. And I certainly haven't gotten as sad as I used to about the weekends they spend at Carl's."

"Dependence on either side—parent or child—isn't good. So this is a beneficial development. You know Kirsten wouldn't have let you join her tonight, whether or not you'd had other plans. If not with me, you might've been out with a friend."

Maggie absently nodded. "Uh huh. If I hadn't been looking so forward to spending the evening with you, I probably would've called Sharon again. And I might've looked a little more carefully at any clues Kirsten gave that she was up to no good."

Evan pushed back onto his heels, away from her. "I didn't intend for you to give up parts of your life for me."

Maggie studied his expression through the thin cloud that formed when his breath met the cold night and detected a flash of guilt there, along with something else…fear? A sickening conviction began to take form in her mind as she replayed the last weeks. She'd thought their mutual affection was something they'd implicitly agreed to leave unspoken, but now she wondered if she'd been wrong and there'd been nothing mutual about it.

"I haven't been entirely honest with myself lately," she said, her voice coming out at a higher pitch as she pushed it through her tightening throat. "But now I see that I'd better be honest with both of us before I keep traveling too far down this rabbit hole. As much as I knew it could never happen — I thought you and I were forming something here." She halted her confession when he backed farther away.

"We are forming something," he said.

"What, exactly?" she asked.

"Friendship."

"Yep. That's what you've been telling me all along." She spoke in a laughing tone, but her voice was bitter. "But you see, I'm operating at a whole other level of delusion over here. I've been telling myself it's only the angel/human thing keeping us from being more, but I get it now. There's another reason: you don't *want* it. Not anymore." She shook her head. "But I continue to twist your every gesture, expression, and word the way I want to see it. I'm such an idiot. I'll never learn. Just like Carl, just like Ray — you're done with me."

"Maggie…don't."

"Don't what? See the truth? Why won't you touch me, Evan? Why won't you even touch me?"

"We agreed — "

"No!" She shot up from the chair and then lowered her voice. "*You* said you didn't want to touch me anymore. I let myself believe it was for the sake of purity, but that's not the whole reason. Even when you kissed me…you had a perfectly logical and innocent explanation. I was the one who chose to fool myself into thinking there was more to it. But you warned me, and I wouldn't listen. Meanwhile, I've been neglecting all my other relationships for you."

"I'm sorry, Maggie." Evan remained rock still, not even a finger twitched in her direction, and she was painfully aware of the earlier times when he'd soothed her heart by resting his head on her chest or tracing his fingers down the side of her face.

"Don't be sorry, Evan. You didn't do anything wrong. But I'm afraid I have to ask you to stay away. Maybe for good this time. I've tried and tried to keep my feelings for you straight, but friendship just isn't enough for me. It's been nearly a year since you first started coming around, and we're still not any closer to figuring out why. Looks like this entire relationship has been nothing more than a lesson in futility. If it was supposed to be anything more than that, I have failed." She walked to the door. "Please, just go."

"I can't."

Her hand clenched the door handle, and she stared down at it. "Unless you're actually a demon and your real purpose is to torture me, you'll do this for me."

"Maggie, you have to understand something. That wasn't a chance fire out there today. I doubt your police will send up helicopters to survey the field, but the charred lines form a pattern. A symbol. One I've seen before."

Chapter 20

Evan wasn't going anywhere after all. As he explained to Maggie on the front porch once she relinquished her hold on the door handle, he'd ignored the symbols once before and wouldn't take them lightly ever again.

Maggie was skeptical. "Wouldn't the fires of hell have been a bit more of a challenge to a team of human firefighters?"

"The firefighters had some help. But I agree; it did seem too easy. The fire's purpose obviously wasn't destruction. It was perhaps a communication of some kind."

"Or a remarkable coincidence."

"I'm not taking any chances. There have been too many coincidences already."

"Well…say the fire is the work of a demon, shouldn't you be out there, looking for it, protecting the community at large? What makes you think it has something to do with me specifically?"

"It was chasing your daughter, Maggie."

A chill ran through her with his words. She had the sudden urge to look in on Kirsten again, and she wished Liam was safely upstairs too. She might want to drive Evan away from herself, but the idea of keeping that extra protection around for her children—just in case—was what made her decide to stop fighting him. When she gave him a small nod, he breathed out in relief as his tensed shoulders eased, sloping slightly downward.

With fear's fingers now gripping her, it was difficult for Maggie to be that near Evan and not run into his embrace, not let his strength and peace become hers. But that wasn't an option anymore. Even if he'd allow it, she needed to stay rational and keep her affection in check for the sake of her sanity. No more relapses. He was her guardian angel, not her boyfriend…and maybe if she kept repeating that to herself, she'd actually start to accept it. Maybe.

"I'm going to bed. Please *don't* come in," she said. "But if you see any flames making a run for the house, kindly do put them out."

That was the last they spoke to each other for the next week. Maggie sensed his presence everywhere, but he stayed hidden for the most part, allowing her the distance she'd requested. Even when he was in her line of vision, he gave up trying to talk to her after she'd ignored him enough times. Steeling herself with bitterness toward him made it easier to realign her emotions, and she knew that allowing him a single kind word or gesture was more than her raw and delicate heart could handle right then.

She 'fessed up to Kirsten that she'd been seeing someone, but explained that she hadn't been sure enough about him to make introductions. She also told her daughter that the relationship was over, which Kirsten seemed to accept. For support, Maggie turned to her sister. Nancy's sons hadn't exactly been saints during the teen years, so she understood and didn't judge Kirsten for the mistakes of the young.

"Carl's attorney spoke with the other kids' lawyers and they're hoping to work something out with the farmer," Maggie informed her sister over the phone. "He assures us that when all is said and done, this will be nothing more than a minor blip on Kirsten's record."

"Thank God."

"Nothing can be settled until after the first of the year, but it's not a bad thing that she has to sweat it out a little bit — she did screw up."

"They all have. And maybe getting in trouble for it early on will help her make better choices in the future. It seems to have worked for my boys."

"I can only hope."

"And pray."

Maggie stayed silent.

"…*and pray*," Nancy repeated expectantly.

"To be honest with you, Nance, praying doesn't seem to have been doing a whole hell of a lot of good lately."

"Um, it's getting Kirsten off with nothing more than a blip."

"No, Carl's attorney is doing that. Look, I'm just going through a little bit of a dry spell spiritually right now. Between Father Tom getting shipped away and…other things."

"Well, I'm going to pray that the holiday season moistens this dry spell. Ew, that didn't sound good, did it?"

Maggie laughed. "No, it didn't."

"So when are you coming to visit? Let's make it soon. I know I'll be up for Christmas in a couple weeks, but that's always so crazy and goes by too fast. I'd love to get you down here and have you all to myself."

"That sounds great. I feel like I just need to get away from everything, even if it's just for a long weekend. Assuming all goes as planned with the lawyers, what would you think of late January?"

"Perfect! Assuming Chicago doesn't snow you in, of course."

"Let's plan on it then."

After ending the call with her sister, Maggie pulled a load of laundry out of the dryer and folded it. It was Saturday, and she was reluctant to admit to herself that she was relieved the kids were at Carl's for the weekend. Things had been strained between her and Kirsten since the fire, with Maggie trying to strike the right balance between stern discipline and maternal nurturing and Kirsten adeptly pushing every one of her mother's guilt buttons. It had been stressful for both of them, and the break from each other was good. Maggie planned to go shopping for a few final Christmas gifts after church the next day and hoped setting her mind to that happy task would bring her heart and nerves back to something more normal. As the weekend had approached, Maggie forced herself to dismiss any fears about the fire being supernaturally malicious. All had been calm since, and she simply couldn't fit one more ounce of anxiety into her emotional basket.

She finished folding and carried the clothes upstairs. As soon as she crossed the threshold into her bedroom, she felt Evan. She'd mastered her poker face and moved about the room putting away her clothes as if he wasn't there.

"I understand your concern about the children overhearing," he said, "but please, talk to me now."

Maggie made the mistake of looking at him. The sincerity and anguish that strained his sublime features cradled her heart even as they ripped it apart. She pressed her lips resolutely together and brushed past him, her shoulder accidentally bumping against his arm. Pulling open a drawer, she shoved a few shirts inside.

"Please, Maggie. This hostility isn't good for you."

She whipped around. "Why are you even still here? Nothing has happened since last weekend—no fires, no possession, no nothing other than tension between me and Kirsten while Carl's the big damn hero. You aren't needed anymore." She moved over to the next drawer and crammed a fistful of socks into it, then turned and stared hard into her empty laundry basket. "Please, just go away."

"I honestly wish I could give you the space and time you need, Maggie."

Gripping the sides of her basket, she said through clenched teeth, "Why don't you, then—and do *not* tell me you don't know."

He was silent for a few moments, and Maggie was about to turn and walk out of the room, resolved to resume pretending he wasn't there, when he spoke. "Something evil is drawing closer to you. It's the only explanation I can give for my inability to leave you. I promise I've tried, but the pull to be with you, to envelop and protect you, is too strong."

Maggie had to force her eyes to stay down as Evan dared a step closer. Her voice shook when she said, "If there's a real danger, I'd rather have you with the children."

"It's not my choice. You're the one I've been sent for."

"It's too hard," she whispered and lifted her eyes, no longer attempting to conceal the desire burning within them. He took half a step back, and Maggie winced. "You see why I need to keep walking away? It's what I do best when I'm not strong enough to handle something."

"You're strong enough, Maggie. I know you are."

Maggie shook her head again. "The only thing that ever made me feel strong enough was you—when you would hold me and impart your bliss. But that wasn't me being strong; it was me borrowing your strength. And now you won't even let me do that. Is my weakness so repulsive that you can't even stand to embrace me?"

"Maggie," he said and reached a hand toward her, but let it drop, balling it into a fist at his side. "The peace you felt came from the Lord. He's the one you need to depend on, not me."

"So the answer to my question is yes." She kept her gaze straight on him, but his image blurred as her eyes filled with angry and humiliated tears.

"Stop," he murmured. "You don't understand. It isn't your weakness that keeps me away. It's mine." His head turned to the side and tilted toward the floor, away from her. "I can't touch you without wanting...more. I have asked — *begged*," he continued as he lifted his face to look at her, "to be reassigned. As much as I don't like the idea of being permanently separated from you, being here has become too difficult for me too. But that doesn't seem to matter to my superiors, because their answer was a resounding no."

Maggie's hold on the basket slackened, but she tightened it, forcing down the bubble of hope that tried to rise amidst all the heaviness of the last week. "I wasn't making it all up?" Evan didn't answer or gesture in any way, but the earnest lock of his eyes on hers told her she had it right. "So you do want me, and the powers that be won't allow you to leave — have you ever thought for one moment, Evan, that just maybe you and I are *supposed* to be together?"

He held his hands up and took a step back. "No. Not in the way we want."

They were right back where they always ended up — nowhere, and Maggie snapped, flinging the laundry basket across the room and shouting, "This is ridiculous! You want me, you push me away, you kiss me, and then refuse to touch me. I'm human, Evan. I am only human, and I can't do this anymore! Decide what you want. Figure out exactly what the hell you're doing here, and until you do, *stay away from me*." She turned to storm out of the room, but he grabbed her bicep, holding her there.

"You have to control your anger, Maggie." She found the incensed tremor in his voice ironic, and turned to look at him, his glowering face only inches away. "This is an extremely dangerous time to give maleficence a foothold. I've told you I can't leave, so what do you expect me to do?"

She gritted her teeth and snarled, "I wish you'd never come here. I wish I'd never seen you, and I wish to holy hell I'd never let you in."

"What do you want me to do?" He tightened his grip on her arm.

"You know what I want."

He grabbed her other arm and pushed her backward until he held her arms pinned to the wall. The force he used shocked her, and before she fully absorbed what was happening his mouth crashed onto her lips and his torso pressed into hers, flattening her spine against the wall. Her body responded immediately, and by the time her brain caught up, she was biting into him with almost as much fury as he was into her.

His hands loosened their hold on her arms, and she pulled them free to wrap around his shoulders and clutch at his hair, pulling him closer. This kiss was unlike any of the others. It was hot and flowing and reached down to every part of Maggie's body. Evan's hands traveled over her, and not in the gentle strokes with which he'd previously caressed. He grabbed and clawed. Fabric ripped as he thrust a hand up her shirt and dug his fingernails into her breast. She let out a muted gasp at the pain.

Pulling his mouth from hers, he huffed, "Is this what you want?" He sank his teeth into her clavicle, and she clamped her lips together to stop from crying out. She saw now that he wanted her to tell him to stop. He lifted his face and asked again, "Is this what you want?"

Stinging tears leaked out the corners of her eyes. "Yes," she whispered stubbornly.

His irises flickered rapidly back and forth over her face as if assessing her sincerity. If being close to Evan meant letting him tear her apart, she'd do it. She'd finally smashed down his barriers and wasn't going to flinch now. His hand trailed down her abdomen and lingered at the waistband of her jeans.

"No!" he shouted and took three quick steps backward, then turned and vanished. But before his essence had fully left the room, he was back, taking determined steps to Maggie. With intent eyes on her, he lowered his palms against the back of her thighs, and gently lifted her to him. She wrapped her legs around his waist and held his shoulders. For several moments, they silently stared at each other. The violence had disappeared from his silvery eyes and the smooth lines of his features, and Maggie understood that he was letting her make the next move. This time it was real. She lowered her mouth to his, and when they made contact, everything Maggie ever knew faded away. There was only Evan.

He carried her to the bed, kissing her the whole way, and laid her down, his mouth leaving hers only to nuzzle away the red marks he'd left behind on her chest. She was hesitant to move too aggressively, not wanting to scare him away again, but her overwhelming curiosity to touch more of his flesh urged her to take a chance. She tentatively slid her fingers under his linen shirt and raked them over the supple skin of his lower back. He shuddered slightly as her flesh sank in, commingling with his.

A tugging below her navel told Maggie he was working at the closure on her jeans, and soon she felt his fingertips melting into the soft flesh beneath her zipper. She walked her fingers up his vertebrae and then skimmed them down his back, tilting her pelvis to entice him ever lower. His hand froze and he abruptly lifted his head, looking down on her with wide, frightened eyes.

"It's okay," Maggie murmured, quickly bringing one of her hands to the side of his face. "We can take this slow. It doesn't all have to happen all at once."

Without a word, Evan was off her, off the bed, and gone.

Maggie sat up and huffed sharply, half exasperated and half exhilarated. The stops and starts were frustrating, but she and Evan were finally getting somewhere, and she was confident he'd be back. She looked down at her torn shirt and smiled. Unclasping her bra, she pulled the straps through her sleeves and slid it off, pleased with the outline of her freed breasts through what was left of the thin fabric. She shimmied all the way out of her jeans and threw them on the floor, removing the obstacles.

There was still no sign of Evan, but she remained steady in her conviction that he'd be back. Everything had been moving toward this point. It only made sense for him to return and finish it. Still, even in her titillated state, she couldn't convince herself that fornicating with an angel had been God's purpose in sending Evan to her. But since the Lord was so irritatingly reticent to reveal his plans, she'd enact hers in the meantime.

It was taking Evan longer to work out his mind this time, and she was getting drowsy, so she pulled on her sleep mask to block the light of the declining sun and lay on top of her covers.

She woke to something tickling the ridge of her bare hip and knew it must be his fingertips, scarcely sinking into her flesh as they ran along it. Smiling, she turned from her side onto her back, reaching to remove her mask, but before she could get to it, his hands clasped her wrists and lifted her arms over her head, holding them to the mattress. His calves brushed against the outside of her thighs, straddling her.

Shifting to hold both her wrists with one hand, he touched a finger to the base of her throat and tickled along her breast bone, tracing a straight line down to the top of her shirt, where he dipped his finger to hook around the fabric and ripped it all the way through to the hem. His warm hand lightly passed over each breast, pushing the fabric away and allowing cool air to lick at her torso. Maggie's every cell was brought to tingling attention when she heard him sigh while no doubt gazing at her nakedness.

This time she wouldn't push. She'd lay back and let him take it as slowly as he needed to—not that she had much choice with him still pinning her wrists to the bed. He moved to one side of her, and with his free hand stroked the insides of her thighs, gradually spreading them apart. He didn't speak. Nor did he kiss her. After a few minutes of silently caressing, eliciting light sighs from Maggie, he rolled on top of her, making her gasp at the sensation of his full chest sinking into hers. Squeezing her thighs into his, she rubbed them along his hips and found that he was completely unclothed. His scent was all spice now, with no trace of his milder aromas.

She felt his lips at her ear, tickling as he whispered, "May I enter you?"

"Always the gentleman," she purred.

He tensed his grip on her wrists and teased her by ducking the fingertips of his other hand just inside the top of her panties, sending his watery vibrations into her but stopping centimeters shy of where she wanted him.

"Say it," he demanded, his voice a sultry octave lower than she'd ever heard it before.

"Yes!"

The sound of fibers rending ripped through the room. Maggie was free, and in the next instant she was screaming as he plunged inside her. She'd always suspected making love to Evan would be amazing, but she never could have predicted such instant gratification. The melding of their flesh was nothing compared to what happened between their sensitive genitalia. These didn't merely sink into each other with the usual cascades—they exploded upon impact. The sensual equivalent of fireworks.

His grunts and growls indicated that he was likewise enjoying himself, but unlike Maggie, he didn't appear to have climaxed. He never slowed for a moment, and even before fully coming down from her first orgasm, Maggie already felt herself climbing toward another. Her moans reached their highest pitch, and he flattened his hand across the small of her back, lifting it and driving her over a peak higher than she ever could have imagined.

She shouted out words, but even as she said them, she knew they made no sense. She honestly felt like she was going insane from the pleasure, yet she didn't want it to stop. She didn't ever want it to stop.

He lowered her to the bed and changed his rhythm to something slower, deeper. It allowed her awareness to reach beyond her interior. She was sweating, they both were, and his abdomen slid across hers with a slapping sound of wetness every time he pushed down against her. He continued to hold her wrists above her head, but like everything else, her flesh there was moist, slipping around in his now precarious hold. She wanted to run her hands along his muscles as they flexed over her, and she wanted to pull his face to hers.

Her hands slipped through his grip, but before they could find purchase anywhere, he grabbed each in one of his own, and rolled to his side, pulling her until he was on his back with Maggie on top of him. He lowered his arms so his elbows were propped on the bed, and Maggie gripped his hands, using them for support and making the most of the new angle. He moved with her, but let her guide the experience.

She was overwhelmed with the desire to look at him, to see those beautiful eyes watching her pleasure. But he clasped her hands to his when she tried to pull away. She was close to climaxing again, so she didn't fight him, instead continuing her rhythmic undulations until he too was groaning.

He dug his fingers into her hand and shifted, flipping them both over so he was once again on top, pounding desperately into her. She peaked first, with him only seconds behind. Lifting his torso, he shuddered, and a scorching blast seared deep into Maggie. She pressed her head back into the pillow and inhaled slowly, attempting to manage the pain through her breathing. As the scalding agony calmed to a smolder, a strange part of her wanted to hold onto the pain — because it belonged to Evan.

As her burning insides began to return to normal, she tried to reconcile the idea of her kind, gentle angel with the beast that had just so thoroughly fucked her. She'd enjoyed every moment of it, but she felt an empty space inside her, like something important was gone. She missed the tenderness, the closeness, the love she'd expected. She again wanted to rip off the mask that separated them and look into his brilliant eyes. She wanted to hold him. But he trapped her wrists at her shoulders while he stroked his tongue over her salty torso, back and forth along one side of her rib cage.

She smiled at his gentle touch. Here was some of the tenderness she was yearning for. His tongue was warm, almost hot, heating her skin and leaving behind a simmering trail in the sweat that drenched her.

He slowly traced his deliberate tongue onto her breast and around her nipple, causing Maggie to inhale sharply as a new spark of desire raced through her. Teasingly, he drew his tongue back down and then up, between her breasts, continuing all the way to the hollow at the base of her throat, where she involuntarily whimpered at having his mouth so close to hers. She wanted to kiss him. But he moved away to flick at her other nipple and then trace along the opposite side of her rib cage.

He was obviously absorbed in his ritual, so Maggie decided to simply relax and enjoy it while she patiently waited for him to come back to her. His tongue curved free-form around her abdomen and naval while her internal burning lessened to a dispersed warmth. Oddly, she found herself craving more heat, more pain.

He finished painting her with his expert tongue and crawled onto her, his face hovering just above hers. His warm breath floated into her open mouth, and she breathed him in, tilting her head and readying her mouth to receive his. Keeping his lips just out of reach, he tortured her. As she sucked in his exhalations, her thoughts grew cloudy, and she realized too late that he was intentionally fading her consciousness. She didn't want to sleep. She wanted to look upon his enchanting face and hold him. She struggled against his influence, but her will was no match for his, and ultimately she slipped away.

Her sleep was deep. She didn't stir or even dream. Only once did anything tickle the remote corners of her mind. In a dreamy fog, she felt Evan close. He was screaming in torment. Maggie wanted to go to him, to tell him everything was okay, but she couldn't move. Then he was gone, and she settled back into the dark. The rest of the night passed in nothingness.

Chapter 21

When Maggie woke, the first thing she did was pull off her sleep mask. Then, she sat up and found herself surrounded by blood red petals. Lifting one, she held it to her nose and inhaled. Roses. Her legs were sprinkled with them, and when she'd sat up, several had cascaded from her shoulders and arms.

So this is what it feels like to be queen, she thought, and then realized she was smirking. Well, why shouldn't she? She'd just accomplished the impossible. She was Maggie Brock: Seducer of Angels.

Feathering the edges of the petal across her jaw and down her throat, she luxuriated in the memory of the ecstasies she'd enjoyed with Evan. Her eyes drooped half closed but opened again when she recognized that her bedroom was in the murky purple-grayness of dusk. Could all of that have happened in the span of just a couple of hours?

The phone rang and as she reached over to pick it up, she looked at the clock. It was only five thirty. "Hello," she said, her voice groggy from not being used.

"My, my, don't you sound sexy." It was Carl.

Maggie chuckled, and even her laugh was sultry.

"Good Lord, Magdelyn. Someone needs to get over there pronto and give it to you good."

"Too late," she crooned.

"You saucy little minx! Is that why you're late picking up the kids? And here I was worried something bad had happened to you."

"What are you talking about?" The haze in her mind began to clear as she glanced again at the clock. "It's still Saturday, right?"

"Are you joking?" A note of concern had crept into his voice, and Maggie stayed silent. "Have…have you been drinking?"

"No! It's just…I'm sorry, I took a nap and am a little disorient-ed—can we start over?"

"Okay, I'm calling because it's *Sunday* evening, and you're over an hour late picking up the kids, so I wanted to make sure everything was okay and see if you needed me to drop them by."

"Shit! I'm sorry. I…I slept too long…" A *day* too long.

Now Carl was chuckling. "Yeah, those nooners'll take it out of ya. Listen, they've got extra clothes here, so why don't I just keep Liam and Kir for the night and bring them to school tomorrow."

"Yeah, I suppose that works," she answered uncertainly. But when she raked her fingers through the pile of petals and considered that Evan must have wanted her well rested for a reason, she became more sure. "Let me just talk to them to make sure they're okay with it and say good night."

"Yes, Mom. I'll get 'em."

The kids were perfectly fine with staying another night at their dad's, so Maggie got a quick weekend update, told them she loved them, and hung up. The room had darkened a few shades while she was on the phone, making the dismembered blooms around her look almost black. She scooped a mound into both hands and held them high above her head, letting them drop one by one.

Her flesh burned at the various points where each floated down and touched like a kiss. Closing her eyes, she imagined her sinful angel biting into her. She dug into the pile and pulled hands-full up her thighs, relishing the penetrating heat. Thoughts of children and schedules and anything other than carnal pleasure left her.

When she brought the petals up to her abdomen, the warmth became a searing pain, and she dropped them in surprise. Looking down, she saw angry red lines across her stomach, reaching up to her breasts—remnants of Evan's tongue-play. She probed one of the lines with her fingertip and found it raw. As much as she adored the souve-nirs he'd left behind, she didn't want the discomfort to interfere with their lovemaking when he returned, so she reluctantly left her nest.

Making sure her soothing oatmeal body wash was in the shower, she turned on the water and stepped into the cool stream. While she gently tended to her wounds, it occurred to her that she should feel guilty about what had occurred between her and the angel, yet she didn't. She was tired of always trying to do the right thing. Who had the authority to say what was "right," anyway? Everything had certainly felt right the night before, and going forward that's what she'd trust—her personal desires.

Stepping from the shower, she rubbed aloe across her front before patting herself dry and pulling on a soft robe. She didn't know how long Evan would keep her waiting, so she decided to make good use of the time and doll herself up while she waited. She'd dried her hair and applied a layer of foundation over her face by the time he appeared, just outside the doorway to her bathroom.

Keeping her eyes forward, she smoothed makeup onto her neck, and when she'd finished, moved her gaze sideways across the mirror to look at his reflection. He'd been watching her, and when their eyes met in the glass, he gnashed his teeth, his upper lip raising on its way to a snarl.

Maggie swiveled on her stool to face him. "What's wrong?"

He averted his gaze before responding in a hoarse whisper. "I shouldn't be here."

"No! No more of that." Maggie stood, taking one step toward him before he held up a hand and warned her with a shake of his head. The resolution in his features and the terrorized flash in his eyes as he briefly glanced up stopped her.

"Come on, it can't be that bad," she said, even while she felt the first tremors of remorse for what they'd done.

He stared at the floor as he spoke through clenched teeth, the muscle of his jaw straining. "It wasn't me."

"What?"

Slowly, he raised his eyes, and the typically warm gray of his irises was now cold stone. "I know you thought it was. That's what he wanted you to think. Maggie…" His angel eyes filled with tears. "I'm so sorry. I didn't realize I was playing right into his plan. This whole time. I didn't know. When I came back it was too late. I saw the mark and…there's nothing I can do. I tried. I promise you, I tried."

Her breath came in rapid bursts. "Evan, what are you talking about? Who is 'he'? How could it not have been you?"

"Maggie, please, I don't have long to explain. The mark of his master—it's on you."

Her hands went automatically to the waist of her robe, and Evan somberly nodded. With shaking hands, she untied the plush sash and let the robe fall open. In the mirror she saw the red lines peeking through.

"Look at it," Evan instructed, his voice harsh.

Her lips trembled as she slid the soft fabric from her shoulders and opened the robe wide. Staring back at her, branded across her body, was the outline of a seven-headed dragon. She was familiar enough with the book of Revelation to recognize it immediately as the sign of the devil.

She screamed.

And she kept screaming, seeing only pulsating redness around her. She was aware of Evan shouting in the background, and for a moment she had the impression he was coming to her, but then she heard other voices. All the while she kept screaming, blinded by the sight of the redness.

When her shrieks subsided, she found herself on her knees on the cold bathroom tile. Her throat burned as Evan shouted her name. Hunched on the ground, she turned to look at him. He was struggling to get to her, but two burly angels, dressed in white linen like Evan's, towered over him, gripping either of his arms to restrain him.

"That's enough," a white-haired angel said, stepping into Maggie's view. He wore a full white robe with a golden rope tied around his waist. He was tall, statuesque, and unlike Evan, his glow extended outward, surrounding him in a pale but visible light. "Take him away."

"No!" Evan screeched before he disappeared with the two angels holding him, leaving Maggie cowering on the floor with the authoritative angel before her. She sat up straight and watched him, daring to hope he'd be able to help her.

The angel stepped more fully into the doorway and examined her, a look of mild curiosity etched into the rigid lines of his elegant features. "Hm," he grunted. "They never look quite like I expect them to."

She bent her head in deference. "Please don't hold Evan responsible for any of this. He always tried to do the right thing. I'm afraid I was the one who kept pushing. But this isn't what I'd intended. I thought it was Evan, which I know is bad enough, but if I'd known who it was that came to me last night, I never would've…"

The angel's features softened, and he regarded her through gentle eyes, his mouth turned slightly downward in a compassionate frown. "You may not have intended to invite Satan's most dedicated and powerful follower in, child, but invite you did."

She bowed her head once again. "There has to be a way, some way for me to erase this mark from my body, my soul."

The angel let out a mournful sigh. "I see the task of fully explaining lies with me. It wasn't you he was marking, per se." A shard of hope pierced Maggie, and she snapped her head up. "He was claiming the womb that carries his heir."

"His heir?" Maggie's belly lurched and boiled, and she instinctually knew it was true, although her brain told her it was impossible.

"I'm sorry, Magdelyn, we can't help you now. *Alea iacta est.* The die has been cast. The best I can do is return to my realm, where I must prepare to deal with what you're now doomed to bring into this world. Be brave, child."

Within seconds, Maggie was alone and trembling. She pulled her robe closed, clutching it high on her chest, and prayed for the mark — and what it signified — to disappear. But her entreaty rang hollow, unable to extend into her heart while her fear dominated. She huddled and shook, her skin icy cold despite the inferno raging beneath it.

None of this could be real. She tried again to pray, to wake up from this nightmare, but that connection now felt lost, severed, and she ached to have it back. Evan had told her many months earlier that willfulness was a harsher sin than weakness, and her determination to have the angel, despite all his warnings against it, had become a pure act of will that night. But even while she accepted that sting of guilt, she knew she didn't deserve to be marked as Satan's property. She'd thought she'd invited Evan into her body, not…this. She hadn't known she was greeting evil with open arms and legs and couldn't recall one single moment when she'd doubted it was Evan.

Just as her indignation and wrath began to rise, it plateaued, overtaken by dread of the indisputable truth of what she harbored in her womb. Its father — or his master — was surely going to come back for her.

Her hands shot up to the marble countertop, and she pulled up to standing, barely able to support herself on unstable legs. The robe had fallen open again, but she refused to look at the malevolent tattoo. Instead she kept her focus straight ahead on the reflection of her eyes. The words "God help me" had never felt more poignant. She *had* to reestablish the connection — had to find a place in God's grace again.

After staring for a moment longer, the answer came to her — Father Tom. He'd given her a warning, cryptic as it was. He'd understood that something wicked was simmering beneath the surface of their seemingly peaceful community. Her legs steadied, and she stood straight. She had to get to the priest. He'd help her.

Terrified of who might be waiting for her, she forced herself to step into her bedroom and was relieved to find it empty. Rushing to her closet, she pulled on the most accessible pair of jeans and a sweater before running out of the room, down the stairs, and to her car, barely thinking to grab her coat along the way.

As she sped away from her house, she wiped her palm flat across both sides of her face and inhaled deeply. Pinpoints of Christmas lights strung along shrubs and porch railings brought Maggie some comfort, but as she left the neighborhood and pulled onto the black, wet street, the bleakness again took hold. She'd cut herself off from the celebrations.

She kept herself calm enough to reach the former seminary and parked in the small lot. Instead of dashing out of the car, she stayed in the safety of her vehicle and studied the large twin wreaths on the front doors of the building. She should be home with her children right now, baking cookies while they decorated the gingerbread house she'd bought earlier that week.

Tears streamed down her face, and her breath caught in small gasps. She couldn't go inside hysterical like this without drawing unwanted attention. She'd been given the direct number to Father Tom's room when she'd called a few days earlier, so she pulled out her phone and steadied her hand to press the right buttons, then clamped her swollen eyelids shut, hoping he'd answer. He did. And she immediately began silently sobbing.

"Who is this?" he asked tersely, but his tone gentled when Maggie was able to convey in gasps that it was her. "Calm down, calm down," he soothed, although she could hear the concern in his voice.

She hadn't intended to tell him anything until they were face-to-face, but couldn't keep this to herself for one more moment. "I'm so sorry, Father. I didn't listen to you. I didn't stay away from the angel." Her sobs interrupted her speech.

"Tell me, Maggie," the priest said in a commanding tone, bringing her around.

She managed to tell him the important points — that she thought she'd coaxed the angel into her bed, but she'd been tricked. She told of how Satan's follower had come to her in darkness, that she'd thought it was Evan and consented to couple with him, and now she was marked as the mother of his child.

Father Tom stopped her only once, asking her to recall the exact words spoken as best she could, and when she finished her tale, he asked, "Who else knows?"

"Nobody. Only the angels, and they said they can't help."

"Where are you?"

"I'm in my car. In the parking lot in front of your building. I can't…I can't come in."

"Don't! Stay where you are. I'll come to you — don't move from where you are."

"Hurry," was all she said before she heard the click from his end.

She reflexively double-checked that her doors were locked and waited for what seemed a very long time before she saw Father Tom ambling around the side of the building. He was in his overcoat, crunching over the frigid ground that had yet to be covered in a true snow. In the darkness she could see his shoulders hunched, his head straining forward, peering at the cars. She waved to him before coming to her senses and opening her door so she could step out and rush to him.

He grasped onto the back of her arm and whispered, "Come along."

Maggie was surprised when he led her back toward the building and along the side. "Where are we going?"

"I'm an old man, Magdelyn," he huffed as he pulled her past the back of the building and toward the forested decline. "In over my head. This is out of my hands now."

Chapter 22

Father Tom continued pulling Maggie along behind the old seminary. She balked when they took their first steps down the sloping hill that led into the shrouded forest, but the priest kept a firm hand on her. "We're going to help you," he said. "And to be blunt, we're the only option left."

Conversation ceased as they had to watch out for every footstep in the dark night, leaving behind the meager comfort of the glowing residence windows. The ground was slick with pockets of icy leaves, and they often had to brace themselves on tree trunks to avoid toppling over. At least moving toward their mystery destination was doing something, and Maggie already felt stronger than she had while slumped on her bathroom floor.

She also knew Father Tom was right—she had no choice other than to trust him. But that didn't stop her from asking "Who's we?" once she'd found her footing. He squinted at her through the shadowy moonlight. "You're not going to like it." Then he resumed his trek down the hill. By now, needing both hands to keep balance, he'd let go of Maggie, but she stuck close.

"I've made mistakes," he confided. "My entire adult life I spent guarding against his ways, trying to shield parishioners from him." They made it halfway down before he leaned his weight on a tree trunk and held a finger up. "One slip. All it takes is one slip for him to gain his hold."

Maggie dug her fingernails into the bark of the tree in front of her and watched the priest's expression sag into a mournful scowl until it appeared pained. Tearing his eyes away, he continued the descent in silence, with her following. When they reached level ground, Maggie went straight to him and put an arm around his shoulders. "You've been a wonderful influence in my life," she said. "Brought me into the fold when I was so, so lost and guided me ever since. You did all you could for me. None of this is your fault."

The surface of his moist eyes glinted under the silver moon. "You don't understand." Pulling abruptly out of her embrace, he moved forward, appearing slightly aimless until Maggie caught up and laid a hand on his back. He stopped and looked at her, forlorn. "I'm the one who lead him right to you."

Before Maggie could respond, footfalls crunched the leaves and twigs just ahead, and a silhouetted figure moved swiftly closer. Maggie's instinct was to flee, but Father Tom stepped behind her and whispered, "Forgive me," before gripping both arms and holding them firmly behind her back.

She moved to free herself, but went numb when the figure moved into the pale light where she could make out the pointed features of Monsignor Sarto. He was cloaked in black priest's robes. Panic instantly flooded her. Her stomach boiled and her breath came in rapid bursts, but for all this adrenaline, her feet and arms couldn't move. She merely pressed back into Father Tom as if she could melt into him and away from her nemesis.

Sarto smirked, moving closer, and Maggie's insides burned hotter with his every step.

"You did well to call me," Sarto said.

When Father Tom spoke, his voice quavered with uncertainty. "You promised not to hurt her."

"I *promised* to take care of her," Sarto sneered. "Which I fully intend to do."

"With a witness present," Father Tom said, the threat in his voice unmistakable. "Stop!" he ordered, halting Sarto's footsteps. The priest's hold on Maggie's arms slackened. "If you move another inch, I'll let her go and throw myself in your way."

Sarto raised an eyebrow. "Really?" His smooth confidence didn't waver. "I suppose this means you no longer wish to keep your secret?"

"My secret be damned!" Father Tom shouted. "I don't know how I ever let you persuade me." His hands shifted on Maggie, and he spun her around to face him. Gripping her biceps, he fixed his gaze beseechingly into her eyes. "I should've told you after you'd stumbled upon us in the church that night. The night I smashed the altar candle. I knew then it was beyond my control. I'm so sorry, Maggie. I honestly thought the less you knew, the safer you'd be."

"Telling her now won't do her any good," Sarto called across the ten feet that separated them. But Maggie noticed he didn't chance a step closer.

Father Tom continued, his focus only on Maggie. "When you told me about the angel, I was afraid, so afraid it was *him*. He'd appeared to me as a regular man, always approaching when no one else was around, pretending he needed to talk, feigning interest in joining our congregation, but in reality he was manipulating me into doing the talking. He let me vent on and on about the monsignor's continuous blows to my precious pride—he encouraged it, fed my frustration. And then he offered to help me. When he was pleased that I'd answered his questions without posing any of my own, he hinted that it was within his power to lessen my woes. The monsignor suddenly eased up, even left town for a few weeks."

Maggie's eyes flicked to the monsignor. His expression grew darker as he listened to the tale.

"That's when I couldn't lie to myself anymore," Father Tom said. "This was no mere parishioner, and the monsignor's change in attitude toward me was no coincidence. But I didn't understand his true nature, nor did I see the harm in continuing on…ah, the lies we tell ourselves. It was only when you spoke of the angel—and I instantly felt the grasp of fear—that I allowed myself to recognize this visitor as something evil. Putting myself into his hands was one thing, but I couldn't allow it to happen to anyone else. So I introduced you to Raymond; I thought I could keep you safe that way."

The revelations were hitting Maggie fast, and her mind was ticking. She kept her focus on Father Tom, the man she'd trusted—the man she still trusted as he clearly proved he was on her side. "When Ray broke up with me for the other woman, he said it was like an angel sent her."

Father Tom nodded. "He *was* an angel at one point."

"This is a delightful walk down memory lane," Sarto said. "But it's not why I'm here—why you *asked* me to come here."

Thomas turned to his superior. "I asked because I hoped you'd show her mercy."

"Mercy isn't exactly what I'm known for." Sarto's upper lip twitched.

"She doesn't deserve this," Father Tom pleaded.

"It's too late!" Sarto shouted. "There is nothing to save her now. I granted you your freedom that night at the altar, but she's given herself completely to the darkness, harbors its newest prince in her womb. I can't release her from what she herself has permanently chosen, and why would I?"

The priest's hold on Maggie slackened. "There has to be another way," he said with no hope evident in his deflated voice.

"There isn't." Sarto's tone had calmed and he sounded almost compassionate. "If there was another way, I'd take it. But handing her over to me is the only merciful thing to do for humanity at large. You know what will happen otherwise."

Father Tom dropped to his knees and began reciting prayers, rocking as he murmured at Maggie's feet. Although she couldn't understand his words, she knew he was praying for her soul, *begging* she surmised by the sounds of his whimpers. She was warm despite the frigid air all around her, and the simmering in her gut jabbed as she watched the priest, her initial wave of gratitude for his intercessions mutating into revulsion. The heat moved, burning her diaphragm, her lungs, and winding its way up her esophagus, ultimately releasing in a low hiss as she bent over the pastor.

He halted his praying to look up at her, and pushed back, sitting on the frozen forest floor with his knees bent in front of him. Maggie watched a flash of fear race through his eyes, but he clasped his hands together and bent his head, resuming his entreaty.

"Spoken like a true bride of Satan," Sarto said, his voice taking on a predatory quality, one that, despite all his previous unpleasantness, Maggie had never heard from him before. Tearing her attention from Father Tom, she saw that the monsignor was smiling. A beam of moonlight reflected off the surface of a long, slender object in his hand, held close to his hip. "You were under my nose the whole time. Always playing the good girl. But when it came down to it, you didn't even put up a fight, did you?" His lip curled, and he took a step toward Maggie, twisting the object so that she could clearly see it was a dagger.

A clammy sweat cooled the heat that had been overtaking Maggie. She flicked a glance toward Father Tom, whose eyes remained closed while he prayed like mad, oblivious to Sarto's approach.

"Father Tom!" she shouted, but he didn't respond. "Please!" She bent over the priest, sliding her hands into his armpits, trying to pull him up. "At least save yourself."

This time he acknowledged her, but didn't move. "I'm sorry, Magdelyn. It's over, there's nothing I can do. I'm sorry, I'm sorry..." He returned to his prayers, openly weeping.

"You needn't worry on his behalf," Sarto informed her. "You're the only one I'm interested in. The entire reason I came here, as it turns out."

She let Father Tom go and stood up straight, taking a step back. Sarto moved closer. His voice was steady, but his sharp features twitched. He looked half deranged, teetering at the loss of control. Everything inside Maggie screamed and flared, urging her to run, to get as far away as possible. But where would she go? She couldn't get away from what had been implanted inside her.

As she witnessed the monsignor's intensity, his mad desire to get to her, she thought back to the burning passion of the night before and wondered if it had been Sarto in another form. Her body revolted at the thought, and she doubled over, retching.

He stopped his approach, at least showing the consideration of letting her get sick in peace. She spit out the final strings, but stayed bent double, refusing to look at him. When she spoke, she was careful to keep her tone deferential, hoping to appeal to any soft side he might have. "I'm not the one you want. It was all a mistake—I wasn't willing. I didn't want this."

"Liar!" Sarto shouted, his voice bouncing off the black tree trunks surrounding them, making Maggie jump and straighten as her instinct for survival forced her to keep an eye on him. "This couldn't be done without your permission. Where did you think playing with angels was going to get you? Stupid, arrogant, human girl. Don't ask for my pity."

He closed the distance between them and smacked the backside of his hand across her cheek, sending her stumbling. Swiftly, he jumped forward and caught her throat in his grip with a sure strength belied by his slim physique.

Maggie's insides flamed. Strangely, she was no longer frightened. Why should she be? She could crack this weakling in two and toss him away like garbage, show him the futility of all his years of study and manipulation. She trapped his gaze in hers and smirked, giving him a small taste of the fun she intended to have with him.

His intensity faltered for a brief moment but rallied as he pulled back the silver dagger and murmured, *"Deus in nomine tuo salva me et in fortitudine tua ulciscere me."*

Maggie clenched her eyelids tightly closed, playing with him, while Father Tom continued to pray. A cool spot amid her burning insides told her she ought to join the priest in his exercise, but she ignored it and let the flames engulf that impulse.

Sarto's arm shot forward, but before the tip of his instrument could touch her and before she herself could bat it away, a whoosh sounded next to her ear, and her assailant was torn from her. She opened her eyes in time to watch his thin figure slam into a thick tree trunk, sending a loud crack reverberating throughout the forest.

The white square of his collar was soon drowned in red as a long, metal spike protruded from his neck. Smaller prongs extended from the tip of the spike, piercing Sarto's throat and holding him to the tree. Rivers of blood cascaded down his now glistening robes. Through the slick mess, Maggie saw the silver hilt of the dagger; the other half of the weapon was plunged into his heart.

The fire in Maggie died down as she watched the man gurgle and his body spasm, his feet dangling helplessly mere inches from the forest floor. Father Tom's murmurs had silenced. She turned to the priest, expecting to see relief, but instead he stared at her, wide-eyed and shaking. Fear again gripped Maggie. What had she done?

She rushed to the tree and tried pulling the pronged weapon from Sarto's throat, but her grip slipped on the blood, and the strength she'd felt moments ago had vanished. She continued her efforts until Monsignor Sarto shuddered and then stopped all movement as his eyes glazed over in death.

Chapter 23

Maggie stepped back from the tree and looked down at her bloodied hands. "I don't understand," she murmured. "How could I have done this?"

A low chuckling sounded from the forest beyond, and a silhouetted figure emerged from the darkness. "You really do have a tendency to overestimate yourself, don't you? I haven't given you those kinds of powers...yet."

It was a man's voice, deep and smooth. As he stepped closer, Maggie could see that he was tall and of a moderate build. The moonlight illuminated enough for her to make out straight, neatly cropped hair framing sculpted cheekbones and full lips. With the way the shadows fell across his face, he looked much like Evan, but with one important difference: he lacked the internal light that made the angel visible even in the darkest of corners.

He continued speaking as he snapped brittle twigs underfoot on his way to Maggie. "Why, only last night you convinced yourself you could actually seduce one of the Lord's heavenly angels."

He was only a few feet away now, fully bathed in the small clearing's silvery glow, but his clothing retained the dreary colors of the surrounding forest. He wasn't dressed in linen, but rather like a gentleman, in a tweed jacket over a black turtleneck. In the broader wash of light, she recognized him—he was the handsome newcomer to St. John's whom she'd first noticed at Father Tom's archaeology talk and then again departing the church on the evening the altar candle had been smashed.

"Please, call me Aedan," he said. "The human name given me by a buxom Irish lass many moons ago."

Even as Maggie's mind rebelled against this imposter who'd taken so much from her, a strange warmth enveloped her as he neared, his presence somehow soothing her, mellowing and sweetening the acrid taste in her mouth. She and this man—this spirit—had a connection, and her body instantly knew him as the being she'd coupled with the night before. Yet the surge of righteous anger that she knew she should be feeling simply couldn't emerge. His calming effect prevailed.

He effortlessly yanked the weapon from the tree trunk, causing Sarto's ruined body to slump to the ground in a heap. The demon turned his eyes toward Maggie and gave her an admiring smirk. "You could've handled him in your own way, I'm quite sure—I felt your fire burning to do so. But I wanted the pleasure for myself. This one's been giving me trouble for a long while now."

"I don't understand…" Maggie said.

"Shh, shh, there's no need to speak, my dear. I'll tell you everything you need to know. He was the Vatican's hitman. Sent here for me. They dismissed the Protégé Prophecy long ago, but kept an eye out for signs, just in case. Sarto was savvy, one of their top experts in demonology, but he had no idea what he was up against. His dealings with my underlings did nothing to prepare him for me."

"But he said he was here to ensure compliance of the…the…" She gave up trying to speak. Her sluggish brain was attempting to absorb too much at once and couldn't properly operate her physical responses.

"He couldn't very well state his real purpose and have the town and all the neighboring counties flipping out. You humans are such fragile things." He touched the tip of his polished black boot to Sarto's temple and shoved it. The monsignor's wide-eyed head twisted on his shredded neck, landing at a grotesque angle. Satan's follower smiled. "He was going to kill you. Nothing personal, I'm sure. He merely wanted to stop my child from entering this world. You see, I'm the protégé in the prophecy—and our child is destined to do wondrous things on this Earth for the sake of my master. Because of your eagerness to consort with those of us who are off-limits, I've been irrevocably elevated to the tippy top of the food chain in the underworld."

Maggie found it difficult to tear her eyes from the monsignor's gory carcass, but she eventually managed to, and her gaze landed on the more appealing aspect of the sly figure next to her. He was smiling sweetly.

"You shouldn't be out on a cold night like this in your condition." He took a step closer and leaned in close to murmur in her ear, "I trust you slept well after the night we had."

"Don't you touch her!" Father Tom shouted. His voice was loud, but it trembled.

The demon's head swiveled toward the priest, who was now standing. "It's a little late to play the hero, old man. Especially considering you're the one who gift wrapped and delivered her to my doorstep."

Maggie took a step back and Aedan reached toward her, but didn't grasp her. Instead he turned his hand, holding it palm up with his fingertips beckoning her.

Father Tom gasped. "You—you *can't* touch her, can you?"

Aedan shot him a malevolent sneer before turning to Maggie and shrugging sheepishly. "He has me on a technicality. I rather bent the rules and only met the requirement half way. I secured your permission, allowing me free access to you for a limited time, but now that your body has been sealed in the name of my lord, I require your acceptance. And why wouldn't you accept? You already carry my child, and I'm afraid Sarto won't be the last man eager to rip out your womb. So without my protection..."

Maggie swallowed, considering the implications of his unfinished sentence.

"There are matters more important than your security in this world, Maggie!" Father Tom shouted.

Aedan hissed, and a ring of flames burst up from the ground to surround the priest. The fire kept a wide berth, but the blazing spires held Thomas trapped. Through the dipping and dancing flames, Maggie saw sweat already beading across his forehead as his eyes opened wide, staring at the walls of his fiery prison. He wouldn't be interrupting again any time soon.

Aedan turned back to Maggie and stated matter-of-factly, "As I was saying, either accept the great honor I've chosen to bestow upon you, or you will most certainly die a torturous death."

Every circumstance surrounding Maggie suggested she should be trembling, cowering in the same fear she'd felt earlier that night, but despite the increasing precariousness of her position, she laughed. A dark, half-hysterical chuckle that allowed her to shove aside fear and deal with what was in front of her. While her seducer watched her mirth, he attempted to endear himself further with an engaging smile.

"Well," Maggie said. "I understand the torturous death part, but what exactly does this 'great honor' entail?"

"First of all, it entails me getting to touch you again—as I recall, you quite enjoyed that." His voice had lowered to a sensual growl. "And secondly, it entails you nurturing my child here on Earth. While you do, you'll be given every indulgence, as will your existing mortal children. Creature comforts, the best of everything, a bounty of friends, a bevy of talents. Whatever you want."

"And after this Earth?"

His lips curled. "You'll be my queen in the afterlife, placed above all human souls in my master's kingdom."

"Why me?" she challenged, causing his sure smile to falter for a moment before recovering into something softer.

"I didn't expect you to come easily, Magdelyn. You're too discerning for that—and you've been unfairly deceived too often, so I'll be nothing but straightforward with you. I came to Prairie Oaks because the town was ripe for me. I required just the right balance of holiness and dedication to sin. Do you know your town has some of the most active churches in the country? Ah, but also present is a strong undercurrent of materialism and competition.

"Trouble was, the women around here are either fully entrenched in their faith, not leaving one sliver of bare thigh or cleavage open for exploitation, or in more cases than not, they've been victims of the evils of this world for so long that they're spoiled goods, unable to give my child a properly prepared and righteous incubator in which to steep his wickedness."

He watched Maggie's brow wrinkle and commented, "Ironic, isn't it? For too long, I assumed any womb would do, so I bedded the brazen and wasted my seed. It never took. Not even with the virgins. I eventually realized it had more to do with the woman than the womb, and it was through infiltrating the church archives in Rome that I discovered the roadmap to success. I needed a woman who'd awakened spiritually—but one who also wavered just enough to give me the opportunity to gain her willing cooperation. That's where your priest came in handy. I was only able to observe so much on my own, and he helped fill in the blanks with his inside knowledge of the parishioners. The information only came in drips and drabs, but the more he gave himself over to me, the more he poured forth.

"I was making progress with some God-fearing women in the area—my calling card at the garden proved quite productive, and the priest made himself useful with his attempts to deflect unwanted attention. It was nice of you to visit, by the way." A smile slid across his lips before he pouted. "Only once? And here I was becoming so smitten with you—all your struggle to do good while you found ways to bend even the most clearly delineated of church rules. I advised your trusted pastor's warning to stay away from the urn. It was seemingly innocent enough advice, though I'd hoped that for you it would prove a temptation. But that didn't work. So I set my minion on legs to get to you and others showing promise.

"A good plan, but as the adage goes, if you want something done, you've got to do it yourself. He nearly had you on that last, valiant attempt though. Who knew you'd grab onto that blasted crucifix at the last minute? I think that's when I decided I had to have you, rather than any of the others.

"Imagine my delight when Father Flambé over there revealed that you'd fallen for an angel. An angel!" He opened his mouth wide in a laugh. "You really are too much. He was wrong in thinking I was the angel, but he was right to know that somehow this was my ticket in. After correcting his attempt to derail me, I had to fully impress upon my priestly servant that *I* was in charge, resulting in the debacle with the altar candle. I hadn't counted on the demon hunter walking in and freeing my servant from my grip. But even that worked in my favor in the form of your growing mistrust of the monsignor and, therefore, the church.

"I had a limited window in which to work before you, too, spoiled. So I threw in a field fire to kick up the tension in your household and bind the angel to you because of the increased threat. I knew that the combination of stretched nerves and having the object of your temptation so close at all hours would eventually pique your desire, leading you to at last drive him far enough away to allow me an opportunity. All I had to do was wait. You came closer to succeeding with him than I'd expected, I'll give you that. But he did reject you and fled far from his temptress, just as I'd predicted."

He moved the side of his face to within an inch of Maggie's. "And you know what happened next." He couldn't touch her, but his hot breath penetrated the buffer, rolling across her cheek. "Taking you was so much more satisfying than I ever expected. Your surprised gasps. Your eager participation. There was even an innocence to your screams of ecstasy."

Maggie stiffened. "Those screams weren't meant for you."

Aedan jerked his face away from hers. "Oh yes, that's right—they were for the angel. The one who rejected you. Repeatedly."

"Because he's good!"

The demon frowned. "Rejection equals goodness? Well then, glad I chose this side. Let's look at your *good* life recently, shall we?" He held up a finger for each rejection he ticked off. "Besides the angel and all his brethren, there was your husband, then the fabulous Raymond—I only brought the girl around; I didn't make him choose her. Then who do we have…ah yes, your BFF Sharon. And how are things going with your daughter these days? She seems more than eager to trade in her old mommy for the newer model. Let's not forget that the good, holy monsignor was going to kill you—rejection doesn't get more poignant than that."

He wiggled his full hand of fingers. "And while all these people rejected you, who was the only one who wanted you? Who pursued you through all the blockades you put up? It was me, Maggie. And I still want you and am here begging you to accept me the way I've accepted you. I celebrate everything about you, including this push and pull between good and evil. Annoying as it is, I find your persistent struggle irresistible. I will want you for all eternity for exactly who you are."

Maggie stared at him, dumb struck, as he made his declaration. It was true. How many times had she been rejected by others while he steadfastly looked after her?

"*He's lying*," a voice said out of nowhere. Maggie's head twitched toward Father Tom, who stood straight with his attention riveted on her through the flames, but the voice had been too low—barely above a whisper—for it to have come from him, and there was no reprimand from Aedan.

"I don't understand something," she said. "One of the angels who came to my room to take Evan away said he had to prepare for what I was to bring into this world. He knew it was your child—why didn't he try to kill me like Sarto did?"

"Angels can't kill humans. It's against the rules. Believe me, your darling Evan would certainly have strangled you himself if it were possible."

"You're an angel," she said with an accusing bite.

"I make my own rules, sweetie."

Her lips curled. The bond between them seemed to be getting stronger, his influence over her growing, and she sensed that he enjoyed this back and forth. What she was doing now was more like flirting than defiance. "But if you can't touch me, you can't kill me."

"Nor do I want to." His charcoal eyes held hers.

"Of course not. Precious cargo." Her hand instinctively stroked the section of wool that covered her ever-boiling abdomen.

His gaze snapped downward and followed her hand longingly. "Will you deny me the right to caress the worthy and beautiful body in which my son resides?"

Maggie watched him and asked coyly, "How are you so sure it's a boy?"

He lifted his eyes to hers, and there was a new tenderness there. He didn't answer, merely stared into her reluctantly receptive gaze. The moment felt as if it could be between a genuinely loving husband and wife expecting their first child.

"What if my answer is no?" she asked, more softly than she'd intended.

"The child will be born, regardless. But it will be much easier to keep both of you safe if you accept my protection. I want to take care of *you*, Maggie. You've never really belonged with them. None of them knew how to properly care for you—you've been taking care of yourself for so long. You must be tired. Let me take care of you now. Please. It's what I want more than anything."

He was saying things to her that no one else ever had. Things that she now understood she'd been yearning to hear. Even while she knew he must be lying, she was no longer sure she'd refuse him. After all, what was left for her outside of him? He'd at least keep her safe from the world that wanted to cast her out. When the angel had said he couldn't help her, she'd taken that to mean she wasn't welcome in Heaven either, and feared she never would be, after this. So why should she refuse the only being reaching out to her?

Aedan watched her internal deliberation and nodded in understanding. "That's right. They don't want you. You've strayed from their ways and teachings too much, sullied your soul with sin." He leaned in closer and whispered, "I'll tell you something I shouldn't — I only get one shot at this. One successful fertilization. I believe in you enough, Maggie, that I put all my trust in you. You'll be my only queen for all eternity."

Father Tom's voice rang out. "The weak must seek his shelter at all times and moments. The truly strong have stepped into the fire, saturated themselves in it, and still tear themselves away to walk toward the light — it's only someone as strong as this who can defeat him."

Aedan glared at the priest, and the flames tightened their circle. At first Father Tom cowered, but then he stood straight, and the flames fell to a low, blue shimmer at the ground. The priest's features had gone slack, and in the odd lighting his eyes seemed to glow. When he spoke, his voice was clear and resounding. It obviously wasn't his. "He didn't choose you, Maggie. I did."

The flames snapped back up to full height, and through them, Maggie saw Father Tom frantically glancing around, bewildered. He didn't have long to question what had just happened — Aedan clutched the forked weapon he'd laid against a nearby tree and blasted it at the priest, catching him in the chest and depositing him directly into the flames. Thomas' howls went up with the snapping sparks, and Maggie had the urge to pray for his immortal soul as she watched his horrendous struggle, but she couldn't. Not in her state of limbo. Eventually the torment ended, and Father Tom's charred body was at last free from the pain of this world.

"How many more have to die before you give yourself to me?" Aedan asked.

"How many more will die if I do?"

"Look, sweetheart, you can cut the good girl act. You chose your side; I won. We can both win, if you'll just stop dicking around!"

She flinched, and his hand went immediately to cradle her face, but he stopped just shy of his goal. "I'm sorry," he cooed. "I'm so sorry. I lose patience easily. You can help me with that when we're together. But I don't have time for patience right now — pink will be showing in the horizon soon, which means joggers and workers in the county building just beyond those trees. I'd rather avoid any more unnecessary bloodshed. You'll see that I'm not nearly as bad a guy as they make me out to be."

She backed away. She didn't want this, it was so clear to her now, but she didn't know what to do, so she mindlessly continued taking steps backward, away from him, away from the influence that had been clouding her mind.

He followed. "This is really just a formality. Face it—you've already accepted me. You can say you didn't know who it was, but that's not true. A small part of you knew the truth, but you liked the feel of me on you and in you, so you pretended it was someone else. You don't have to pretend anymore."

She'd stumbled through the forest and then moved into an open expanse, jerking around to find that she was directly behind the county building. Her mind clicked to the angel stone she'd visited there, and she instinctively ran to it, slipping on the frosty grass along the way but keeping her balance until she reached the circular patio. Turning back toward the forest, she expected to see Aeden casually striding across the lawn since she'd heard no heavy footfalls directly behind her, but he already stood at the edge of the pavers.

"I don't accept," she said. "I know I've probably closed the door on my chances for an afterlife anywhere else, but that doesn't mean I'll make things easy for you. Others will come for me! And this time I won't fight when…they try to…kill me…" Her voice became small and died away when the trees along the perimeter of the forest seemed to move. The shadows grew in bulk and emerged from the tree line. Horned demons. She gasped and looked back to Aedan, who'd shed his human form. Red eyes glared at her from a blackened, spiked head as he tensed his clawed fingers. His inhuman voice was a shrill, hideous hiss. "Well, my dear, I hardly promised to make things easy for you either."

Invisible tugs pulled at her arms and legs, edging her forward. She forced a step back and stood squarely on the angel medallion. The tugging stopped, but she felt nips pinching through her coat and at her hair. The demons crouched and stepped closer, and the nips jabbed at her in greater frequency as a growing roar, like rushing wind, swirled inches away. But she wasn't pulled away from the stone; it seemed to be protecting her from the demons' summoning powers.

Aedan reverted to his human form. "It didn't have to be like this," he said, his voice again smooth and enticing. "It still doesn't. I can make all these horrible creatures disappear with a snap of my fingers, and you and I can carry on as we wish." Maggie stood resolute. "Or," he continued, "you've got these guys as your babysitters for the rest of your human life."

As the creatures crept closer, their force became stronger. Maggie clamped her eyes shut, and even though she expected no answer, she prayed. She asked forgiveness for her willful disobedience and for mercy to be shown to the world.

"Lean back. Rest in him."

This time she realized the voice had come from within. And she wanted to trust it. But leaning back would mean moving away from the medallion and getting swept up in the demons' cyclone. It would mean relinquishing her desire to cling to the stone's protection and instead trust this unseen voice. It would mean freedom. She could give up her struggle to choose and instead leave her fate in God's hands.

Clamping her eyes shut, she inhaled and leaned back. Immediately, the swirl of air surrounding the medallion caught her up, and high-pitched whooping erupted from the lawn. Despite her fear, Maggie relaxed her muscles, accepting that whatever happened to her would be the Lord's will. She wasn't lifted or brought closer to the celebrating demons. Her feet held fast to the stone.

The burning in her abdomen boiled to an unbearable heat. All at once, the triumphant whoops went silent and Aedan let out a wretched cry. Maggie screamed as scorching pain ripped through her, but kept her eyes closed and lifted her arms over her head, giving glory to her Heavenly Father.

And then all went silent.

Chapter 24

Something nearby beeped. The mechanical noise was the only thing Maggie could focus on. Everything else remained in a dark haze, her thoughts disconnected. During her more lucid moments, she became frustrated with this state of helplessness. But eventually, the internal voice that had spoken to her in the forest returned, encouraging her to relent on her tightened grip, to trust the power she'd been praying to most of her life, to surrender to a deep sleep.

Her next awareness came in the form of a familiar blend of scents that she struggled to place. Floral and musk. Freesia and…Carl. Her heavy eyelids lifted to see his profile as he stood by the window, next to a vase overflowing with a vibrant garden of stems and petals. Even from that angle, his face looked haggard, with creases of worry carved into his forehead and around his mouth. She let her eyes close again, and the next time she opened them, he was gone.

"Hey, nice of you to join us," a young woman in scrubs said, her dimples going deep with her wide smile.

Maggie's return to consciousness brought with it ice chips and a tray of hospital food, lots of questions from the doctor and nurses about how she was feeling, and then more questions from a detective who was attempting to piece together what had happened in the woods that night. Her answers were honest; she remembered very little. Only that she'd been frightened, she wasn't sure why, and she'd gone to see Father Tom. At the edges of her mind, she recalled flames and a glimpse of the enraged monsignor. After that there were creatures and sensations that could only have been in her dreams. All of it felt like a dream.

"Can't Father Tom tell you what was real and what wasn't?" Maggie asked.

The detective frowned and glanced toward the nurse. "Does she have any family here or friends that can talk to her?"

"Her ex-husband's been here for most of the time since she was brought in yesterday morning. He had to leave for a few hours but wanted us to call when she woke, so he'll probably be back soon."

"What do you mean 'talk to her'?" Maggie pushed herself up to sit, but was silenced by a sharp jab in her abdomen. Settling back into her pillow, she attempted to manage the pain with deep breaths—spurring the recall of another memory. Something horrible had happened, but as soon as her mind grasped onto a sliver of detail, it slipped away. Tilting her head to glare at the detective, she asked, "What happened out there?"

"The investigation isn't complete, but as best we can tell, you were simply in the wrong place at the wrong time." He closed his notebook and left, and the nurse encouraged Maggie to relax, giving her something for her pain.

Maggie slipped back into a light sleep, and was roused from her nap by Carl gently rubbing his thumb across the back of her hand.

"Nice to see those eyes again," he said, the gentleness in his deep voice cascading over her.

"Where's Father Tom? Why won't anyone tell me anything?" Her drowsy eyes swept around the bright room, and she saw that she and Carl were alone.

He reached with his free arm to slide a chair over and sat in it, taking her closest hand into both of his and leaning his elbows on the mattress so he could press his lips to one of her knuckles and then onto the next. "Can you let me enjoy having you back first? Just for a moment?"

His blue eyes were soft, almost like liquid, and Maggie's hand tightened inside his. "Please?" she whispered. "Tell me."

"He's gone, Mags. The night you went to see him, he got caught up in some sort of satanic ritual. Victimized. Burned."

"Burned?" The priest's screeching rang through her memory. "Why? *Why!*"

"Shh," Carl murmured. "If this going to upset you—"

"Upset me? Of course this is going to upset me!" She tried to wrench her hand from Carl's grip so she could push herself up, but he held fast, and when a nurse appeared in the doorway, he nodded her off.

"If you want me to tell you the rest, you've got to promise you'll remain calm."

"Fine." She huffed, quelling her temper but quickly realizing that she preferred rage to her swelling sadness. "He's dead?"

"Yes. And the monsignor too. They actually think that's why the cretins came here. Turns out the monsignor has a background in dealing with the occult."

Maggie stayed silent. This piece of information was something she knew. Because of the...demon. Remnants of her memory began to take shape. She clamped her eyelids shut, and Carl joined her in silence for several moments before speaking again, his tone cautious and his voice low.

"There's something I haven't informed anyone else of yet," he said. "I wanted to speak to you about it first. When I called you Sunday, the night this all happened, you said you'd had a, eh, *guest*. Was that true? Did he have anything at all to do with this?"

She creased her forehead and kept her eyes resolutely closed as she recalled the conversation. Suddenly, the pieces fit together and she remembered everything. But how could she even begin to explain any of it to Carl? She needed Evan.

The nurse stepped into the room. "Excuse me, Ms. Brock, you have another visitor."

A tall, slender man in a dark woolen overcoat appeared in the doorway. Below his coat Maggie noted denim, and despite her grief, she smiled and almost laughed at seeing her angel dressed this way. Evan's pale eyes, concentrated only on her, were earnest, but they sparked at her grin.

"This is him, I take it," Carl grunted, sitting back in his chair and dropping Maggie's hand.

"Oh, yes, I mean no," Maggie said, her eyes flicking between the two. "Carl, this is Evan. Evan, Carl."

Evan nodded his greeting and kept his hands around the small cluster of holly he held. An agitated silence fell upon the room, and when Maggie's attention wandered in Carl's direction, he locked his eyes on hers. Through her steady gaze, she attempted to assure him that Evan was trustworthy, but she could see by the tensed crinkle at the corners of her ex-husband's eyes that he only half believed her.

"I'll let you two talk," Carl finally said. "But I'm going to be right outside the door. Are you feeling well enough for me to bring Kirsten and Liam by later?"

"Yes, please!" Maggie said. "Are they okay? Have they been scared?"

"A bit. But the doctors have never listed you as in critical condition so I didn't see the need to freak them out any more than they already are by what happened to the priests. They only know you needed to come here as a precautionary measure."

Maggie nodded as Carl kissed the tips of his fingers and touched them to her forehead. Then he bent down anyhow and pressed his lips there too. Straightening up, he walked around the bed, and repeated, "Right outside the door." When he passed Evan, he glanced at the small bundle of greenery in the angel's hands, and then smirked when he purposefully shifted his eyes toward the much larger arrangement perched at the window.

The nurse exited the room after Carl, and as Evan stepped toward Maggie, her eyes travelled over his dark clothing. "Nice getup," she teased.

His mouth twitched into a grin. "I'm blending." Stopping next to her bed, he held her gaze, and both of their smiles faded.

"Tell me none of that really happened—the demons, the monsignor, Father…" Her throat clenched and she couldn't finish.

"It all happened. I'm so sorry, Maggie." He set the holly on her bedside tray so he could trail his fingertips down the side of her face. She let her eyelids close, and her tears flowed in straight lines down to the pillow. "I can't explain everything now, not here, but your body has had the time it needed to recover from its trauma, and you'll be released tomorrow afternoon. I'll come visit you in the evening."

"Trauma," she said, her eyelids lifting. "The spawn. Is it…is it…"

"Gone. I'll explain everything tomorrow. Rest well, and enjoy the reunion with your children."

When Evan was gone and Carl left to get the kids, Maggie called her sister and talked her out of making a special trip up since they'd be seeing each other soon for Christmas. Then Maggie spoke with her parents, who were relieved to hear their youngest daughter's voice sound so strong. They'd also be making their annual trip to Chicago for the holidays.

Evan was right, and Maggie was released the next day. The doctors were still unclear about what had happened to her, but concluded that her unconsciousness and loss of memory had been her body's natural coping mechanism. The reason for her abdominal pain was more confusing, but it had subsided, so they simply told her to see her doctor if it returned, the emergency room if the pain was severe.

Within an hour of arriving home, Maggie received a visitor. "You'll stop at nothing to get me to cave first, won't you?" Sharon chided, carrying in a casserole dish covered in tinfoil and a container filled with cookies. "Why do you look so great? Don't you know you just got home from the hospital? And sit down!"

"I've been telling her the same thing," Carl said.

"Oh, stop it," Maggie said. "The only thing that happened to me was that I couldn't handle the situation and blacked out, but I've rested and now I'm fine. And I'm so happy you're here." The second Sharon had set the food on the counter, Maggie threw her arms around her.

Sharon squeezed back. "You know I love you."

"I don't deserve it, but yes, I know. I love you too, and I'm sorry."

"Guess I should let you ladies kiss and make up in private," Carl said. "Unless you want me to stay and watch…"

"Goodbye, Carl," Maggie said, pulling away from her friend and giving him a kiss on the cheek. "Thanks for the ride home and for *everything*. I've got it from here."

Carl said his goodbyes, and then Maggie gestured for her friend to join her on the couch.

"That was an awfully friendly smooch," Sharon said.

Maggie smiled. "He's been amazing. We seem to have finally smoothed out all the rough spots—I even spent Thanksgiving with him and Melissa."

"So he's still seeing the bimbo?"

"She's not a bimbo, but yes, they're still together." They went on to discuss their daughters' legal issues, their plans for the upcoming holidays, and inevitably, what had happened in the woods. Maggie stuck to the same story she'd told the police and Sharon informed her that the newspapers were reporting no more signs of the satanic cult in the area. It was assumed that they'd moved on and that the monsignor had been their target.

Sharon didn't stay long, and Maggie and the kids had a quiet evening. After assuring her children she'd be okay alone in her room that night and settling them into their own beds, Maggie had fallen immediately asleep. When she next opened her eyes, it was after two a.m. Evan sat beside her on the edge of the bed, and she immediately pushed herself up to be eye level with him.

"Where would you like me to start?" he asked before she could even speak, having learned to dispense with formalities when Maggie's mind was cluttered with questions.

"With the demon's heir. What happened to it?"

"When you trusted our Father with your fate, he granted you his protection, and you were held back from the demons' grip. But Aeden feared what his son might become if left in the care of a woman who answered to the Lord. He wouldn't allow it, so he continued to beckon his child forth. What happened inside you was a separate battle between good and evil. Aedan continued to crush his only chance at procreation relentlessly against the fortified walls of your womb until its prophesied life was cut short. Because of your faith, Satan lost his prince."

"The doctors didn't say anything about a pregnancy or miscarriage."

Evan shook his head. "It was so small. Too new and supernatural; they'd not pick it up on the equipment available to them."

"What about its father? He must be furious with me—do I need to be prepared for him to come back?"

Evan waved his head back and forth, a smirk playing at the corners of his mouth. "The decision to deny or accept him was yours alone to make, but once you made your choice and gave yourself fully to the Lord, my brothers and I were free to step in. We took care of them."

"Killed them?"

"Nearly, and then we cast what was left of their sniveling life forms back to their master. The torture he's sure to inflict for their failure will be far worse than being extinguished entirely. It's doubtful he'll ever liberate any of them long enough to visit this realm again."

Maggie nodded, staring down at her blankets and absorbing what he'd told her, trying not to imagine what Satan's punishments might be. When she was ready for more she looked back to him. They sat very close, only inches away, but neither of them seemed inclined to touch the other. "How much about Aeden did you know ahead of time, and why didn't you warn me?" she asked.

"I knew nothing of his plans. Not until the night I found you with his mark. That's when I was enlightened. The reason I became visible to you was so that I could be both a temptation and a guide. My divine propensity against lust was lowered, and while I grappled with the confusion and anguish that caused, I was distracted from the ways my struggle was fostering your growing physical desire for me, providing Aeden with the pathway he needed to implant his prophetic seed. At the same time, my spiritual guidance was meant to give you the fortitude to beat him in the end.

"God trusted you to meet the challenge, and I was only an in-strument." His tensed features softened, his natural light seeming to almost throb, beaming on her. "You did well."

Maggie let her sorrow, her guilt and anxiety, subside for a mo-ment, and allowed herself to bask in his glow, feeling the truth of what he said.

"What about now?" she asked. "Your propensity. I don't know if it's just because of everything I've been through, but…it feels dif-ferent. I'm still—I feel a connection to you, but it's not the same."

His eyes narrowed as he took her in, and his mouth tightened into a small frown. "How do you mean?"

"I don't know. I just, I feel *steady*. Like I could be okay just sitting here with you, talking for hours, not touching, not wanting more than just this."

A bright smile burst across his beautiful features. "My libido has been renewed to where it belongs. I'm as angels are meant to be." The shining shards in his silvery eyes were more brilliant than ever, but Maggie was happy to simply admire them, and didn't mind that they no longer burned on her.

"And I'm apparently a huge sucker for unbridled angel-lust," she said, "because you *really* had me mesmerized."

Evan chuckled. "I suspect it wasn't just my vibes influencing your affections."

Maggie quirked an eyebrow. "What are you talking about?"

"When you were trying to manage your feelings for me, you deflected onto Raymond. It's quite possible you'd also been deflecting onto me all along."

"The ol' double deflect," Maggie said, scrunching a teasing nose at him, but then her expression morphed into something more serious. "Carl?"

The angel tilted his head, raising his eyebrows in confirmation.

"But what was between us was so different from what I ever had with him."

"You weren't directly substituting me for your husband, but your emotions, your lingering feelings for him, may have been looking for a place to land, and they found me. Understand that I don't know this for certain — it's just a theory."

"A theory that doesn't exactly do me any good. I don't want these 'lingering feelings.' I need to get over him for good."

"You need to trust the Lord with your heart the way you trusted him with your life and soul two mornings ago. Stop trying to control what you feel and just feel it. He won't leave you bereft. The answer will come in his time."

She scowled, not completely understanding what he was telling her to do and not in the mood to try to figure it out. She had other things pressing on her mind, the question she'd been afraid to ask since she'd remembered what had happened. "Can you tell me anything about Father Tom? Is he happy?"

The angel placed both hands on her shoulders, his light pulsating into her. "Immeasurably."

Maggie's relief came out in a sharp exhale and she fell into Evan, who wrapped his arms around her and held her close as she laughed and cried at the same time. "I'm so happy he's made it to a better place, but I don't know if I'll ever get over the guilt of knowing he was killed so brutally — because of me."

"His own actions brought him there as much as yours. Like you, he made missteps, but they led him to where he needed to be. It was his fate."

Maggie stayed pressed to him, listening to the even rhythm of his heart and pleased to see that her own maintained a smooth, platonic pace. "Will you go away now that your purpose in my life is fulfilled?" she asked.

"I don't know."

Pulling her head back, she leveled a stern look at him. "Well, one thing you can know is that I'm going to continue to exercise my summoning powers for as long as they work."

He brought his hand up to tweak her nose. "I wouldn't dream of trying to stop you."

Chapter 25

On the day of Thomas Reardon's funeral, weary circles darkened Father Dominic's eyes, and he wore a vaguely lost-looking expression. But as he performed the rite, surrounded by a sea of deep red poinsettias and white-lit Christmas trees, a quiet strength entered his visage. Carl joined his family for the service, with Liam and Kirsten sitting between their parents. The children were stoic and rigid at first, but began to sniff as the ceremony continued. Father Tom had become a respected fixture in their lives, and it would be difficult for them to grasp the reality that he was gone.

When the final commendation began, Liam crawled onto his father's lap, and Carl clamped his arms around his son while sparing a hand for his daughter's shoulder. Kirsten's head slumped, and Maggie immediately caught it and pulled it to her, pressing her lips to her daughter's hair and letting her own tears freely slide down her cheeks. The chain clinked as Father Dominic shook the golden vessel of billowing incense around the casket, and Maggie silently whispered a final prayer for her beloved priest and friend.

She felt especially in tune with the celebration of Christmas that year and showered love onto her parents and her sister's family as they gathered together. Carl joined them all for a few hours on Christmas Eve. Maggie had been making such good progress in accepting that the marriage was definitively over, but having her ex-husband so close these last few weeks, and having him be so wonderfully supportive, had been a setback so she considered it a good thing when he spent Christmas Day with Melissa, thus extinguishing any false hope. It had been more than a year since those two had started dating, and Maggie steeled her nerves to be prepared for the announcement of an engagement at some point during the holidays. But that didn't happen.

Two weeks into the new year, the kids were sleeping while Maggie stayed up, paying bills and making a few updates to the parish website. St. John's was still waiting for a new pastor to be appointed, so Maggie, Brenda, and Father Dominic were scrambling to keep things running in the meantime. Just as she turned off her laptop, her cell phone rang and she saw that it was Carl. "Hey there," she said.

"You still awake?"

"No."

"Smart ass. I guess what I should ask is, are you alone and is this an okay time to talk?"

"Sure." She shoved the computer aside and clamped her eyes shut, bracing herself for *the talk*. "What's up?"

"I'm just around the corner; see you in a few." He clicked off, and Maggie swore under her breath. It was going to be more difficult to hide her true reaction in person. She went to the mirror near the front door and practiced a few different spontaneous smiles. If he didn't pay too much attention to her eyes, she'd be okay.

He tapped lightly on the door, and she swung it open, gesturing him down the hall to the great room so their voices wouldn't travel up the stairs. Maggie settled onto one of the island stools and swiveled to face him. "I repeat: what's up?"

The lines on the sides of his mouth creased as he gave her a small, tense smile and remained standing. "I like that we've become friends in the past year. We never paid enough attention to that part of our relationship when we were a couple, and I'm really happy that we've been able to look past all our issues and get to this point."

"Me too."

He stood there, just looking down at her with that awkward smile frozen on his face. Maggie almost felt sorry for him.

"Is this what you came to talk about?" she asked. "Us being friends?"

"Not exactly. But I do want you to know how important that aspect of our relationship has become to me, and I don't ever want to lose it."

"Don't worry. Nothing you tell me right now is going to make you lose my friendship. I'm an adult, I care about you too, and I'm not going to let a good thing die just because you're moving on with your life."

He tilted his head and scrunched his eyebrows in question, studying Maggie. Then his expression relaxed, and his eyes sparked. "Melissa's a wonderful woman. So easy going, fun, loving. Sexy."

"She's a peach, Carl. No need to convince me."

He sauntered over, suddenly a little too at ease in Maggie's opinion, and lowered onto the stool next to her. They sat side by side, both of them looking forward rather than directly at each other. "Things became more serious between us after we got back together last spring, and we've reached a point where…well, Missy was expecting a ring this Christmas."

Maggie held her breath, but when Carl didn't continue, she prompted, "And…"

"And I gave her an iPad. I had no idea she was expecting an engagement ring until the tears were spilling out and she explained to me that electronics are the kind of gift you give to a good client or a brother, not a woman you're romantically involved with. And then I blew it again on New Year's Eve, which is when she'd apparently convinced herself I'd been planning to propose and that the iPad was meant to throw her off."

Maggie crossed her arms and didn't even try to hide her amusement when she turned to him. "So you've come to a woman for help. Here's a tip: on February fourteenth there's this holiday called Valentine's Day. You'd better show up on her doorstep that *morning* with either a big, fat ring or a leather strap and handcuffs so she can take you inside and beat some sense into you."

Carl looked at her sideways and smirked. "I see I'm not the only one who's clueless." To the furrow in Maggie's brow, he responded, "Missy and I are done. For good. The reason I never picked up on any of her cues is because I don't want to marry her."

"Oh," was all Maggie said, unfolding her arms and letting her hands fall to rest on her thighs as she leaned back against the counter and again turned forward.

"Like I said, she's a wonderful woman, has a lot going for her. It's not like I never considered making a life with her, but every time I added it all up there was always one important quality missing. And as it turns out, it's the one thing I can't live without." Maggie's eyes flicked to him, and he twisted his neck so he could look back and meet her gaze. "She's not you."

Practicing her smiles had been a complete waste of time, and Maggie's mouth dropped open as her eyes tensed in confusion. Carl turned on his stool to face her, swiveling hers so he could mold his knees to either side of her. Her jaw moved up and down as she struggled for what to say until Carl stopped her by gently grasping her hands.

"I don't expect a response right away," he said. "In fact, I'm not even sure I want one. I know I've hurt you, and I know I missed my second chance last spring, but I've been praying that it won't be my only one. I told you we needed to think about the kids, and whether or not they could handle it not working out; what I didn't say was that I wasn't sure I could handle it either. Splitting up the first time was devastating; failing a second time...I was too afraid to risk it, especially after we both finally seemed to be doing okay.

"But when I walked in and saw you in the hospital room, that fear suddenly felt like nothing compared to the idea of losing you entirely. The doctors said you were stable, but you slept so long, it gave me time to worry that they might be wrong. I don't want to live in a world without you, Maggie. And then that guy walked in and I saw the way you smiled at him..."

His hands slid down hers so that he was only lightly touching her fingertips, and his mouth tensed into a straight line. "I honestly just wanted to get through the holidays quietly, and I knew you needed time to get over your ordeal before I brought any of this up—I should probably have given you even more time, but I don't know where things stand with you and this Evan, and I didn't want to wait until things got more serious between you."

"We're just friends. Evan and I."

"That didn't look like the kind of smile you give to 'just friends.'"

"Things got confusing for a while, but sincerely, he's not a factor."

Carl began running his fingertips along the bones at the back of Maggie's hands. "I'm glad to hear that. But I take it from your tone that there are other factors."

"You're not the only one who gets scared. What if all you're feeling is relief that I didn't die? What if, a few months down the road, we forget all about this newfound friendship and slip back into the same old patterns?"

"What if we 'what if' ourselves for the rest of our lives and then suddenly it's too late?" Maggie frowned, and he took her face into both his hands, the deep blue of his irises focused unflinchingly on her. "I'm scared too, but you're worth all the risks, Maggie. You're worth it. That's the only thing I'm sure of. Is that enough?"

"Why couldn't you have been so sure eight months ago?"

His eyes didn't waver. "That wasn't the right time for us. Maybe I needed to have it easy with someone else to fully realize that wasn't what I wanted. Who knows why?"

Maggie let her eyes drop but slowly brought them back up to him, conceding, "Guess I had a few things to go through myself."

They stared at each other, and Maggie's terror must've shown because Carl broke the silence to say, "I didn't come here to pressure you into making any choices tonight. I just wanted you to know where I'm at—and I'll be in the same place weeks, months from now. As long as it takes."

She nodded as much as his hold on her would allow, and his rugged, handsome, wonderful face blurred as a sheen of tears welled in her eyes. "I've never stopped loving you," she told him, her hands moving to grasp onto his legs, just above his knees. "And God knows I tried. So that's got to mean something, doesn't it? But I do need time to think about this, if you're honestly willing to give it to me."

"Of course, of course." His voice got misty, and he pulled her head to rest at the crook of his neck while he peppered kisses onto her forehead. "Whatever you need. I love you. I'll wait forever if I have to."

Maggie let him hold her for a bit, and then she pulled back and wiped her eyes. "Early day tomorrow. So I should probably walk you out. We'll talk again this weekend, okay?"

"Okay." He wiped his thumbs over her remaining trails of tears and gave her one last kiss on the top of her head before sliding to his feet and holding a hand out to her. They walked together toward the front door with Carl leading, and on the way, Evan's words strummed through Maggie's head: *Stop trying to control what you feel and just feel it. Trust.*

When they were just beyond the bottom stair, she squeezed Carl's hand and stopped. He turned, and she held her a finger to her lips, pulling him all the way back to the great room. Once there, he didn't even get a chance to ask her what was going on before she threw her arms around his neck and crushed her lips to his. His mouth was stiff at first, but quickly yielded and they melted into each other, with no words needed for Maggie to let him know that her choice had been made.

The necessity of breathing eventually caused them to reemerge, but they continued to pelt each other with tiny kisses. "Thanks for giving me the time I needed," Maggie whispered in between.

"No problem," Carl said, lightly touching her lips with his and then going in for something slower and more penetrating.

They moved to the couch, kissing and rubbing noses, and giggling every once in a while. But it would be a few weeks before they retested the lock on Maggie's bedroom door. The circumstances of the past year had served many purposes, not the least of which was to bring Maggie's family back together. As she and Carl snuggled on the sofa that night, a reel began playing in her mind—of family vacations, graduations, anniversaries, and holidays—but she stopped it. She had no idea what was ahead for them, and she was certain it wouldn't all be happily ever after, but she knew this was right, and as for the rest, she'd just have to trust.

The End

Acknowledgments

And now for the very best part—in which I get to count my blessings. Immeasurable gratitude to the following people, none of whom I deserve, but all of whom I'll keep:

Colleen Wagner, a constant source of strength and encouragement. Brandon, who persisted in saying, "Mom, you should get *Three Daves* published," long after I'd given up on the idea. Mia, who patiently and earnestly listens—if angels could be human, they'd all be her. Rick, for not stopping me, even when he thought (knew) I was crazy. Frank and Joyce Keough, whose pride by far eclipses any embarrassment over their daughter's naughtiness.

For this book in particular, I thank Kathy Jaffer for inviting me into her home for the coolest Bible study group ever—our early discussions were the seeds from which this story grew. John Wharem, who was willing and able to wade through the muck of my first draft with an objective eye and sage advice and who has prayed me through many a meltdown since. Leslie Waterson, who gave me Prairie Oaks. Patti and Kevin Foss for generously pre-reading and providing feedback. Kelly Keough, who's been a particularly wonderful cheerleader as well as a willing ear. Suze, the girl wizard, whose steady, rational voice pulled me up during my lowest moments.

Elizabeth Harper, rock star visionary, who's taken a chance on me more than once. The Omnific team of editors and marketers who lent their skills to this book: Emma Taylor, CJ Creel, Coreen Montagna, Micha Stone, Amy Brokaw, editor Jennifer DeLucy, who saw what I myself could not, and publicist Traci Olsen, for her perpetual enthusiasm even when I know I'm being a pain in the bum. I'm especially grateful to the amazing Kimberly Blythe, head editor, who didn't hesitate to take on more than was her due and was truly a blessing to this story and to me.

To the book club hostesses who were so welcoming and fun, they made me want to write another book just to get invited back again, especially Colleen Miller-Owen, Cindy Downey, Jane Kramer, Colleen Sabol, Connie Whitesell, Jean Myers, Meg Schreiber, Linda Zacchea, and Judy Dainko. The staff of Eastern Illinois University, who've been beyond supportive with *Three Daves*, especially Janice Hunt, Dr. Allen Lanham, Karen Whisler, Jana Aydt, and Arlene Brown.

And to everyone in my life who still talks to me and graciously ignores the months and months of being neglected while my head is in the clouds and my fingers at the keyboard.

About the Author

Writing wasn't something Nicki set out to do; it just sort of happened when she realized writing reports was by far her favorite part of her investment consulting position. She traded stock allocation and diversification for story arcs and dialogue and now weaves creative writing time into her busy life with her family in the Chicago suburbs.

Nicki writes with two goals in mind: #1 to keep the characters realistic, even when their circumstances are anything but, and #2 to make the reader feel. Her other published works include contemporary romance novel, *Three Daves*, and short stories "Sway" (available as a single), "I Don't Do Valentine's Day" (part of *A Valentine Anthology*), and "Impressionism 101" (included in the debut issue of *Insatiable: The Magazine of Paranormal Desire*).

→Young Adult←

Shades of Atlantis and *The Ember Series: Ember* and *Iridescent* by Carol Oates
Breaking Point by Jess Bowen
Life, Liberty, and Pursuit by Susan Kaye Quinn
Embrace by Cherie Colyer
Destiny's Fire by Trisha Wolfe
Streamline by Jennifer Lane
Reaping Me Softly by Kate Evangelista

→Historical Romance←

Cat O' Nine Tails by Patricia Leever
Burning Embers by Hannah Fielding

→Erotic Romance←

Becoming sage by Kasi Alexander
Saving sunni by Kasi & Reggie Alexander
The Winemaker's Dinner: Appetizers and *Entrée*
by Dr. Ivan Rusilko & Everly Drummond

→Anthologies and Singles←

A Valentine Anthology including short stories by Alice Clayton, Jennifer DeLucy,
Nicki Elson, Jessica McQuinn, Victoria Michaels, and Alison Oburia

It's Only Kinky the First Time by Kasi Alexander
Learning the Ropes by Kasi & Reggie Alexander
The Winemaker's Dinner: RSVP by Dr. Ivan Rusilko
The Winemaker's Dinner: No Reservations by Everly Drummond
Big Guns by Jessica McQuinn
Concessions by Robin DeJarnett
Starstruck by Lisa Sanchez
New Flame by BJ Thornton
Shackled by Debra Anastasia
Swim Recruit by Jennifer Lane
Sway by Nicki Elson
Full Speed Ahead by Susan Kaye Quinn
The Second Sunrise by Hannah Downing
The Summer Prince by Carol Oates
Whatever it Takes by Sarah M. Glover
Clarity by Patricia Leever
A Christmas Wish by Autumn Markus

coming soon from
OMNIFIC PUBLISHING

The Winemaker's Dinner: Dessert by Dr. Ivan Rusilko

The Englishman by Nina Lewis

Tangled by Emma Chase

16 Marsden Place by Rachel Brimble

Sleepers, Awake by Eden Barber